sweet TOOTH

PERSEPHONE AUTUMN

BETWEEN WORDS PUBLISHING LLC

sweet TOOTH

USA TODAY BESTSELLING AUTHOR

PERSEPHONE AUTUMN

BETWEEN WORDS PUBLISHING LLC

Sweet Tooth

ISBN: 978-1-951477-91-2 (Ebook)

ISBN: 978-1-951477-92-9 (Paperback)

Editor: Ellie McLove | My Brother's Editor

Proofreader: Rosa Sharon | My Brother's Editor

Cover Design: Kate Farlow | Y'all. That Graphic.

BOOKS BY PERSEPHONE AUTUMN

LAKE LAVENDER SERIES

Depths Awakened

One Night Forsaken

Every Thought Taken

DEVOTION SERIES

Distorted Devotion

Undying Devotion

Beloved Devotion

Darkest Devotion

Sweetest Devotion

BAY AREA DUET SERIES

<u>Click Duet</u>

Through the Lens

Time Exposure

<u>Inked Duet</u>

Fine Line

Love Buzz

<u>Insomniac Duet</u>

Restless Night

A Love So Bright

<u>Artist Duet</u>

Blank Canvas

Abstract Passion

<u>Novellas</u>

Reese

Penny

STONE BAY SERIES

Broken Sky—Prequel

Shattered Sun

Fractured Night

Fallen Stars

Stolen Dreams

Raptured Souls

STANDALONE ROMANCE NOVELS

Sweet Tooth

Transcendental

In Knots For You

POETRY COLLECTIONS

Ink Veins

Broken Metronome

Slipping From Existence

Poisonous Heart

Beneath Wildflowers

PUBLISHED UNDER P. AUTUMN

STANDALONE NON-ROMANCE NOVELS

By Dawn

CONTENT WARNING

Sweet Tooth is a steamy romance story with light suspense. Graphic content and sexual violence in certain scenes may trigger some emotional distress in some readers. If you are sensitive to sexual violence, this story may not be for you. The graphic scene(s) is/are possible to skip and still understand the story.

Please use your personal judgment before proceeding.

———

Every 73 seconds, an American is sexually assaulted.

1 out of every 6 American women has been the victim of an attempted or completed rape in her lifetime (14.8% completed, 2.8% attempted).

About 3% of American men—or 1 in 33—have experienced an attempted or completed rape in their lifetime.

9 out of every 10 victims of rape are female.

Majority of sexual assaults occur at or near the victim's home.

Statistics from RAINN*

If you or anyone you know has be a victim of attempted or completed sexual assault and/or violence, there is help available.

- Chat online or find resources at https://www. rainn.org
- Call 1-800-656-HOPE (4673)

Both are free, confidential and available 24/7.

To the woman who sparked this idea… thank you.
I only met you once, but will never forget you.

CHAPTER 1

"So, did Mr. Williamson cop a feel today?"

Startled, I drop the pink paper-lined plastic tray layered with various dental tools. The mouth mirror and jacquette scaler fall off and clang on the counter. I spin around and spot Karen holding a light blue tray loaded with her hygienist tools.

"Oh my god, Karen." I slap a hand to my sternum and press hard over my racing heart. "You scared the crap out of me."

A pained smile stretches the corners of her mouth as she scrunches her shoulders. "Sorry, sweetie, I didn't mean to scare you."

I remind myself Karen has a deep-seated thirst to learn everyone's business. I breathe deeply through my nose and exhale slowly through my lips. Then, I focus on the tray of instruments and place them in the sanitizer.

"Make more noise next time you leave your station. Shuffle your feet, cough, laugh—something. Announce your arrival, stealth ninja."

I don't scare easily, but my last patient has me jumpy. Good old Mr. Williamson. Hence the question Karen asked as she snuck up in private detector mode. Mr. Williamson is one of *those* patients. The patient or customer we have all experienced once in our career. The one we avoid or work extra hard to shorten their visit. In this office, that patient is Mr. Williamson. And I just sat through a painful thirty-minute cleaning with him inches away.

"Are you avoiding my question, Tami?"

Avoidance is the best policy when Karen asks questions, but she need not know that.

I lift my head to meet the death stare Karen burns through my skull. She squints at me with her stern mother glare that intimidates most people. And I swear she sucks the answers from my head via osmosis. I purse my lips and grind my molars, and the pain lances up my jawline to my temple.

Karen has several lovable qualities. A tender heart and an eagerness to help others. Maternal instinct courses through her, head to toe. But she has several unlovable characteristics too. The most notable of those traits? Karen is a gossip queen. *The* gossip queen. One worthy of a golden sash and jeweled crown. She gossips enough that everyone grows speechless in her presence.

I suppose this happens to occasional women when they become empty nesters. They fill the void with something or someone else. Karen packs her days with the dirty details of patients and celebrities. If I need the inside scoop on who dates who, Karen is the woman to ask.

"Swear I'm not avoiding." I shuffle away from the machine and she steals my place. "I was giving my heart a minute to settle. No one would complain if you stomped out of your station. Unless you were trying to be a sneak."

"I am sorry," she says as sullenness lines her eyes. Her usual perky demeanor steps back for a split-second. "I'll make a better effort. Swear it wasn't intentional."

"I believe you." I lay a hand on her shoulder, give a light squeeze, and convey silent forgiveness. "Mr. Williamson was his usual self today."

She peers up from her tray and stares at me. Silence is how Karen asks for more details. She worked on Mr. Williamson for years before It's A Bright Day Dental hired me. I remind myself she has been in my shoes. Sat on my stool. Hovered over him with sharp implements as he did things which should have gotten him kicked out. The dentist dismisses those random touches as loneliness. That he misses his deceased wife.

I don't discount his loneliness, but no justifiable reason permits his behavior.

"I don't understand why doc lets him return." Karen shakes her head. "I mean, he has to believe us, right? Or is he that ignorant? He did attend college for years to become a dentist."

I lean against the wall and shrug. "Who knows doc's train of thought? Guess it could be worse. At least he only touches my leg. Not any specific part. I try to be polite and shirk him off. Tell him I need to shift the chair or grab a different tool."

Karen nods and puckers her lips with unsaid questions. "Yeah, I suppose. Guess it annoys me more than anything. I spent years in school to learn this trade. Patients should respect and treat me as a professional. I help support their health. Never expected to tackle this nonsense."

Our profession is respectable and I understand her frustration. People choose professions for a variety of reasons. A high percentage choose careers for money. No one will ever hear salary complaints spill from my lips. Although, fellow hygienists earn more outside this office. Others select their occupation to help people. Improve or keep a patient's health. Then, a small sliver of the population of the dental industry hygienists and doctors love teeth. Love to study and touch them. The ones giddy to transform a mouthful of crowded teeth into a perfect smile. Or those who fill in the empty slots of long-lost molars with artificial replacements.

Where do I land in the mix? Not one of the tooth enthusiasts. They are an anomaly. A rare breed. The second category is more my style; to help people. In college, I spoke with my professor regarding my future. It was then that I found my niche.

"Any plans for the weekend?" Karen snaps me back into focus and I return my attention to her.

"No plans yet. Same old, same old. Might check the city events page online. Should be lots to do. What about you?"

Karen juts out her lower lip for a split-second. Her eyes drop to her hands, then meet mine. "Not sure. The twins are settling in their new apartment. They packed up and left home so fast." She shakes her head and sighs.

Karen loves motherhood more than wifehood. And she misses her boys. A lot. Anyone paying attention noticed her mood shift when she spoke of them.

"Why don't you ask if they need help. Sweeten the deal and order pizza. They have to miss you, and free dinners."

"I don't want to be one of those helicopter parents, though." Her eyes drill deep in my soul. The crinkles at the corners of her eyes hint at concern. She fears scaring the boys away further.

I reach out, clasp her dainty wrist and give a gentle squeeze. "Don't act overeager and I'm sure everything will be fine. Explain how overwhelming it was the last time you moved. Offer to unpack or clean and in return feed them dinner. They'll jump on board for free dinner and cleaning help."

Karen beams for the first time since startling me. Those boys are her breath. Her reason for living. She would stop a meteor collision to save them. On occasion, Karen reminds me of my mom and the obstacles she overcame for me. A larger-than-life woman that handled several roles. I pray I can fill her shoes one day.

Karen rests a hand over mine and taps a few times. "Thanks for the advice, Tami. I needed to hear that. I've wanted to reach out, but didn't want to nag. Never thought to offer free food."

"You're welcome. Happy to help." With one last squeeze, I release her arm and hitch a thumb over my shoulder. "Need to clean my station. I'm ready to call it a day and start the weekend."

With that, Karen springs into action and bolts in the opposite direction. "Me too. Thanks again. You're the best!" Her voice fades as she enters her station, but not her enthusiasm.

Deep breath in through the nose, out through the mouth.

I mumble, "No, Karen, thank you. For not prying more than usual today." Whatever saint graced me with a less-than-noisy Karen, I will pray to them tonight. And tomorrow.

Lemon-scented sanitizer perfumes the air as I wipe my workstation. With each spritz and wipe, I advance toward the three-day weekend. Long weekends are one of several job perks. Most dental offices work four days a week. Long weekends grant time to recoup from the tedious, poor-postured, body-aching work. Hunching over people strains my back and neck. Ask my massage therapist.

I collect my purse from the employee lounge and head for the exit. Before the door closes, I wave goodbye to Karen and the receptionist. As soon as my feet hit the pavement, the California sun warms my skin. I tilt my head back, close my eyes, and absorb the golden rays.

God, I love this state.

Thank goodness all the patients are long gone. If I met Mr. Williamson in the parking lot, it would be a painful nightmare. I toss my purse across the truck bench seat, crank the ignition, and hum at the body-rattling engine roar. *This weekend will be great.* After I check for cars, I throw the truck in gear and drive off to my little slice of paradise.

CHAPTER 2

MAX

After ten minutes of driving circles around the parking lot, I locate a fucking parking space. Nic told me this place is fucking busy. Understatement of the century. But Nic refused to shut his pretty-boy mouth. Said this bar is one of the best in Los Angeles. I trust his judgment, but only I decide if this place is worth my time or money. If the number of cars and lack of parking are any indication, this place has promise.

I cut the engine, step out of the car and open my text history with Nic. I type a quick message of my arrival. Before I lock the screen, my phone chirps with his response. His message says to meet him near the entrance.

Hundreds of men and women line the wall near the entrance of The Sophisticate. Everyone dressed to the nines and eager to gain entry. I weave through the crowd and scan faces until I spot Nic close to the front. *Thank fuck.* My patience not worth the test of an hour-long wait in line.

I zigzag between patrons and survey the crowd as I catch up with Nic. Several women garner my attention and twitch my groin. The probability of warm sheets and sweaty sex tonight is high. And I capture a mental photograph of women who toss smiles my way.

"Hey, bro!" Nic slaps my shoulder when I approach.

"What's up, brother. This place is a fucking madhouse. But the fine ass women make up for the madness."

"Wait until we're inside. This place is insane, in the best way. If you think women out here are hot, wait and see who they let in. Selective. Very selective." He emphasizes the tail end.

"Then why the fuck are we still standing here?" I narrow my gaze and raise my brows in question.

He shakes his head, then faces away from me. "Right. Let's go."

We slither through the crowd near the front doors and enter a shorter line. A rush of excitement heats my skin as the line lessens one by one. As each person approaches the bouncer—a beefy, tall man, possibly ex-military—they receive the ultimate stare down. Grown men shrivel under his scrutiny. After the patron passes his visual assessment, he asks for identification. Even those more than old enough to enter. Once he approves that inspection, he asks a question. Your answer determines your fate of entry.

This place isn't just high class. They test you to prove your worth. Prove to the owner, and his scary henchmen, you are notable enough to be in their presence.

What the fuck question validates a person's worth?

Nic and I inch closer to the velvet rope and I swear the bouncer asks a man his profession. *Is that the secret question? Is that what grants access to The Sophisticate?*

My palms dampen as I question whether or not I will make

it inside. Not as if my career doesn't hold significance. But I am no fucking doctor, attorney or CEO.

As we approach the bouncer, he hooks the thick velvet rope to a gold post and prepares for his next inspection. He surveys Nic head to toe, then mimics the action with me. After his visual violation, he extends a hand and says "ID" for the millionth time. Nic and I hand over our licenses as the bouncer's jaw tics from the five second wait. The length of time he studies each license concerns me.

What the hell takes this long? Not the math to determine my age.

A grunt echoes in his throat. Followed by a smirk as he hands us back our licenses. He zeroes in on Nic. "What's your profession?"

Nic doesn't need his peacock feathers fluffed further, but his spine straightens as he thrusts his chest forward. "Male model." Confidence bleeds from his pores and he sparkles under the minuscule limelight.

"And you?" The bouncer hones in on me.

"Nutritionist/dietician coach and a CrossFit trainer."

I have no desire to *fluff* and *pretty* myself like Nic. He loves the spotlight and cameras on him. Loves when people ogle or request photos of or with him. My body is far from mediocre—my ass hits the gym several days a week—but I dial back my vanity compared to Nic.

The bouncer eyes us again before he reaches over, unhooks the rope, and permits entry. "Thank you, gentlemen. Enjoy your evening."

We nod and step past the rope as the cacophony of well-wishers roars in the background. Mr. Intimidation's inspection was an intense start to the evening, but thank fuck it is behind us. Bring on the hype of The Sophisticate.

My shoes clack the walnut floor as we venture down a

lengthy corridor. Pale cream, rustic browns and a bold red decorate the space. Oil and water paintings, as well as charcoal and pencil drawings, stare back at us through glass and wood. The art varies from world-renowned classics to new original pieces. Past the artwork, we near a colossal wooden archway with intricate embellishments.

As we step through, the venue morphs into a nightclub and bar. The Sophisticate doesn't resemble other bars and night-clubs. The walls a cream, natural stone and the surface uneven. Two separate bars run the length of the room—on opposite sides—the wood top a glossy black. Liquor bottles rest on glass shelves. Between the two bars are small, round tables that add to the motif. Three oxblood leather chairs tuck under each table with a candle at the heart for subtle illumination. Soft jazz floats in the air and I question if the music is live or recorded.

The Sophisticate has soft lighting with an amber glow throughout. At the far end of the room, I spot two bouncers more intimidating than the doorman.

I tap Nic on the bicep. "What's back there?" I point past the men to a black stairwell that disappears below the floor.

"Not sure, man." He studies the men and shrugs. "People went down the stairs last time I was here. Think you have to be invited, though."

I grunt my obvious displeasure. Another rope to pass. What valuable secrets lie beneath us? Do those secrets warrant another quiz for passage? Lay them on me. If they want a background check, I will grant them permission.

Two men guard the stairs. Whatever lies at the end of those stairs is worth more than the bar.

Nic leads us to the bar and I survey the room. Determined,

I search for anyone who will grant me access into the best part of this establishment.

We slide out stools and sit as the bartender approaches. A man clad in a long-sleeve white button-down, black vest, black slacks, and a black bow tie with a polished smile.

"What can I get you gentlemen this evening?"

"Gin and tonic, please," Nic orders.

"Scotch, neat. Thank you."

The man retrieves appropriate glassware and pours our respective drinks, then places them on a red cocktail napkin. We sit in silence a moment, sip our drinks and sweep the crowd.

The Sophisticate is unparallel to similar establishments. The men and women that line the bars and occupy the plush chairs aren't just anyone. These people are handpicked. They exude affluence and elegance and a sense of superiority. In The Sophisticate, you won't find drunks or people high out of their fucking mind.

I empty my glass and the bartender replaces it without question. Nic rotates on his stool and takes in the room again. His eyes dart from one place to the next over and over.

"So, man. What do you think?"

"Much better than The Well. Don't think I'll look at bars the same again."

"Now you know why I wanted to bring your ass here. Whole different caliber of people. You won't *want* to go anywhere else."

We shoot the shit as we sip our drinks. Nic and I hang out often—once or twice a week. Our usual routine involves random bars or strip clubs in the Los Angeles area. Nic joined a photographer at The Sophisticate last week. Since then, he won't shut up. Like a little bitch, he blathers on over this, that, and the other.

But now I comprehend the attraction.

If I hook up tonight, I will meet a new caliber of woman. Women here aren't bimbos in search of a good time. These women are classy and modest and respectable. My typical plan of attack may require a makeover.

"Gentlemen." A middle-aged man approaches us in a pristine tailored suit and extends a hand my way. "Name's Rocco. How's your evening so far?" He shakes my hand, then Nic's.

"Great, thank you. I'm Max and this is my friend, Nic."

"Good to meet you both. Welcome to The Sophisticate. I don't recall meeting either of you before."

Nic jerks his chin toward me. "It's his first time and my second. This place is amazing. You've done a fantastic job."

Rocco slides his hands in his pockets as he smiles wide. "Thank you. I appreciate compliments. This place is my lifeblood. A longtime dream of mine."

"Well, it's amazing."

Nic fans out his peacock feathers again. Always on stage, ready to flaunt himself at whoever pays him attention.

Rocco's eyes dart between the two of us as a *v* bunches his brow line. "I like you two. And because I like you, I have a proposition to make you gentlemen."

Intrigue surges inside me. When I glance to Nic, he mirrors a virgin getting off the first time. The urge to slap and shake him makes my hand twitchy. He needs to man up. *Fucking pansy.*

"What would that be?" Fascinated as hell, I restrain my curiosity better than my counterpart.

"We have an exclusive section within the club. A little more..." He pauses a moment and chooses his next words with precision. "A little more intimate. A little more of a visual display." The description methodical and selective.

Rocco's evasion has me clueless. Wild guess? The exclusive section is an artsy extension. Maybe that is what is down the stairwell. Once I consider this, I accept his proposal.

"I'm interested," I voice, but don't speak for Nic.

"I'm in, sir."

Did the word *sir* just slip from Nic's fucking pansy mouth? I internally cry-laugh at his idiocy. Ready to call him a pussy on a moment's notice. But I bite my tongue and stash it for later. He never uses common courtesies. Ever.

Rocco steps back, removes his hands from his pockets, and gestures us to follow. Nic and I gape at each other, slide off our stools and amble behind Rocco. With each step forward, we shorten the distance between us and the bouncers guarding the stairwell. Electricity hums in my veins as new energy courses throughout my body. An unmatched exhilaration.

I lean toward Nic and mumble close to his ear. "What do you think is down there, man?"

He runs a hand over his shaved, dark brown scalp, down his face and stops at his chin. "I haven't the slightest, brother. Whatever it is, must be fucking worth it. If they only have one guy at the door, two has to mean a whole hell of a lot."

Rocco stops inches from the two men. When we reach them, authority rings loud as Rocco speaks.

"Chad. Pete. I'll be inviting Nic and Max into P.I. tonight." Rocco faces us then continues. "Gentlemen, there are rules you must follow while in P.I. First and foremost, don't touch the ladies. Any of them. What happens outside my walls isn't my business. Inside my walls though... Second. If you are told to leave, you will never be allowed to return. To P.I. or The Sophisticate. Lastly. Be gentlemen. If you present yourself as such, you'll be offered a membership. Do either of you have any questions before I step away?"

Nic stands stock-still with a shit-eating grin plastered across his face. I swear to god he is an idiot at the worst times.

After the full rundown, only one question comes to mind. "I have just one. What is P.I.?"

A megawatt smile stretches Rocco's face. "It's your new Private Infatuation."

Our shoes tap against wood as we descend a dimly lit stairwell. At the bottom, Nic and I enter an extensive hall and trek forward. Ahead, I discern the faint glow of lights. A slow bass vibration echoes through my bones and I shiver. The lights and music beckon me. Shine brighter and thump harder with each step forward. I spot the silhouette of another bouncer.

Jesus, is this place Fort fucking Knox?

As we approach the bouncer, he shuffles to the side and permits us to enter. "Welcome, gentlemen. I assume Rocco relayed the P.I. rules?"

His sharp words more a statement than a question.

"Yes, he did."

"Have a good evening." Then, he resumes his post.

This place is better guarded than any other nightclub. Insane. Before I voice as much, I amble toward the flashing lights and music. In a blink, I puzzle out why P.I. has bouncers in every nook and cranny.

P.I., or Private Infatuation as Rocco calls it, isn't an upscale nightclub. Although, I am certain the majority of their business occurs during the hours of sundown to sunup. P.I. is so much more than a nightclub. This place is the sweetest version of heaven on planet Earth.

Nic and I drift over to a vacant table near the bar. The seat is barely warm when a tight body with blonde hair walks up and introduces herself as Nina.

"What can I get you gentlemen to drink?"

Drink orders placed, I ogle Nina's plump ass as she walks to the bar. The only fabric on her skin is a skimpy, red lace thong. The material barely forms a triangle at the junction of her thighs. I fixate on her a moment as she leans on a charcoal blacktop bar. A moment later, I lose my shit.

Behind the bar, the female bartender appears to be in the same wardrobe. She shakes a drink and her voluptuous tits bounce. I face forward and glance at Nic, struck speechless.

"Bro, I don't know what we did to deserve this, but I never want to fucking leave."

Nic opens his mouth to respond, but gets interrupted by the boom of a man's voice over the music.

"Good evening, gentlemen. And let's not forget the few ladies in the room. Thank you for joining us in P.I. tonight. Hope you are enjoying your evening. Up next... everyone's favorite sweetheart." A cluster of men near the longest section of stage applaud. A wolf whistle cracks the air behind me. "The sweetest thing you'll see all night. Ladies and gentlemen, I give you Candy."

The lights extinguish and the club is blanketed in darkness. Only small lights over the bar illuminate the club. A buzz filters through the air and captivates the audience. A deep bass pierces the silence and vibrates the ground before it resonates in my groin. The seductive melody lilts around us, a single, soft light highlights the center of an H-shaped stage. As a deep chord strikes, a thin, muscular calf with an olive complexion peeks out from a black curtain.

As the song picks up tempo, Candy steps into full view.

Most strippers I have watched wore stilettos with four-plus-inch heels. Some of the spiked accessories vinyl, others leather. They range in color; some bright and thigh-high.

But Candy is in a league all her own.

Feet bare as she glides across the stage and torques her body. Toenails painted a hot pink that pops against her exotic skin. Mesmerized, I unabashedly scan every inch of her body —toe to top.

Without question, her physique is irresistible. Toned calves. Muscular yet feminine quads. Abdominals that women and men envied. A killer rack, perfect for her body type. A heart-shaped face with voluptuous lips, the perfect nose, and eyes that charm snakes. She wears a wig with curls that brush her mid-back in layers of cotton candy pink, blue, and purple.

Body clad in leather, small triangles cover her magnificent tits and the apex of her thighs. The material matches the color on her toes as if planned. Black straps wrap around her torso and cage her like a wild animal. But the way she glides across the stage says otherwise.

Candy dances like no woman I have seen. Her muscle definition and overall flexibility indicates she takes care of herself. And is aware of every line and curve and uses them to her advantage.

She floats from one side of the stage to the other. Body fluid with the music and addictive as hell. Her back bows as fingertips roll down her abdomen in a physical siren's call. Every bend at the waist, the way her ass pops out… Jesus, my cock twitches like a prepubescent boy. The pole presses between her shoulder blades center stage as her hands slide up and grip the post. Her body sways as she bends her knees, dips lower and spreads her legs wide.

And when she rises to full height, somehow, the pieces covering her tits have loosened. Her bare breasts exposed for every horny man—and woman—in the room.

No one makes a sound. Everyone as equally lost in the visual display. My hand slides under the table and squeezes my dick through my pants before readjusting myself and shifting in my seat. My cock more ramrod and hard than ever.

I have fucked my share of women, and I am not shy to admit facts. That said, no other woman has gotten my dick this hard. Has made me *hungry* enough to consume every inch of her. And I haven't touched her.

Fuck.

As if the gods hear my inner turmoil, the delicious torture shifts. Tantalizes me further. Before I register what has happened, Candy stands nude before the audience. Not a lick of fabric to conceal her delicious skin. Her body stuns me thoughtless for a moment.

Gorgeous skin, not one hair follicle visible. Her hands skim from the swell of her breasts, down her abdomen and land between her legs. After a clench of her thighs, she removes her hands and continues her routine across the stage.

Earlier, I was wrong. When I thought I was the hardest I had ever been. When I thought I had never been more turned on. I had been mistaken. Because right now. In this exact moment. There is a high, embarrassing chance I may blow my load. Without so much as a hand or finger on my cock.

I have no clue who this woman is—this sweet little piece called Candy—but I hunger for more of her. The way she calls out to me feels surreal. The urge to have her skin under my fingers, to trace her perfect toned body, to memorize the heat between her legs, and experience the tightness of her core as I plunge into her...

Fuck. One song will never be enough. Candy is pure magnificence.

And then, as if unable to handle the torture further, the stage light cuts out. Candy disappears from view. The room blanketed in absolute silence before it erupts in loud whistles, hollers, and applause.

How many of these people have seen Candy dance more than just tonight?

I feel bereft. Jealous. Envy spikes my bloodstream as I take in the crowd. Why have I just found Candy? How have they seen her more?

My pulse pounds behind my ears as my skin heats and my blood pressure rises. I scan the room with narrowed eyes, ready to pounce. And it surprises me that my reaction is one of ownership. As if Candy already belongs to me.

She should belong to me.

As if someone hears my tempered thoughts, a hand taps my shoulder. I turn and see Rocco behind me with bright eyes and a broad smile.

"Gentlemen." He nods to me then Nic, who I forgot was there. "How are you enjoying your time in P.I.?"

My mind fumbles to best express how I am a changed man. Addicted seems acceptable. But I don't want to sound like a pussy after one dance. No need to worry about that, though. Nic fluffs his tail feathers and speaks up before I open my mouth.

"Rocco. Thank you, again, for the invitation. I'm speechless. This place is amazing. You really know what you're doing, man. I haven't seen a place like this."

Nic prattles word vomit like he wants to suck Rocco's dick. I shake my head at Nic, but he doesn't notice.

"Glad to hear you're enjoying it." A genuine smile lights his face. "I'd like to extend a new invitation to you both. If you're interested in returning to P.I.—and let's be honest, who wouldn't be—we can set you up with our exclusive membership. Thoughts?"

Exclusive membership? He has my full, undivided attention.

P.I. is the perfect combination of heaven and temptation. Hell… I watched one woman dance across the stage, take off her clothes (if you can even deem what she was wearing as clothing), and seduce me in a way I never knew existed. All within five minutes. If given the chance to see more of Candy… what is there to think about?

"Where do I sign up?" My brain to mouth function is on hiatus. And I don't give a fuck.

Rocco's throaty laugh at my knee-jerk reaction garners the attention of others. "Candy sweetened the deal, huh?"

"I never thought I had a sweet tooth, but it appears I do."

"If you'll follow me, gentlemen, we'll get you taken care of."

And within minutes, I have a new addiction with endless access.

CHAPTER 3

TAMI

The morning sun slices through the shutters, beams bright on my face, and wakes me from the best sleep. I live for weekends. No alarm clock. No regimented routine. Weekends are chill and when I feel most myself.

Arms stretched over my head, I starfish and make sheet angels under the covers. Fingers to toes, my muscles stir to life. I glance at the clock on the ledge and grumble at the time. Just after ten. Time to motivate and get in my morning run before Amber and I go for brunch.

I flop the ivory afghan to the side, scoot to the foot of the bed and amble to the dresser. I slip on a thong and running shorts, then struggle a solid two minutes with my sports bra.

Whoever created sports bras… bless you—your design to keep the girls in place while women exercise is wondrous. And fuck you—for making it so damn challenging to get in and out of these tight-ass contraptions.

Once I have my hair secured in a ponytail and my teeth brushed, I do some light stretches. On my way out the door, I tell Amber I am going on my morning run.

I open my workout app, select my running playlist, crank up the volume, then tuck the phone in the bicep band on my arm. For the first quarter-mile, my feet pound the pavement in a slow jog. Once warmed up, I enter my stride until cooldown. I switch my route daily and love the change of scenery. Not that it varies much in different directions.

Sweat drips down my temples as the app breaks through the music and a robotic voice says I have run thirty-five minutes and hit three-and-a-half miles. My goal is three to five miles per run. Distance has always been my thing, but not in extreme ways. Let's just say, you won't spot me in a half-marathon.

Sorry, bucket list.

Turning down the next street, I decide to run back toward the apartment.

The streets and sidewalks bustle with people from all walks of life. Parents with children. Couples walking hand in hand. Small clusters of women laughing and enjoying the company of one another. Cyclists and runners getting in a workout before the summer sun becomes too intense. People in the park with their dog. Others coming and going from storefronts.

The city is alive and beams with thousands of happy faces. The buzz radiates off them as I pass. The hum energizes and motivates me to push harder.

The last quarter-mile, I slow my pace and start to cool down. At the front door, I slip my phone from the band, stop the app and dart inside for a quick shower.

Amber sits on the couch with a mug of coffee between both her hands. She lifts a hand and waves.

I pop my earbuds out and point toward my room. "Going to take a quick shower, then I'll be ready."

"Cool. How was your run?"

"Good. Glad I got up when I did. Would've had to wait till later otherwise. And running in the heat sucks."

Down the small hallway off the right side of the living room, I enter my bedroom and en suite bathroom.

Our apartment has a unique layout. The main communal areas—living, dining, and kitchen—are in the center of the space. The bedrooms and bathrooms sit off to either side. The concept is fantastic for roommates. If either of us has company or comes home late, we don't hear the other in their room.

I strip out of my workout gear, crank the shower and step under the hot spray. For a minute, I stand limp and let the heat soothe my muscles. The heat relieves the ache as I hang my head. But relaxation time is up.

Inhaling a deep breath through my nose, I close my eyes and hold it a beat. Just a few more seconds. As I exhale, I snap into action.

Amber and I go to Cora's Coffee Shoppe for a late breakfast. One of the other hygienists in her office raved about the food—literally wouldn't shut up—and insisted everyone check it out. So, we ventured here to see what all the fuss is about.

Located on Ocean Avenue, not far from the Santa Monica Pier, the restaurant is a thirty-minute drive from our apartment in Rosemead.

We find a place to park and walk toward the entrance. The closer we get to the door, the more I smell heaven. Potatoes, fresh bread, citrus, and maple float in the air, and my stomach grumbles. I pat the ferocious beast. "Soon," I mutter.

The late-morning crowd packs the small restaurant. Light

chatter heard over music. And after a quick table scan, I assume a long wait time. But luck is on our side and the hostess seats us on the covered back patio. At a small, round table, the hostess hands us menus and says our server will be with us momentarily.

I survey the extended patio and gaze up at the wooden arches above us. A thicket of vines and flowers shade us from the sunny day. The patio full of lush greenery that hides patrons from cars and passersby. Strands of Edison bulbs hang above us and illuminate the shaded expanse, more so later in the day. In the center of our table is an ensemble of condiments —hot sauce, sweetener packets, and shakers. The vibe is laid-back yet chic.

I love the place already.

After a tedious glance at the menu, we order our breakfast when the server returns. Without a doubt, Amber and I will visit again. Not only is it cute, but the menu has every possible breakfast option.

"So, how's work been? Any better?"

I sip my water and shrug. "Not horrendous, but I wish the doctor cared about the employees and patients more than his own pocket. Don't get me wrong, I'm happy to have a job. But I might see what else is out there."

"I hear ya. But hang in there. Something else waiting in the wings. There's always demand for hygienists. Just a matter of finding a good practice to work in. I'll let you know if I hear anything."

"Thanks, Amber. You know how much I appreciate you. I just want to feel respected for what I do. I may not be the doctor, but I busted my ass in school to get to where I am today. We both did. And I hate feeling like I'm just another girl working in the office. Not to mention some of the patients I have to put up with. For crying out loud, I'm over getting groped by old men."

Amber stares at me with judgmental eyes. Her unspoken question over my final statement sits on the tip of her tongue. To add injury to insult, she justifies her *oh really* stare down.

"Are you serious right now?"

I look away from her and stare off at nothing in particular. Her bitterness puts me on edge, but I don't want to argue. My repeated attempts to make her understand the difference in her judgment exhausts the hell out of me.

And who gave her the right to judge me? What makes her more superior than me? Absolutely nothing. We are equally educated in a respectable profession. What I choose to do outside of dentistry is my business, not hers. And I do my best to keep it away from home—which I succeed at ninety-nine percent of the time.

I meet her gaze and soften my expression. A quiet plea on my tongue. "Can we please talk about something else?"

She narrows her eyes and studies me a moment, assessing my mood. Content with what she sees, she veers us toward a different topic of conversation.

"Julia's boyfriend started using a new gym. He loves it. When she told me, I thought of you and how you might like to try somewhere new. Especially once the heat becomes unbearable."

Thankful for the neutral topic change, I prompt for more information. "What gym is it? What did he say about it?"

I love the gym, but the chain establishment I use only has basics. No extra classes. No personal trainers. No frills. Just the most utilized exercise equipment. It keeps me fit, but I need progress. I don't need to be some buff beauty. Just want a balanced workout regimen.

"The place has machines, weights, and trainers. It's mainly CrossFit, but has extensive hours. Want me to text her?"

Happy for the shift in her mood, I smile. I love this Amber. The Amber I knew in college. A woman mostly hidden now. But a woman who still adds colorful highlights to her hair. Those stripes of pink and teal in her shoulder-length blonde tell me she is still in there. The Amber I love.

When we were in college, Amber lived more. Was more herself. She ventured out into the world, smiled nonstop, and laughed endlessly. Not long after graduation, she met David. With David, Amber became someone else. A stranger. The longer she stays with him, the less lively she is. When I voiced my opinion, she said she was growing up. I disagree.

Which is why I have made it my life's mission to not let the fire in her fade away forever.

David isn't all bad and has several qualities that weigh in his favor. As a pediatrician, he has a well-established, thriving practice. Without issue, he provides for Amber. He is financially stable—a large, sparkling reminder of his wealth sits on Amber's left, fourth finger. And, most importantly, she loves him. Every time he tries to stir up shit, I reiterate his good qualities in my head.

That said, I still keep an eye and ear open for anything off-putting.

Since David, Amber doesn't radiate the same light from years ago. Sure, she smiles and laughs, but they feel forced. Especially with him in the room. I want her to want to smile. I want her to want to laugh. Without thought or care. Without concern for other people's opinions.

"I would love that. If they have a website, that works. If I go, would you go with me? Maybe workout after work."

Although we work in two different dental offices, they have similar hours.

She plucks her phone from her purse and winces. I almost miss the rejection. Her fingers tap the screen as she types out a message to Julia. Done with the text, she opens another app and scrolls. Her avoidance is a dental probe to the heart.

Does she not want to spend time with me? Or is David in her head with his harsh authority, harping about expectations?

Honestly, it wouldn't shock me if he'd want Amber to let herself go. To become less attractive. Then, she wouldn't outshine him when they go out. Sure, David has the fancy degrees in ostentatious frames on his office walls. A lot of people are impressed by his status or title.

But Amber radiates beauty and warmth. Her beauty understated, but noticeable when she enters a room. She takes care of herself, primps on a regular basis, and makes the most conservative attire breathtaking. Overall, her smile—her genuine smile—is what ensnares people.

I want her genuine smile more often.

"Julia said it's called CrossFit AF. She sent me a link. I'll send it to you." Her eyes remain downcast as she taps on her phone.

"Cool. Tell her I say thank you." I want to ask again if she will go with me, but a wad of cotton clogs my throat. This is Amber. My friend. So, I swallow down the scratchy lump. "Want to check the place out with me? Maybe go together Tuesday, after work?"

"I don't know. Sounds like a great place, but I think David has plans for us already. Maybe another time."

Her voice a bit vacant; eyes not meeting mine. I don't want David to smother out her light, but I don't know how to prevent it. One way or another, I have to try.

"Maybe another time. After we finish breakfast, want to check out the shops nearby? I saw some super cute furniture and clothing stores a block away."

Her eyes light up and a spark from years past sneaks in. Sometimes, the little moments, like eating at a chic restaurant or wandering vintage stores for hours, make all the difference. It doesn't take much to make Amber happy. Glad I still make her smile.

"I'd love to."

Just then, our server arrives with two massive plates of food. We stare down at our plates with wide eyes. Then, we dig in.

Right now, life is pure bliss… at least for our stomachs.

CHAPTER 4

MAX

I drop the barbell and it hits the floor with a loud thump, clanging as the weights smack from the impact. Sweat seeps from every pore. A pleasant burn in my muscles. The familiar adrenaline high in my veins. I needed that workout before I teach the beginner's class. Thank fuck, I finished with minutes to spare.

As with any job, there are pros and cons. Getting the workout my body needs is a challenge when I train people who have either never exercised or want to try something new. Most people fit into one of the two categories. On occasion, I get thrown for a loop and eat my words. But those moments are far and few between.

I also need to snap out of this fog and get my head in the game before class.

For the last two days, I resided in la-la land more often than not. My brain seems to have forgotten its primary function. Or how to process life at normal speed.

Since Nic and I were invited into P.I. on Thursday—and

purchased a membership without a second thought—I have returned nightly. Sat at the same table and stared at the stage in awe.

Candy has most certainly become my very own private infatuation. Thursday, Friday, and Saturday, I walked out of P.I. with a granite dick and throbbing blue balls. Each night, I fisted my dick like a symbiotic life form. Jerking with intensity while cold water rained down my back. And each night, I went to bed without relief. Hell, my shower got more fucking action than me.

Since Sunday, the fog cloud in my mind has grown thicker. Denser.

When I walked down the dark corridor into P.I. Sunday evening, I learned the most disappointing news. Candy works three days a week. The three days I had already seen her.

And now, my head is all over the place. Each minute is the longest hour of my life as I wait to see her again. Candy is more than an infatuation. She is the drug-loaded needle and I am the vein. Begging for the next hit.

Fuck. My. Life.

Not sure what it is about Candy that has me so addicted. So needy. But I do know one truth. I am fucked.

I need clarity. Something to slap me across the face and say *wake up, motherfucker*. A reality check.

Thank fuck for working out. Being at the gym provides a different form of release. And a different high. Helps me locate some form of lucidity and provides the perfect distraction. When I am in the zone, nothing fazes me.

After putting the weights back, I drink water and grab a piece of fruit. As I finish my apple, a small group with confused faces walks through the front door. They scan the gym, equipment, and other members. One of them legitimately looks frightened by the concept of working hard to be healthy. Another pales at how many people are in the gym.

"Somebody help me," I mutter to no one.

This will be a slow fucking night. Although working with beginners is a pain in the ass—mainly because they have no drive, yet—it is also the most rewarding. For those who stick it out, I enjoy watching their transformation into healthier versions of themselves. One of the many reasons I work in this industry.

I plaster on a toothy smile, approach the group and attempt to put them out of their misery.

"Hi everyone, I'm Max. You here for the beginner's class?"

Two men nod as if they have forgotten how to use words. The woman speaks up, tells me their names, and indicates they are here for my class. A family trying to get into shape together. *How fucking cute.* Cue the vomit.

Although I should, I won't tell them one or two of them are doomed. Anytime families join the gym together, almost always, only one follows through and keeps training. Typically, the person who suggests they join is the last one standing. They're the one with all the ambition. Which is why they will see it through to the end, and beyond. The same exact scenario has played out hundreds of times.

"Great," I say with false excitement. "If you follow me, I'll show you where we'll be working out tonight."

I guide them past several people in full workout mode. Lifting weights. Pull-ups and push-ups. Battle ropes. Looping on the rings. Others doing circuit training routines. Bodies of all shapes and sizes. Some just out of the beginner's program. While others are longtime veterans and doing their own thing.

All of their capabilities astound me. And they sweat their asses off and love every second.

Leading the trio over to an open mat space, I direct them to hang out while I wait for others to arrive. I expect at least two more people, according to the sign-up log. One male and one female.

I take my phone from my pocket and note another ten minutes before class begins. I scroll through emails and respond to client messages from earlier in the day.

As I type the last line of an email, I glance up and spot a woman walking in the door. As if it never existed, I forget the email. Locking my phone, I stuff it in my pocket. My legs operate of their own accord and head in her direction.

"Hey, I'm Max. How can I help you?" I extend a hand in her direction as a genuine smile curves my lips.

"Hi," she says with a smile in her voice. "I'm here for the beginner's class. Tami. It may be under Tamara." She takes my hand and shakes with more strength than I expect from her semi-lithe appearance.

"Pleasure to meet you, Tami. We're expecting one other person, if you'd like to wait here with me."

I sure as shit am not walking her over to sit with the scared shitless family. Glancing over at the trio, I notice the woman rubbing the pale-faced man's back as his chest rises and falls rapidly. Always a challenge, I restrain the urge to roll my eyes and say something snarky and unprofessional. Besides, I want a few moments alone with this one. Tami is a sight for sore eyes—and a sore cock.

"Sure. That's fine." She retrieves her phone from the bag slung over her shoulder and checks to make sure she silenced it.

Something about Tami feels familiar. I stare at her from the corner of my eye, but can't put a finger on how I may know her. Usually, I remember faces and names in my line of work. But neither strike a chord in my memory.

The peace in my veins as we stand here, silent, befuddles me. Her energy reminds me of a Tibetan singing bowl. A quiet, intense power that vibrates deep in your bones the longer you stand near it. A strange tranquility blooms hot beneath my pecs, and I don't know how to feel about it.

Tami is stunning, to say the least. Dark, wavy locks secured back into a ponytail. Prominent cheekbones accentuate her light olive skin and heart-shaped face. Curves in all the right places. Not too short. Not too tall. Plus, it appears she works out on a regular basis. Not that I plan to jinx things, but why is she *here*? She doesn't need a beginner workout class.

"So…" I start, trying not to come off as eager. "Beginner's class? You might do better in an intermediate setting."

She shrugs as a half-smile plumps her cheek. "Yeah, I'm new to this whole CrossFit thing, but I've been working out for years. Just want to try something different. Hoping to get a more rounded workout. Better to start at the beginning, don't you think?"

If starting at the beginning means I get to see her, I sure as shit won't tell her no. "It's a good idea. Then you get a better grasp of how it all works."

She nods, opens her mouth to respond when a man walks up to us, interrupts our conversation and pisses me off.

"Hi, I'm Don. Here for the beginner's class." Don shoves his hand forward and inserts himself between me and Tami. I stare down at his hand and groan. I really want to refuse his handshake. Part of me wants to teach the man how rude it is to interrupt conversations.

But, like the professional I am, I reach out and shake his hand as I curse him in thought.

"Nice to meet you, Don. If you two would like to head back to where the three people in the fluorescent lime green shirts stand, we'll get started."

Don drops my hand and walks away, his scrawny stride a bit eager. I gesture for Tami to follow. She steps around me and treks across the gym with a more casual pace. After a few steps, I fall in line behind her and revel in the glorious view of her ass as it sways left to right in her yoga leggings.

I shove a hand in my pocket and adjust myself discreetly. Ten minutes ago, I thought tonight would be a bust. Turns out, this will be the best damn class I instruct. Even with the lime green trio.

***

Fastest fucking hour of my goddamn life. And no lie, I enjoyed every fucking second of staring at Tami. When she bent at the waist. Squatted. Lifted. It really didn't fucking matter. She has a sinful body. Every testosterone-laced molecule inside me begs to feel her soft skin against mine.

Whenever opportunity struck, I corrected her technique. God, I have never wanted to assist someone as much as I do her. Any chance I get to touch her, I sure as fuck am taking it.

"Great first class everyone. You all did good. The workouts get easier with time, just keep at it. Stay on track and attend classes. And if you need motivation, make sure you reach out. Ask family or friends, but if you need motivation from someone else, we're always here to help." I pray the only person to reach out is Tami. "You're excused. Drink a lot of water, your muscles will thank you for it. Also, remember you'll probably be sore in the morning. Although it doesn't feel fantastic, it's a reminder we're doing good things for your health. Have a good night."

I pick up my water bottle from the mat and take a swig. My eyes trail off to where Tami riffles through her bag and retrieves a towel and bottled water. The other four from the class head toward the exit while Tami rests on the mat and cools down.

This is an irresistible opportunity. A chance to speak with her again. Alone.

I walk over, crouch down beside her and gesture to the mat, asking permission to sit. She swipes the towel over her nape, then nods and takes another swig of water.

"You did great. I know you're unfamiliar with the routines, but you might see more benefits from the intermediate class. There's less guidance, but I can help." I pause to sip my water. "The intermediate class starts in about ten minutes, if you'd like to hang around and watch. You don't have to participate, unless you want to."

Gold flecks sparkle in her green-rimmed, hazel eyes as she studies me. Her teeth capture the corner of her lower lip and hold it prisoner. The visual is a direct connection to my dick. My favorite appendage jerks in reaction and I have to remember how to breathe.

Fuck.

My dick has one goal on its agenda. To get laid. And soon.

Normally, I don't have this many fucking problems with my cock. Sure, it flaunts its appreciation for beautiful women. But damn, there has never been a time I couldn't contain it. Right now, my cock resembles a caged animal that escaped. Hungry and out of fucking control.

Get it the fuck together.

As it stands, I fuck a different woman on the regular. Monogamy has never blipped on my radar. The idea of fucking the same woman every night holds no appeal. For years, this has been my life. Sex three to five times a week. A different woman in the sheets each time. Variety is the spice of life.

Until I laid eyes on Candy.

Candy is the first fucking female to get me so fucking hard, it pains me to stand. Not to mention how much it hurts to walk with a steel rod pinned to your thigh. No matter how many times I jacked off—no matter how many times I came— it made zero difference. As if my cock knows the only genuine relief comes from being inside the source.

And to be honest, Tami only adds to the problem. Soon, my balls will be a permanent shade of midnight blue if I don't fuck soon.

"Yeah, I can hang around for the next class. I don't have anywhere else to be." Her words a blessing and a fucking curse.

"Great. Everyone should be here soon. We usually meet here and then get into the nitty-gritty. You can leave your things here, if you'd like."

For the first time in days, a legitimate smile spreads across my face. Like I said, there is something so familiar about this woman. Maybe I knew her years ago. *Maybe I fucked her years ago.* No, I sure as hell would remember fucking her, even if time changed her.

"Perfect."

As she puts her towel and water in her bag, I glimpse a tattoo on the inside of her left wrist. Two or three inches in length with not much width. Can't be sure, but it looks like a lollipop. The type you see on large dowel sticks. A long rope of rainbow swirled sugar that wraps in a circle. Interesting. My curiosity gets the best of me and I open my mouth before I stop myself.

"What's that?" I point at her wrist.

She flips over her forearm and peers down at her wrist. Definitely a tattoo.

"Oh, that? It's kind of an inside joke." I cock my head and narrow my eyes at her, curious. "I'm a dental hygienist. Sweets are a big no-no. Just a little humor. Plus, it usually stays hidden when I wear my watch."

"Dental hygienist, huh? I suppose that can be an equally gratifying and disgusting career. Just like mine. Like many, really."

She laughs, but holds back. The sound not quite what I imagined coming from her. Light, a bit musical, a beacon.

I don't recall a time when I wanted to hear a woman laugh again. Most women laugh with me out of artificial pretense. To flirt or get something from me. But that isn't the case with Tami.

Tami laughs and I want a repeat. Can laughter be attractive? Hers is, and then some. Warm and whimsical. A bewitching invitation. It radiates authenticity not often heard in the world. Her laugh is cute and fits everything I know about her so far.

"It has its moments. Suppose every line of work does. I enjoy helping people, though. Getting them into better health. A healthy body starts with the mouth, ya know." Her laughter erupts again.

"More dental humor?"

"Yeah, sorry."

"Don't be. You have a great laugh."

And before I blink, I make things awkward. Not one-hundred-percent, but enough to where neither of us says anything further. Not until the next group trickles in, takes over the mat, and I excuse myself.

Seriously… fuck. My. Life.

CHAPTER 5

TAMI

"See you Monday, Karen. Have a great weekend."

"You too, sweetie."

Snagging my purse and duffel bag, I head for my truck in the back of the lot. Cranking the engine, I listen to the purr of Tiff's engine and close my eyes briefly. A low vibration thrums beneath me as the engine rumbles. Of all the things I own, this truck sits on the top of my favorites list. Over the years, I have done so much work to restore her and she repays me every time I hear the roar under the hood.

Heading out of the lot, I drive toward the city, practically bouncing to get another workout under my belt.

After watching the intermediate class on Tuesday, I decided the beginner's class would only hold me back. The level of activity and weights in the intermediate is more up my alley, and exactly what I need to help maintain my tone and strength. The only downfall to switching is the time the class starts.

Starting at a later time, the class cuts into the center of my free time and makes it more challenging to get things done.

One way or another, though, this will pass and balance will take over. A few more classes and I will walk into the gym with confidence; do the routine on my own without instruction or guidance.

Parking Tiff, I grab my bag from the passenger seat and head for the entrance. I beeline to the women's locker room, and swap my scrubs for a sports bra and some yoga leggings. After a swig from my water bottle, I cram my duffel into one of the available lockers and exit the locker room, ready to warm up.

As I step out on the main floor, I only spot one other woman working out. I pray to whatever higher power listens to me. *Please don't let this place be one where every male stops and stares the second I stretch.* I blow a kiss to the heavens, seal my silent words, and walk over to a vacant area with yoga mats.

Taking a moment to get my head where I need it—clear and focused—I take a deep breath and start the yoga routine I have practiced years to warm up my muscles. Halfway through the routine—my ass to the heavens in downward dog —my skin hums. A warm, irrefutable energy wakes me head to toe. I avert my eyes and spy a figure in my periphery. I flow into cobra and peer up at Max standing close enough to touch. Like every hormonal male on planet Earth, his eyes hone in on my frame and curves.

The manner in which his eyes roam my body… hunger, ache, and need scorch his irises. Sure, I have witnessed it hundreds of times. An unfortunate—and occasionally uncomfortable—side effect of caring for your body and having curves.

With Max, the lingering, obsessive gaze feels different. I try to decipher each stare. Each unasked question. And before I pinpoint the difference, I lose traction. But I still feel it. Floating in the atmosphere like humidity, clinging to my skin.

When it dawns on him my eyes haven't strayed—his haven't left me either—he snaps out of his foggy state and smiles. Before I blink, his professional mask slips back into place. "Hey, Tami. Hope you haven't been here too long. Still have another ten or so minutes until class begins."

"I haven't. Headed here from work. Thought I'd get in my yoga warm-up time before class."

"Good plan. I'll let you get back to it. When you're done, we'll be starting at the pull-up bar." He gestures to said bar.

"Perfect, thanks."

Still in cobra, I stare after Max as he retreats and heads for the small office in the far corner. Ogle the way his calves flex with each stride. Gawk at the ropes of muscle on his biceps. Drool over the flex of his glutes with each step forward. Max has an admirable body. Not just from the muscle and sinew beneath his skin, but also the way he carries himself. With confidence and appeal.

A trim, tall frame, but not one that towers over me. His light brown skin accentuates the musculature of his legs and arms in all the right ways. Arm and leg porn have never been my gig, but I sense a new opinion forming. I bet my savings Max is more exquisite underneath his muscle tee and basketball shorts.

From elbows to pecs, his biceps are artfully decorated with Japanese designs. Other men with tattoos never made me break out in a sweat, but on Max... his tattoos are hints of sin sprinkled atop an already alluring package.

Going through a few more poses, I refocus my attention and settle my mind. I zero in on prana and breathe with purpose. At least that is what I tell myself.

My reason for visiting the gym is not to gape or be ogled or flirt. I come here for a change of pace. To learn new exercises and strengthen my regimen.

Standing up, I bring my hands into prayer position and peer toward the office. Through the windows facing the workout floor, Max busies himself with paperwork as a hand combs through his spiraled, brown and golden locks. My eyes trail the angle of his jaw, the pout of his lips.

Damnit, Tami! Get your head in the game. You are not here to date. You don't do the dating thing and you know why. In the end, it never works out.

After a momentary mental slap session, I shake my head and circle back to the reason behind why I am here. Once in the right headspace, I stroll to the pull-up bar and wait for others to arrive. Soon, men and women clamber around me, eager to begin.

Max strides out of the office with his confident, competent mask in place. His eyes scan everyone in the group before resting on me—longer than anyone—and a smile lights up his face. Just before he faces the group to speak, I swear he winks at me.

"Good evening, everyone. I hope you've done warm-ups. We'll be jumping right in tonight and starting with pull-ups. If anyone hasn't warmed up yet, I suggest you do so while everyone else begins."

For a split-second, I question his tone and the way he intends it. As if he degrades anyone who steps up to the bar unprepared. By now, most of the people in this stage of the game know to warm up before class—either arriving early or doing so ahead of time. *Is this his way of complimenting my dedication?* Certainly hope not. Although arrogance has its place, it isn't a trait I find attractive.

After the first man drops from the bar—Roger, I think—Max flaunts his cockiness further. "Make sure you all warm-up beforehand. This is what I want to see."

He steps up to the bar, grabs hold and proceeds to do one pull-up after another. The rate of speed both obscene and captivating. Can't tell you how many times he hoists himself above the bar because I get lost in the definition of his body and how it flexes and tightens with each movement. The corded bicep muscles harden and contract with each ascension. Deltoids lock tight. Ankles latched together and kicked out behind him. After three or four minutes, and countless pull-ups, he lets go and lands with a thud.

"That's what I'm looking for. Let's focus, people."

What the hell crawled up his ass and died?

His current attitude heats my cheeks. Pisses me off. Fact… I can do enough pull-ups to shut him up. Or maybe chill him the fuck out.

So, I step up to the bar, slide the grips onto my hands, and jump up to grab hold. Engaging my biceps and core, I cross my legs together at the heel and lift myself up. A few pull-ups later and I fall into rhythm. When a slow burn rips through my arms, I drop from the bar and my feet hit the mat with a light slap. Stumbling back a foot or two, I am met with cheers from more than just the people in my small group.

Looking around the gym, almost every set of eyes is on me. The attention not lost on me. But in a place like this, I don't expect to be the center of attention. We are all here for the same purpose. Why am I the one on a pedestal? Other women here have more muscle mass than me.

Embarrassment heats and stains my cheeks as I mentally cower at the crowd of eyes on me.

I slide the grips off my hands, step away from the bar, and

go grab my water. I need a moment away from the crowd. Away from the countless pairs of eyes judging me. I gulp the water and wipe sweat from my brow, then return to the group and keep myself hidden in the back.

Max saunters beside the group, observing and coaching the current person on the bar. I don't remember hearing a word the entire time I was up there. *Did he not coach me?* Surely my form needs some tweaking. Yes, I have great upper body strength, but every one person needs direction.

"You were pretty amazing up there." I jolt as Max startles me. How long has he been next to me?

I try to play off the slight jump with arm stretches across my chest before I face him. "Thanks. I've been doing basics for years—running, biking, push-ups, pull-ups, sit-ups. Pretty religious about it."

"Well, it shows. Definitely appreciate anyone who takes care of themselves. So many people say they want to be healthier, but they want it handed to them on a silver platter. A lot of them don't want to put in the effort. They still want to eat the grease and trash, but look lean and strong."

I nod. His words couldn't be truer. Many women I have known over the years want to have their cake and eat it, too. "You sound like more than a fitness coach."

A smirk tugs at the corner of his mouth. "Because I am." He faces me and all I see are his vivid, green irises. They consume my vision, penetrate deep, and swallow me whole. But I snap out of my haze when he continues. "Health is my life. Practice what you preach, right?" My brow scrunches at his evasive answer. Confusion must register on my face. "I'm also a nutritionist/dietician. Exercise is great and all. But if you don't fuel your body with what it needs, it doesn't really matter, does it?"

His question seems rhetorical, but I nod anyway. After several beats of silence, he steps away and steps toward the front of the group. Strangely, the moment he stalks away, pain perforates my solar plexus. The sensation a minor blip on my radar. Almost indiscernible. An inexplainable spasm. Like an unexplored void beneath my sternum.

The remainder of the hour flies by. I do my best to focus on the workout and not the sight of Max. More than a few times, he stares at me. He attempts to play it off by telling the group how proper technique should look or feel. If you aren't conscious of accurate movement in specific muscles, your form should be corrected. As true as his words are, he uses them as a substitution for his visual perusal.

Honestly, though, being ogled is familiar and typical.

I get my bag from the locker room and exit the gym. Looking down at my wrist, I check the time. Still have time to shower before meeting up with Indigo and grabbing a quick bite before our evening. Just as I reach my driver's side door, a hand touches my shoulder.

I spin around, ready to beat whoever is behind me with my duffel bag, and spot Max with his hands up in surrender. "Sorry, didn't mean to startle you. I called your name, but I guess you didn't hear me."

He called out to me? Am I so lost in thought I didn't hear him? I need to snap the hell out of it. Now.

"Sorry, didn't hear you. Lost in thought. I'm meeting up with a friend soon."

"My fault. I tried to catch you before you came outside." I study him a moment as his hand pushes through the few inches of hair atop his head. "I wanted to see if you had any plans, but you already answered that question. Do you want to grab dinner sometime?"

So, I wasn't imagining things earlier. He had been observing me. Not simply for the sake of critiquing my technique. He had been checking me out. Openly. Which now has me questioning what everyone else in the group thought about said observation. The last thing I need is judgment. Or drama.

This is one of several reasons why I don't date. I don't do drama. And I definitely don't deal with judgment. I can't. Not in my life.

"As nice as that sounds, I'm going to decline. Thank you, though."

"*Seriously?*"

I stare him in the eyes. His face dead serious and his expression saying so much without speaking a word. He isn't mad. More like I bruised him, or perhaps his ego. Yes, Max is gorgeous. No doubt he has women throwing their panties at him on the regular. But I don't wear panties—for the most part—so that won't happen here.

"What's that supposed to mean?"

"I saw you check me out. Probably about as much as I did you. Can tell you're interested. Your body language speaks volumes." He cocks his head to the side and waits for me to respond.

Yes, every word he speaks is fact. I won't deny myself these truths. But I won't share that little tidbit with him. With every guy prior, history has proven relationships just don't work in my favor. Nothing will change with Max. It doesn't matter if the spark between us is something wholly new.

"As true as some of that may be, I don't do the dating game. Never works out."

"So, you're not denying it?" I shake my head and his voice stops me before I answer. "And you won't have dinner with me? What if I said we could grab a bite as friends? Not as a date."

"As nice as that sounds, when has a friendship between a man and a woman ever remained platonic? Next to never. Especially since I know you don't just want to be my friend. As flattering as the offer is, I'll pass."

I unlock the door to my truck and toss my bag across the bench seat before hopping in myself. I crank the window down and take in Max, actually seeing my vehicle for the first time. As with most men, he is entranced by the antique automobile.

"I never pegged you as a lover of classic cars."

I crank the ignition and see his eyes light up at the sexy rumble of the engine. "There's probably a lot about me that would surprise you."

"I won't deny that. But how will I ever know if I can't even have your friendship?"

This man will not give up easily. If even possible, his persistence makes him sexier. "I don't know. We'll have to wait and see where life leads us."

And then I drive off, staring at Max in my rearview mirror as his unmoving body grows smaller and smaller. Max is nothing short of delicious torture. Something to fuel my future fantasies. Someone who will be on my mind often. Which might be a problem. But I haven't decided yet.

CHAPTER 6

MAX

Tugging hard on my cock, I brace against the cold tile as hot water sprays down my spine. My imagination teeters back and forth between Tami working out in the gym yesterday—the contours of her body, her erection-inducing contortion during yoga, and sweat glistening in her cleavage—and Candy as she glided across the stage last night—perfect tits and perky, taut nipples, voluptuous ass, and a tight as sin waistline. One more jerk and my body convulses, releasing and splashing the tile with my seed.

Fuck. I need to get fucking laid. Again. Soon. As in yesterday.

My cock has a requisite. Is used to getting off—not via my palm—almost daily. But since laying eyes on Candy… *Fuck.* The last woman I wrestled in the sheets with—three days ago, to be exact—didn't cut it. She moaned my name at all the right times. Her tight pussy clenched my cock like a glove. But relief was nowhere in sight, even after I exploded inside her. And she was a smoking hot piece of ass. Although she didn't hold a candle to Candy, she was hot nonetheless.

What the ever-loving hell is happening with me?

Never has a woman gotten in my head like this. Ever. Maybe, just maybe, Tami is the distraction I need. Maybe she will give me the release I so desperately need. The one which will tame the beast between my legs. Tami is beyond gorgeous. She may not have every curve, peak, or valley Candy does, but she is pretty fucking close. And right now, close is going to have to fucking cut it.

Stepping out of the stall, I towel off and dress in a pair of basketball shorts and a tank. I towel dry my hair then toss the terry cloth in the laundry pile.

Giving myself a mental pep talk, I tell myself repeatedly I won't let Tami leave the gym today without agreeing to a date. Not that I actually want to *date* her. *Dating* isn't something I do. With any woman. Sure, I sweeten them up with dinner first, but the only reason I spend time with a woman is for the end result. What follows after dinner. My dick inside them. That is all. Nothing more.

Not to say I would never go back to the same woman twice, but they are conscious of my endgame. And if they aren't… not my problem. Several of the women I fucked reside on a secret list in my memory. A list reserved for the occasional repeat. Some of the sweetest faces, with the quietest demeanors, are the freakiest in the bedroom. As the old adage goes, never judge a book by its cover.

Kink makes sex even better, but not having a perverse bone in your body isn't a deal breaker for me when it comes to pussy. As long as a woman isn't clingy and she understands my motives, it is all good.

Leaving the locker room, I stroll around the gym, smiling and greeting several people who have been coming here longer than me. My level of respect for long-term patrons is tremendous. Gyms are a dime a dozen in the city, but these people choose this place because we give a damn. The smile I don and my word of thanks to each of them is one-hundred-percent genuine. Without them, my job wouldn't exist.

As I pass a group of guys doing deadlifts, I spot Tami. Exactly where she was yesterday with her body in pigeon pose. Her sports bra doesn't cover much as is, but I openly stare as her tits thrust forward while one of her ass cheeks juts out. And without any further aid, my dick hardens again.

Goddamnit.

Somehow, someway, Tami needs to agree to a date with me. If I have to act like a pussy to get her, at this point, I will fucking puss out. I suck in a deep breath—mentally telling my dick to chill the fuck out—and walk in her direction.

A few more steps, I recognize the moment she senses my proximity. Whether aware or not, her body instinctively reacts to my presence. Every damn time. A slight hesitation in her flow, stiffening of her spine or held breath. I notice every little move she makes.

She shifts poses and is now in a wide-angle fold, her legs spread, ass in the air, and bent at the waist. *Jesus fucking save me.*

An idea springs to mind as I approach her on the mat. "Mind if I join you? I haven't stretched yet."

Turning her head so she faces me, Tami eyes me a moment before gesturing to the space beside her. "Be my guest."

I go through my normal routine of stretching, eyeing her when the opportunity presents itself. After a few minutes pass, she finishes her warm-up and I take the opportunity to spark conversation.

"I notice you've been doing yoga as your warm-up each day. Did you previously take a class? You seem familiar with the flow of it all."

Sipping her water, she studies my face a beat. Her brow pinches as she reads and scrutinizes every captured detail. "I practiced yoga a couple years in college. I loved it, but didn't want to limit myself to only one form of exercise. Don't get me wrong, it does amazing things for the body, but I want more on top of it."

"So now you just mix it in with whatever other workout you're doing?"

"Yeah, I suppose so. It's great for keeping me limber. And I think many people don't realize how much strength or flexibility you actually need to do some of the poses. I compare yoga to three-dimensional, live art. I've seen yogis do astounding things with their body." Awe passes over her face as she recalls specific memories. Tami speaks with sincerity. And, unbeknownst to her, gave me a small piece of the Tami puzzle.

"If yoga isn't your main form of exercise, what else do you do? Besides starting CrossFit?"

I keep her talking. Show her how interested I am in *her*—not just her body, but also her mind. Because the truth is what it is. Of course, I still itch to trace every inch of her skin with my fingertips, but that isn't the only reason she intrigues me.

Something else about Tami sparks my curiosity. Calls out to me in barely audible whispers, but remains hidden in the background. I have no clue what the hell it is, though.

What I do know is whenever Tami steps in proximity of my internal radar, a low-frequency vibration sets off in my bloodstream. A low hum. A wild current of energy on the cusp of explosion.

I don't understand the buzz, can't grasp what it means, but something about Tami makes me feel more alive. Baffles me. Makes me question myself.

But what perplexes me most? The fact I never want the zeal to disappear.

"I do a lot of running. On average, I run five days a week. Probably around five miles each run. Other than that—push-ups, pull-ups, core work, biking. Pretty much anything I can do without major equipment."

"Pretty impressive. Honestly don't know many women who can do half that. Hope you feel what you're doing here is valuable. We do a lot of what you just said, but it's all about growing from point A to point B, whatever those points are for you. Really, they're just a measure of each person's individual goals."

I do, and don't, want to keep talking exercise with her. On one hand, she seems at ease with this line of conversation with me. Openly talking and letting me in. On the other hand, I yearn to know other aspects of her, physically and otherwise.

Question is… how do I transition from professional conversation to personal and intimate? This type of exchange isn't something I do with women. With most women, I have one item on the agenda. Fucking them. Genuine conversations excluded.

I won't deny fucking Tami is one of the top items on my to-do list, but there is something different about her. And it drives me insane. Scrambles my thoughts.

Her presence alone lights me on fire. The closer I physically get to her, the hotter the flame. The idea of touching her, *really* touching her… I shake my head as a volcanic river pulses under my skin. To trace my fingertips down her skin from the hollow of her throat to her navel. Skim the edge of her panties. Inhale her delicious pheromones…

Bam! My cock springs to attention.

As I finish the last of my stretches, she responds to my

compliment under her breath. "Thanks. I'm sure there are plenty of women here much more impressive than me."

The group gathers their belongings and heads for the exit. Tami is off to the side with the strap of her duffel across her body as she stashes her water bottle and retrieves her keys. An idea strikes. Something we can discuss other than exercise.

I sidle up beside her. "Great job today. How are you feeling?"

Catching her breath, she answers, "Good, thanks. Never realized how intense CrossFit was, but I think it's exactly what I've needed."

"Glad to hear. Can I walk you out?"

Confusion mars her face, and her eyes beg to ask why. But surprisingly, she doesn't. "Yeah, sure."

I let her lead the way, enjoying the view as I pull up the rear. As soon as we step outside, the warm, summer air sticks to our sweaty skin. I shield my eyes from the sun and inch closer to her. When her truck comes into view, I take the chance at starting a more personal discussion. "So, what inspired you to own a classic?" I point toward the baby-teal-colored pickup truck.

She glances at me with a heartfelt smile brightening her face. "Honestly, I have no idea. I saw Tiff one day—"

"Tiff?"

She laughs. "Yeah, Tiff. As in Tiffany." Her stride falters as she stares at me. As if I should know the reason behind the name. But I have no fucking idea. Finally, she relieves my misery. "As in Tiffany blue. The iconic color used by the jeweler that has been around since the early to mid-1800s. Please tell me you've heard of them?"

The faux-shock on her face right now is fucking adorable. A mix of serious and making fun of me. It takes every ounce of strength to not drag out the moment. To see if she will figure out some other way to tease me. But I won't. Because as much as I long for this blip of time to continue, I also want to provoke other parts of her. Parts she can't ignore.

"Yes, I'm fully aware of Tiffany's. Not that I'm a frequent patron of their business."

"Well thank god for that. I was psyching myself up for how exactly to explain a legendary store. Maybe another time." She tips her head back and laughs; the chortle a direct line to my aching balls. And for a beat, I memorize the infectious resonance. How it settles in places I didn't know existed inside me.

"Well, Tiff is a fine motor vehicle. And the way she sounds, you must take great care of her."

She beams from ear to ear. And for a blink, I lose myself in the dark green rims of her hazels. They shimmer and stir up an odd sensation in my chest. A gravity I relish and fear in unison.

"I appreciate the sentiment. It's not easy owning a vehicle that hasn't been manufactured for over sixty years. They don't make 'em like they used to."

"I'll second that." We reach her truck. Her fingers guide the key into the lock and twist before she opens the door. Time speeds up as she slips in and rolls down her window. But I'm not ready for her to leave yet. "Tami, please reconsider my offer. Have dinner with me."

Her fingers flex around the steering wheel before she meets my gaze. The corner of her mouth tics as a hint of a smile plays on her lips. "I wish I could, but I've got plans. Sorry."

"Do you have plans *every* day?"

A smirk tugs at the corner of her mouth as she shrugs. "What can I say, I'm a busy lady. You'll just have to keep trying. Perhaps one day, I won't be so tied up."

My thoughts dive headfirst into the fucking gutter—not an abnormality. Visions of her bound to my bed filter in—wrists and ankles knotted to the four posts, eyes shielded with a blindfold, body writhing for my cock, mouth begging for my touch.

Fuck, fuck, fuck.

At least I'll have a new visual when I step into the shower later.

"Well, I suppose I'll have to ask you every day going forward."

She throws the truck in reverse. A toothy smile plumps her flushed cheeks. "I look forward to it."

And then she drives away. Leaving me in the parking lot. Just me, my hard-on, and a million new fantasies.

The only way I know to forget Tami is to see Candy. At this point, I have no clue which I am addicted to more. Both of them stunning. Both of them seemingly unattainable. Because of Candy's profession, I don't doubt for a second she gets propositioned. Often. Probably heard every reason under the sun for why they want time with her.

My reasons would be nothing new.

What did I actually know about Candy? Nothing except what my eyes told me.

She has an incredible body—one she spent countless hours perfecting. She wears colorful wigs (I haven't seen the same wig twice) to disguise her true identity outside the walls of P.I.

I suppose, for some women, disguises come with the job. A façade to mask what they do so they can maintain a private life. Never know who might see you in public or, better yet, who might follow you home. Male or female, the idea is terrifying.

No sense in denying I am hot for Candy—and Tami—but I would never follow a woman. Once you earn creep or stalker status, no woman will step within one-hundred-feet of you. Not to mention it fucks up any chance at having a career. The stalker/predator stamp is a one-way ticket to a sexless and lonely life.

When it comes to Tami... I can't peg that mysterious woman down. Everything in her body language—the flux of her voice, the way her body gravitates in my direction, how her breathing spikes and eyes dilate—screams attraction. But she fights it, tooth and nail. Her denial perplexes me. Perhaps her past keeps her from trusting anyone or moving forward. Or every guy she dated was a prick, like me, and only wanted a good fuck before ghosting her. Fuck if I know.

All I know is she has taken up permanent residence in my head.

Yes, she is the perfect visual for when I need to blow off steam. No lie—I get off time after time with her front and center. Tami is attainable, and not in the same breath. She plays hard to get just to see if I truly want *her* for more than what lies between her legs.

The more she plays, the more I ache for her.

And for the first time in my fucking life, I have no fucking clue what to do.

Which leads to my current situation. At the same table in

P.I., alone. Beer in hand while I bounce my knee and wait for Candy to take the stage. Only she holds the power to distract me now.

My eyes hunger to roam her silky skin. To follow her lines and curves as she dances. To salivate over the fantasy of sucking her nipples between my teeth. Daydream about her breasts smashed to my chest. Flesh to flesh in a mess of heat and sweat and limbs.

As if the heavens hear my plea, the lights dim down. The occasional flicker of candlelight the only illumination in the club. Then the emcee announces her.

An upbeat, seductive song silences those still sharing conversation. The stage curtains part enough to see her silhouette. Her body glides forward in the darkness as the curtains shut behind her. A stage light sparks to life and beams across her backside as it faces the crowd.

As if practiced, the audience audibly gasps in unison—me included. Her hair every confectionery color ever created—hot pink, brilliant orange, bold teal, sunflower yellow, chartreuse, and a striking violet. She wears a one-piece—a corset and boy short combo—which consists of fabric strips caging her torso. And when she faces the audience, I eye her head to toe. A single one-inch strip hides each of her nipples and apex. I swallow hard, and adjust myself. Her attire is not the reason everyone gasps. Every inch of her skin shimmers from a thin layer of body glitter. The sparkle from each fleck accentuates every arch and swell and bow of her body more.

I follow her as she drifts across the stage. My eyes locked on her every move and I lose myself. The exact reason I came here tonight.

A topless server stops at my table, my gaze still on the stage, and asks if I need a refill or want any other services. I decline another beer, but ask about the additional services. And that's when life shifts. The moment I learn about paid lap dances.

Other clubs offer lap dances, but I hadn't assumed the same for P.I. The women and clientele here are not your average strip club crowd. I don't doubt they told us about the additional services when Nic and I purchased memberships, but I zoned out after seeing Candy and heard none of it. Now, though, I slap myself for not doing this sooner.

I pay to receive a dance from Candy. The server closes my tab and directs me to a separate area of the club. The space still visible, through thin layers of material, to the main floor.

How did I not see this before?

The server directs me to a bench, tells me to wait, and Candy will arrive momentarily. She reminds me I am not allowed to touch her with my hands, arms, face, mouth, or anything the dancer deems uncomfortable. If I disobey, I will be escorted from the club. Not even allowed to return to The Sophisticate.

I wipe damp palms on my thighs and silently scream at my cock to calm the fuck down. My knee bounces as I sit on the cool black leather. My breath more erratic than a teenage boy getting off for the first time.

Calm the fuck down.

The sheer curtains at the entrance part and I spot a head of colorful hair. The way she ambles in my direction—the sway of her hips, her silhouette against the colorful lights, the way she carries herself—feels oddly familiar, but I dismiss it and mentally prepare myself for what will happen next.

Candy stands feet from me, no longer nude. A baby pink, silk baby-doll negligee clings to her breasts. The soft material barely covers her nipples, drifts down her torso and stops at the junction of her thighs. She inches closer and I notice how the swoop of her bangs masks her brows and one of her eyes.

I hiss when she crawls on the bench, slides a leg over one of mine, then the other, and straddles me.

"Hey there, handsome." Her voice is liquid cotton candy. Pure, sweet, sugary, and mouthwatering.

I swallow hard and try to lock eyes with her as she evades the action. A buzz surges in my bloodstream. It starts as a low simmer before zinging through my fingers and toes, limbs, and core before a volt shoots to my cock. Music plays all around us, but I don't hear it. A strange sensation flickers in my chest—a foreign, yet familiar warmth—and I attempt to shake it off.

Tonight is about Candy.

The distraction of her over me, pulsing and gyrating and giving me a gift I will not soon forget. She rises from my lap, faces away and bends at the waist. Pure male heaven smacks me in the face and I refuse to look away. Her fingers glide up her legs before she straightens, slides her hands up her sides, and lifts the negligee over her head.

Facing me again, my jaw drops and I am dumbstruck. No words. Not one. Breathless. Speechless.

Candy stands completely bare a foot away from me. Her body sways and rolls to the beat of the music I have yet to hear since she walked in my direction. Her legs straddle mine again, her arms rest on the back of the bench behind me, her body rubs against mine in a pulsating rhythm. A rhythm which could get me off in seconds.

Before I breathe a normal breath, her glorious tits smother me. Circle my mouth with such intensity, I almost give in to temptation and wrap my lips around them. But somehow, I manage to restrain myself like a good little boy. Honestly, I have no idea where I unearth the strength to resist temptation. Perhaps the desire for more has me on good behavior.

Just as my cock reaches the cusp of release, she pops up from my lap, bends forward, and presses her lips to the shell of my ear. "It's been fun, handsome. Hope I get to see you again." She nips my earlobe with her teeth, biting with gentle force before suckling a second. My cock jumps at the contact then cries at the loss. Her ass shakes side to side as she saunters off.

Holy fucking shit.

Top priority—a cold fucking shower. Now.

CHAPTER 7

TAMI

I turn and jog down the street to my apartment; the summer sun licks my skin and evaporates some of the sweat. Briefly, I tip my head back and absorb the beautiful, cloudless day. Perfect weather to lay out and tan. The idea lingers as I slow to a fast walk a block before home. And before long, I commit to the idea after a bite to eat.

I unlock and open the door, and all but ram into Amber as she blazes past me.

"Where you headed?"

"David wants to go to the beach. It's such a nice day. Plan to picnic and hang out for a few hours. Want to tag along?"

A hopeful glint crosses her face and a pang amplifies in my solar plexus. It's difficult to pinpoint why it bothers me. The sensation resonates deep, surrounded by marrow.

Does she want me to tag along so she can play peacemaker between the two of us? This would be nothing new. Or is she not wanting to be alone with David? Has he done something to make her uncomfortable? God, I hope not. At times, David is difficult to read.

I love the idea of hanging with Amber at the beach, but I don't want to spend time near David. Something about him makes me antsy and churns my stomach. I haven't been able to narrow it down, but I can't shake the feeling. Around him, it seems as if I can't inhale a full breath.

"Thanks for the invite, but I've got a few things to do. Maybe next time. Keep me in the loop, yeah?"

"Sure thing." She tosses her beach bag over her shoulder and heads for the door. "See ya later, T."

"Bye. Have fun!"

As soon as the door lock engages, I yank off my sweaty clothes. When I have the apartment to myself, I tend to wander in my birthday suit.

I throw my clothes in the hamper, head back to the kitchen and grab a protein shake, a bowl of diced fruit, and head for the patio off my bedroom. One of the best parts about being on the third floor of our building... top floor. And none of the buildings nearby stand as tall or taller.

I step out on the oversized balcony, nothing between my skin and the sun, set a towel on the lounger and bask in the sunlight. I snag the paperback I always leave next to my lounger and get lost in the words.

Four lengthy chapters later, my skin simmers from head to toes—partly from the sun, partly from the saucy scenes in the romance novel.

"Going forward, I need something less erotic while I sunbathe," I mumble to myself.

Back inside, I jump in a cooler than normal shower and do a quick rinse before I go to the gym. As my hands run down my body, my mind wanders. My head and body hot from the sex scene I read moments ago.

Fingers dip between my legs. Within seconds, I get lost in a world of sensation and succumb to my arousal. Two fingertips circle and flick and add pressure to my swollen clit. I prop my foot on the tub ledge as the water beats along my spine.

"So close," I mutter. My eyes roll closed as an image of Max flits across the back of my eyelids. *Circle, circle.* The same two fingers dip inside as I tilt my hips forward. My free hand glides up my abdomen, clutches a fleshy breast and squeezes my nipple.

My breath comes in short bursts as a new form of heat pierces my skin and spreads like a forest fire. I pinch my nipple harder as my body peaks and clenches my fingers. The orgasm explodes in a violent rush. Has me lightheaded and whimpering. My legs tremble and I grab the inset shelf to stay upright. Slickness coats my fingers as satisfaction tingles in my veins.

I drop my foot from the ledge, brace both hands on the cool tile, and work to calm my ragged breathing. I let the water douse and cool me a minute before I exit and get ready to see real-life Max. Not sure what it is about him—the slight asshole persona, how he carries himself, the tattoos on his upper arms and chest, or how he engages me like he hasn't craved anyone else before.

Whatever the reason, his attraction for me burns white hot. The closer he is, the hotter it burns. A flame I thought extinguished years ago. What is it about Max that sets me on fire? What has me *almost* willing to ignore my no-dating rule?

Wish I had the answers.

Dressed, I toss the duffel over my shoulder and jog down the stairs to Tiff, waving to one of the neighbors as I drive off. My thoughts swirl in a hot spirographic mess of emotions. Before I get to the gym, I need clarity. Before I walk through those doors, I need to set my head straight.

Fingers crossed, the effort won't all crumble away the moment I see Max.

At a red light, I flip on the radio, connect my phone via Bluetooth, and hit shuffle on my favorite playlist. Tiff may be a 1955 classic Ford F100, but she has been fully refurbished—still classy, yet modern. When the light turns green, I set my phone down and get carried away with the music.

The long drive flies by and soon I steer into the lot with one of my favorites by The Weeknd blaring through the speakers. Before I cut the engine, I crank up my window. I glance across the lot and spot Max staring in my direction. I give a cordial wave and smile. But he just stands there, head cocked as his sunglasses-covered eyes study me.

My chest tightens. My breath shallow and nowhere near enough. Something in this exact moment feels… *off.*

Does he know? Not a chance. Right?

Slipping out of my truck, I take my things and head over to where he still stands like a statue. The closer I get to him, the more his posture shifts. An *I know something you don't know* smile lights up his face. His eyes still shielded behind his tinted lenses.

There is no possible way he knows. Not a chance in hell. Just do you, Tami.

"Hey. This your ride?" I ask, pointing at a sexy as hell black car.

He glances over his shoulder and stares at the car a moment. "Yeah, I had to come out and grab my water bottle. Interesting choice of music." He points toward my truck.

What was playing? I drop my eyes to my phone, light up the screen and check which song had been playing. When I read the track title, a million thoughts pass through my head. Is it the crude lyrics? He doesn't peg me as someone who would be bothered by expletives. Actually, the more I stand here and ponder the reason why, it is probably something simple. He likes the song.

Shrugging, I answer, "I pretty much like all music. What I listen to depends on my mood that day."

He cocks his head again as the corner of his mouth twitches. "So, you're feeling like a little vixen today, huh?" A mischievous grin spreads across his face and it sparks the kindling in my core.

Is he flirting with me? Seems to be the case. Well, if that's how he wants to play this, I have no problem entertaining him.

"Honestly, my vixen tries to make an appearance every day. Sometimes she just needs a little inspiration."

I start walking toward the gym entrance, leaving him to trail behind me and watch me as I go. I don't know exactly what lit the match inside me. Maybe something to do with yesterday. Perhaps it has something to do with the fact I haven't had sex with someone other than my hand or BOB in far too long. Or better yet… maybe it is the simple fact I know something he doesn't and I hold the upper hand.

All the way to the door, I give him a show he won't soon forget. When I hit the mat inside, I immediately begin my warm-up routine. I make sure to bend and contort myself in all the perfect positions for his torturous viewing pleasure.

Class starts a few minutes after I finish and leaves neither of us time to trade any further banter. But I have plenty more in my arsenal and am ready to tease him for a torturous length of time.

Throughout the session, I manage to find every possible way to pop out my curves. I wait to see if he will correct my form when I intentionally set my back or limbs in the wrong placement. But he doesn't.

Does he not see my form? He has to. I know him better than he knows me. Kind of.

Class ends and I chug my water as everyone heads out. Soon, I grab my things and follow suit. Just as my feet leave the mat, a hand wraps around my bicep and halts me. I spin around to catch Max holding me. His vivid green eyes smolder with an unspoken statement. I drop my eyes from his, glance to where his hand grips me, then meet his once more. He unwraps his fingers when I narrow my eyes.

"Can I talk with you a moment?" he asks.

"Yeah, sure. What's up?"

"Walk with me." His words more a statement than a question before he saunters toward the office.

Following in his wake, he opens the door, steps inside the office and gestures for me to do the same. Before I get a word in edgewise, the lock on the door engages and he closes the blinds facing the gym. I have no idea why he brought me in here, but it is not as if thirty plus people didn't see us come in here.

Unsure of what to say, or why I'm here, I start at the bottom of the totem pole. "Everything okay?"

He tilts his head to the side and studies me a moment. His brilliant bottle-green eyes alight with mischief. A smirk toying with the corner of his lips. "Was that fun?"

Confused, I follow up with a question. "Was what fun?"

"You know what I'm talking about. Don't play coy with me."

"Actually, I have no clue what you're talking about. You whisk me in here, lock the door, and shut out any potential onlookers. I really don't know *what* to think right now."

"So, you're going to stand there and pretend like you didn't just spend the last hour pushing your tits out. Or flaunting your ass in my face. *Seriously?* I pegged you as smarter than that."

For a breath, I relish in the fact all my attempts at being seductive and flirtatious worked. That I got under his skin. That he *had* been watching me, noticeably or not, throughout class. But the last words to exit his mouth have me backpedaling. Did he just call me an idiot?

"Excuse me?"

"You heard me. Not sure if you were putting that show on for me or someone else. But if it *was* for me, all you had to do was ask, sweetheart. As much as I enjoyed watching you toy with me, all you had to do was ask for my attention and I would've gladly given it to you."

As much as I enjoy how he couldn't keep his eyes off me, I suddenly feel turned off by his over-confident, self-assured cockiness. His behavior just as much a turn-off as a turn-on.

I spin on my heel and step toward the door. "Fuck you."

"I know you want to, sweetheart. Like I said, all you have to do is ask."

Does he think I don't know what he does most nights of the week? That he is a player with one goal.

"That's just it. I don't want to ask."

"Well, I'm not going to beg for it. You can count on that."

Before grabbing the handle, I turn to face him. "We'll see about that, *sweetheart.*" And then I walk out without another word.

He has no clue I have an advantage up my sleeve. He doesn't realize I know about his evening rendezvous in the dimly lit floor of a certain night club. That I know his tastes and desires better than he does. Know exactly what he wants. Because in the dim lights of the nightclub, he has no control.

CHAPTER 8

MAX

If I seriously have to watch her stick her ass out one more time, I will lose my shit.

Just as the thought crosses my mind, she starts doing burpees. Her hands hit the floor, feet kick back, body tight as hell in plank position. As I restrain myself from staring at her, she brings her feet back to her hands, bends at the waist for longer than necessary, and stands with her ass upright for all to see. My dick twitches in my shorts and I mentally tell it to settle the fuck down.

Before I realize what is happening, she pops up, jumps, and lands on the floor with a thud. Her tits jiggle in her tight as fuck sports bra and I groan. As much as I appreciate every one of her curves, seeing them now is a new form of hell. Sex deprivation hell.

This happens another twenty-four times. I try to avoid ogling the show she puts on, but then I realize I am not the only voyeur. The guy I pretend to assist, Jack, is equally distracted by the view. My eyes scan the gym and I count six more sets of eyes glued to Tami's tits and ass.

As the group continues going through the routine, I make a larger effort to put myself on the opposite side of everyone. Trying to grant myself a visual buffer. At times, it works. But not the entire time.

And then something shifts.

Tami wanders over to a set of parallel bars, lifts herself up, and maneuvers like a gymnast. Being on the bars isn't part of our lineup, but I don't interrupt her. Watching her glide between the bars like she has done it years—over and under, twirling in a routine only she knows—mesmerizes me. Her movements continuous and fluid. *Is she a gymnast?* Not quite sure what this visual display is, but it seems less technical and more provocative with each twist or turn.

After her time on the parallel bars, I zone out for the rest of class. Something niggles me in the back of my mind. Every time I look at Tami, it feels as if I know her. Really *know* her. Déjà vu washes over me and I can't explain the reasoning. The way she shakes her hips, the way she acts and carries herself— it strikes something in me, besides my dick.

I spend the remainder of class time trying not to look in her direction. Instead, I distract myself with thoughts of Candy. About seeing her later. Perhaps paying for another lap dance. The visual distraction I need. Actually, what I need is to get laid. *Fuck.* How many days has it been now? Five, at least. Which is a goddamn lifetime for me.

Every woman, since setting eyes on Candy—and Tami, for that matter—doesn't seem to fulfill the ravenous hunger growing inside me. My balls ache, feeling bluer than the Pacific, and probably just as cold to be completely honest.

The last woman I fucked—Trish, I think, but couldn't care less if it's not—was merely a warm blow-up doll. She moaned at all the right times, screamed my name too many times with overenthusiasm for me to believe she actually got off. Not like I really care anyway. To my recollection, no other woman pant-screamed *yes* that many times during sex. As if she had secret aspirations to be a porn star. And let's be real here... the only reason I came was because I fantasized about Candy and her tight-ass body. Hell, I almost belted her name when I came.

I need relief before my balls shrivel up and die. So, I have to make another play at Tami.

Tami is not the extraordinary woman I have developed an unhealthy obsession ogling a few nights a week. But she ranks in a close enough league that I no longer give a fuck.

Class wraps up and everyone makes their way out. Now is the perfect opportunity to make my move. She picks up her water and starts for the exit.

Reaching forward, I grip her bicep and stop her from leaving. When her eyes meet mine, I swear they heat for a split-second before they shift to where my hand holds her. As our eyes meet again, I drop my hand. Her eyes ask me what the hell I want.

"Can I talk with you a moment?"

"Yeah, sure. What's up?" Her tone nonchalant.

I don't want to have this conversation in the middle of a crowd. "Walk with me." More a command than a request. Because I don't have time for any more games.

I lead us to the gym office, close the door behind us, twist the lock and shut the blinds. From an outsider's perspective, it wouldn't surprise me if people think I brought Tami in here to fuck her. I give two shits what other people think, though.

She crosses her arms over her chest, clamps down on her biceps and closes herself off to me. "Is everything okay?"

I simply stare at her a moment and try to get a read on what her endgame is. As good as I usually am at reading people, her mood is indecipherable right now. So, I opt for a different card in the deck, remembering her little charade out there earlier. "Was that fun?"

Her brows pinch together. "Was what fun?"

So, this is how she plans to play the game. "You know what I'm talking about. Don't play coy with me."

Her response quicker than I expect. "Actually, I have no clue what you're talking about. You whisk me in here, lock the door and shut out any potential onlookers. I really don't know *what* to think right now."

Is she playing hard to get? Can't be sure. "So, you're going to stand there and pretend like you didn't just spend the last hour pushing your tits out. Or flaunting your ass in my face. *Seriously?* I pegged you as smarter than that." She has to be pulling my leg. How can she not know why I pulled her aside?

A flash of amusement lights her eyes, but then fades just as quickly. "Excuse me?"

"You heard me. Not sure if you were putting that show on for me or someone else. But if it *was* for me, all you had to do was ask, sweetheart. As much as I enjoyed watching you toy with me, all you had to do was ask for my attention and I would've gladly given it to you."

As horny as I am right now, I will find a glory hole to get off if necessary. I just need some goddamn relief from the ache in my balls. Personally, I would rather her be my form of relief.

Obviously, I said something to piss her off because she spins to face the door and walks away from me. "Fuck you."

I can't help myself. "I know you want to, sweetheart. Like I said, all you have to do is ask."

She halts in place. "That's just it. I don't want to ask."

Stand your ground, Max. Keep the upper hand. "Well, I'm not going to beg for it. You can count on that."

She turns to face me, and mischief twinkles in her eyes. "We'll see about that, *sweetheart*." And then she disappears out the door.

Goddamn. Son of a bitch. Motherfucker.

Do not go after her, Max. Do. Not. Fucking. Do. It.

Three deep breaths later, I bolt from the office and jog out into the hot, sunny Saturday air. My eyes sweep the parking lot and spot her getting into her truck at the far end. I jog over to her, hoping to catch her before she drives away.

"Tami!" I wave in her direction. "Wait! Please."

I don't know when I became such a *please and thank you* bitch, but apparently it happened.

She catches sight of me running toward her and shakes her head. Her eye roll visible from a distance. "What is it that you want, Max?" Irritation laces her voice, but I ignore it.

"Sorry. I don't know what came over me in there."

Where the hell did that come from? Fucking pussy.

"Apology accepted." A small smile graces her plump lips.

Resting my hands on the open frame of her window, I toss out another attempt at getting on her good side. "Sometimes I lose all sense of focus when you're around. And with you bending and jumping in there… let's just say you probably put every male in a stupor today."

She tilts her head to one side and studies me with her eyes hidden behind her large-framed sunglasses. Like she is searching for something which may or may not be there. A devious grin slowly stretches her face. And the length of time she remains silent makes me more uncomfortable by the minute.

Finally, she decides to bless me with some form of verbalization. "Well, well, well. If I didn't know any better, I'd say what's happening right now is your version of begging." A chuckle resonates in her throat.

My blood heats as I realize how right she is. "What can I say?" I shrug. "Guess I didn't quite know the power you held over men." My words meant to be flirtatious and I hope she regards them as such.

She faces forward and nods as a soft laugh leaves her lips. Instantly, I imagine what she would look like with her head bobbing over my cock. But I snap out of my daydream when I hear her mumble what sounds like "power to the pussy", but can't be certain.

"Sorry, what?" I ask, wondering if she will repeat herself.

"Nothing. Was just thinking out loud."

She loses focus as her eyes stare off at nothing in particular and her lips plump in a sultry pout. Seeing her profile like this, with the sun beating from above and the wind blowing the baby hairs around her face, I can't help but take stock in how absolutely stunning she is.

Before I register what I am doing, my lips move of their own accord and words I never thought I would say leak out. "Tami, I'd really love to get together and have dinner with you. Sorry I was an ass earlier. I can't help it sometimes."

It is official. My dick now speaks for the rest of me.

"Can't tonight." Her words break my degradation. "I have plans already."

She didn't say no. Thank fuck! "No problem. How about tomorrow night?"

Behind her tinted lenses, I see her eyes peek up. "Tomorrow should be fine, if that works for you."

"Tomorrow is good. I know this amazing little Italian place not far from here. I can pick you up or we can meet there.

Whichever you prefer." I silently plea for her to ask me to pick her up, my chances of getting laid higher with that prospect.

"Sounds delicious. I'll meet you there, if that's okay? Mondays always start early for me, so it'll probably be better in the long run."

Her words deflate my chances of getting laid, but I keep telling myself that date one leads to date two. I won't make the same offer next go around.

"No problem. Do you have your phone handy? I'll give you my number and text you with the time and address. The place is pretty low-key and relaxed."

She hands me her phone and I input my contact info, sending a text from her phone to mine afterward. When I hand it back to her, she smiles and throws her truck into reverse. "See you tomorrow, *sweetheart*." A gorgeous smile lights up her face.

I might have a snowball's chance in hell of fucking her tomorrow, but that sure as shit isn't going to stop me from trying.

CHAPTER 9

TAMI

Taking the day off from any form of exercise, I opt to lay out on my patio and soak up as many rays as possible. The sky a perfect shade of blue today. With only a few clouds floating across the sky now and then. I glance down the midline of my body where my olive skin darkens little by little. I decide to flip on my stomach to avoid any chance of redness. Luckily, sunburns almost never happen thanks to my Italian mother.

And although I told myself I wouldn't read anymore smutty romance books while I was stripped bare and baked in the sunlight, I can't help myself. Women love romance novels —so why shy away? Besides, I have never worried about anyone spotting me nude on my lounger. What difference does it make if I lay out here, in all my glory, read a chapter of steamy romance, and take care of myself?

As if on cue, I turn the page and read how the hero and heroine can no longer keep their hands to themselves. I devour every last word of the scene, flip over on the cushions and slide my free hand between my thighs. The page describes length and girth and hardness, and how the hero continues to tease her opening. I close my eyes for a beat and Max flashes across my closed lids.

I imagine his breath hot on my neck as he stands behind me. *Circle.* I imagine one of his arms wrapped around my waist as the other hand latches on my breast and pinches my nipple. *Circle, circle.* Imagine his hand gliding down my abdomen, dipping between my thighs as he coats his fingers with my arousal and rubs my clit. *Circle, circle, dip.*

My daydream wanders deeper. Fantasizing about his hands, his mouth, his cock. How they would worship me. How they would trace and lick and consume my body. Rough and animalistic. And with that fantasy dancing in my head, my orgasm swallows me and leaves me gasping for oxygen. Heat ripples in waves across my skin.

Slipping my bookmark in place, I set the book down and stare at my hand as it pumps between my thighs. Honestly, it has been far too long since I last had sex. And I can easily have sex with Max tonight. Without hesitation. But I want to make him work for it. Really work for it. I may not be the prize every man thinks I am, but I know my worth.

I lose myself in my fantasy once more, promising to get up and start getting ready soon. Shutting the world around me away, I picture Max's hot, sweaty body at the gym. The cocky grin he wears on his face as he ogles my body. Without much effort, he inundates every thought I own—him, us, what could be—and my body detonates again. For a while, I lay like a limp noodle in a lust haze with an unfading smile.

Standing at the vanity in my bathroom, I dry my hair and add product to help tame the frizz which will inevitably make an appearance if I don't. Done with my hair, I step into a pair of fire-engine-red lace panties and snap the matching strapless bra into place. I may have already decided not to sleep with Max tonight, but that doesn't mean I can't feel like a brazen goddess when we are together.

I zip up the back of the dress which bears the same fiery color as my lingerie. A devilish smile stretches my cheeks tight as I run my eyes over my ensemble. There is no way he will be able to resist me all evening. Heat simmers low in my belly as I close my eyes a moment.

Back in the bathroom, I add a touch of makeup to highlight my natural tones and a hint of nude gloss. After a quick spritz of perfume, I slip on a pair of black heels, grab my clutch, and head out the door.

After plugging the address for the restaurant in my phone, I back out and let the map guide me through the city. Traffic is lighter than typical as I drive the streets of Los Angeles. The less than crazy commute garners me little time to mentally prep for the evening. Years have passed since my last date. Years.

Driving on autopilot, I flashback to the last guy I went out on a date with—Benny.

Benny was smoking hot. Like a rock god. His hair ink-black; long enough to spike but not too long. His arms sleeved in tattoos and a piercing in the corner of his lower lip that begged me to suck it. He said the dirtiest things to me when we had sex, which turned me on immeasurably, and knew how to use his tongue as if his life depended on it.

But sexy as sin wasn't the only thing Benny had going for him. Nope. After we had seen each other a couple months, he started acting strange. As if a switch flipped inside him. I had always been into all kinds of play in the bedroom, but the first time he cuffed me to the bed and left me there for eight hours straight (he literally left my apartment), I decided it was time we went our separate ways.

That didn't sit so well with him. He started following me everywhere and threatened to beat the shit out of anyone who looked at me in any way he deemed unworthy. He would bang on the door at four in the morning, drunk off his ass and screaming for me to let him in.

Needless to say, I had to file a restraining order and carry mace on the regular. It just goes to show, never judge someone by their outward appearance. It took a couple months for Benny to flip the way he did. To this day, I still have no idea what triggered the whole one-eighty nor do I care.

Benny is at the top of the list—as far as reasons go—as to why I don't date. Going through that experience... let's just say I never care to encounter a repeat.

And until this moment, I hadn't realized how attracted I am to men with tattoos. Huh? Until now, I had totally forgotten about Benny's tattoos.

I park my truck in the lot of Angelo's Italian Bistro and check my appearance in the mirror before I step out of my truck. Thankfully, my hair is still behaving itself. Dropping my keys in my clutch, I walk toward the entrance and spot Max encased in dim light under an awning, strands of tiny, twinkling lights dangle above him.

His head down as he focuses on his phone. He hasn't seen me yet. Hasn't caught me observing him. I take a minute to absorb his non-I'm-trying-to-impress-this-woman appearance.

Dressed in all black, he looks sharp. Mouthwatering. The perfect complement to his warm, light brown skin. Black slacks and a button-down, the top two buttons left undone. His tight curls tamer than usual as the golden tones accentuate the darker ones more under the lighting.

As if he senses me standing here, staring at him, he peers up and locks onto me in the darkness. I smile and amble in his direction, stopping inches away from him.

"You look stunning," he states with a hint of undertone.

"Thank you. You look pretty handsome yourself."

He slips an arm around my waist, and it glides down to rest on the small of my back as we walk inside. We step up to the hostess and Max tells her our reservation. It is not lost on me when she ogles the length of his body then sneers in my direction. The disgust in her eyes does strange things to me. Evokes unfamiliar emotions in my chest.

And without thinking, I rotate in Max's grip and face him. I skim a hand across his chest as I lean in and whisper, "I don't know why I waited so long to agree to this."

My words are innocent, but the display is anything but. He faces me with a smile bright enough to light a city block. He chuckles. "Some things are worth the wait, baby."

The hostess rolls her eyes, yanks the laminated menus from the holder and barks at us to follow her. She seats us in a back corner of the restaurant with only two other tables within five feet of ours. Secluded and not at the same time. When the server arrives at the table, we order a bottle of wine, a bruschetta appetizer, and our meals.

We talk with ease, discussing work and what we enjoy doing outside of those hours. There is still no doubt in my mind Max believes he holds the title of a Greek god—and let's be honest, I could stare at him for hours and not be sick of him.

But something else lies there. Deep. Hidden. Something magnetic. Gravitational. Electric. I could stand in the middle of a thousand people and I would *feel* Max nearby. His aura is that potent.

But he is a player. Not a trait someone drops with the snap of a finger. So, for now, I plan to keep things simple. Leave out the possibility of crazy and heartache. Because I can't handle them. Not now. Not ever.

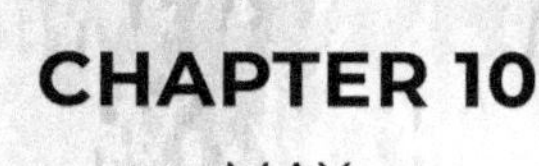

CHAPTER 10

MAX

Arriving at the restaurant ten minutes early, I opt to stand under the awning by the entrance and wait for Tami. Unlocking my phone, I scan through emails and respond to a few while I wait. Finished, I text Nic and tell him I finally scored a night out with Tami. His response... *I hope you get laid, bro.* I laugh. *Me too.*

A quick scan of the lot and still no sign of Tami. So, I scroll through social media. Same old shit, new post. Honestly, the only reason I maintain accounts is for work.

Just as I close out the app, a volt of energy zaps my bloodstream. I stow my phone then scan the dark lot. Mere feet away, Tami stands stock-still and studies me.

Between the cars, she visually peruses my body. Devours me with her addictive hazels. I swallow down the salacious hunger building inside me. Tell myself to save that hunger for later.

Gorgeous in a vibrant red dress, I ogle how it hugs her every line and curve. How the color accentuates the olive tone of her flawless skin in such a way my balls cinch. God, I ache to map every peak and valley and winding road of her body. To hear her purr as I rev her body higher.

She shakes off her statuesque pose and saunters in my direction. The sway of her hips provokes the bulge in my pants further. Her stride falters as she stands a breath away. And I can't help what spills from my lips. "You look stunning." Hunger and honesty lace each word.

Her eyes crinkle at the corners and a glow lights her skin at my compliment. "Thank you. You look pretty handsome yourself."

For some reason, I feel like a nervous twelve-year-old with a crush. The jitteriness irritates and fascinates me.

I itch to reach out and touch her. Before I second-guess myself, I throw down my gloves to temptation and slip an arm around her waist. Warmth radiates through my palm as I slide my hand down to rest on her lower back and guide us in the restaurant.

At the hostess stand, I spew out our reservation to the girl behind the podium. She openly checks me out. Ogles me without shame. Not the first time this has happened. Certainly won't be the last. But in this moment, with Tami at my side, the female attention turns me off. And when the girl curls her lip at Tami, I start to open my mouth and put the girl in her place.

But Tami beats me to the punch.

With a slight twist of her body, Tami presses her front to my side as she brushes her hand over my chest. When her warm breath cascades along the shell of my ear, my dick twitches against my zipper. Her lips dance over the rim as she whispers, "I don't know why I waited so long to agree to this."

I don't know if her motives are strictly to piss off the little thing behind the podium, but I give no fucks right now. With a light laugh, I face her. "Some things are worth the wait, baby."

Jealousy radiates off the young girl, her eyes roll heavenward at our display. She all but stomps as she leads us to our table. A back table that conceals us enough to have intimate conversation or, if I feel ballsy enough, get a bit freaky. I may test the waters to see how Tami receives the idea.

We place our order and transition into basic conversation—her talking about the dental industry and her roommate, me telling her about the dietician side of my life and about hanging with the guys a few nights a week. I leave out the fact I visit a strip club at least three nights a week and have an unhealthy obsession with a sweet piece of ass who has me horny as fuck.

Sometimes, less is more.

The more Tami talks, the more enthralled I become with her. She is the whole package—beauty, sex appeal, brains—wrapped with an intricate bow.

Since when have I given a fuck about whether or not a woman has any form of intelligence?

If anything, the fact she has a good head on her shoulders should have me running the opposite direction. Women who think always want more than I am willing to give.

But I don't run.

Nope. I let her reel me in closer, more than okay with being baited and hooked on her line.

Tami is an addiction I don't quite understand. Incomprehensible. I have never longed for a woman the way I long for Tami. Do I want to fuck her? Hell yes, I do. Do I want more than just a simple dirty fuck? The thought lingers in the back of my mind a minute. When I don't answer my own thought quick enough, I know I am up shit creek without a paddle.

Motherfucker.

Our food arrives and I memorize every move she makes. How she leans closer to the table, her breasts brushing the wood. The way she closes her eyes and inhales the aroma wafting from her plate. How delicately she places her napkin in her lap before picking up her cutlery.

She slices into the chicken breast resting on a bed of pasta, pierces the meat then twirls a hefty portion of the linguine around the tines. Somehow, she fits the entire forkful in her mouth and I immediately wonder how wide her lips will spread. How much will fit in her mouth, her throat.

Her eyes close as a low moan rumbles in her throat. The reverberation mixes with the visual and I bite the inside of my cheek. I want to shove the food to the floor, throw her atop the cloth-covered wood, and have my way with her. Full display, in front of every set of eyes in this restaurant.

"Confession. I wish I was that forkful of marsala," I tell her without shame.

Her eyes pop open and twinkle when they meet mine. That twinkle laced with a hint of humor and a dash of desire. And it penetrates me from feet away.

"Maybe if you behave, you can be." Her tongue sweeps along her bottom lip before she bites down.

My dick stiffens beneath the white linen. Begs me to take this date next level. *Believe me, I'm trying.* At this point, I will do whatever necessary in order for this date to not end when dinner does.

"What exactly is involved in your version of behaving? Can't really follow the rules if I don't know how to play."

A teasing smile spreads wide on her face. "You mean you don't know the rules? And here I thought everyone knew. Hmm..." She taps her lips with a finger, the polish matching her dress. "I don't know. I figured a man as attractive as you would know how to play the game."

She taunts me intentionally. And it turns me on tenfold. "Guess I'll have to wing it and see if the way I play is correct. Who knows… maybe I'll get lucky." I waggle my brows and she laughs, loud enough to garner attention in our little corner.

"You never know." She smirks and takes another bite of her meal.

Our banter continues throughout dinner. By the end of the evening, I want to haul her to the back of the restaurant and have my way with her. But I don't. Instead, I pull out her chair, take her hand, and stroll out of the restaurant toward her truck.

Next to her truck, I lazily drag my fingertips down her arm and take her hand in mine. A chill, almost undetectable, tremors through her body. Knowing I evoke this type of shiver warms me in a newfound, familiar way.

I lift her hand to my lips and press a kiss to her knuckles. Peeking up at her, I radiate every ounce of heat coursing through my veins. From head to toe, an inferno roars inside me for her. And I can't picture her unaware. At this point, I will grovel. Do whatever necessary to continue the evening. Any goddamn thing.

"Tami…" I inhale deeply. "I had a really great time tonight. More than I thought I would. Thank you."

She tilts her head to the side. Her eyes scan my face and read me like a book. "I had a great time, too. Thank you for the date."

The air around us grows thick and heavy with desire. I inch forward. My lips hungry to feel the softness of hers. To taste her. I lean in, watch as her eyes close, and seal her mouth with mine.

So soft and warm. Her succulent lips play in time with mine. Slowly opening and begging for more. One hand slides to her hip and grips firmly while the other cups her cheek and draws her in closer. I dart my tongue between her lips and pray she reciprocates.

Fire and lust and hunger course through my bloodstream. Every molecule of her infiltrates me. But the moment the tip of her tongue brushes against mine, I go into sensory overload. And in a blink, I am as good as done.

CHAPTER 11

TAMI

It has been an interesting evening, to say the least.

Throughout our date, we tease nonstop. Hidden innuendos thrown left and right. To say the banter isn't enjoyable, would be a lie. The date has been more than I expected. Between unearthing every possible way to eat my dinner like a wanton seductress to saying anything and everything that can be interpreted "the wrong way", I have been officially torturing Max for over an hour.

The continual torment is fun and I have bitten my cheek to hide my laughter so much I have permanent teeth indentations.

On occasion, I pucker my lips and moan in pleasure while I eat my chicken marsala. My inner hussy steps up to the plate as I suck the pasta between my lips and lick the sauce away with overexaggeration. When relief washes over his face as I close my mouth and chew, I decide dessert is a must.

Just can't help myself.

A wicked vixen exists inside me and she gets off on the

agony I put Max through. Practically purrs at the idea. And when my cannoli arrives at the table, I chuckle softly.

No joke, I would pay to watch this from the sidelines.

I pick up the cannoli, bring it to my lips and lick the tip of the sweet ricotta with unhurried precision. His attention locks on my mouth and the erotic way my tongue laps at the sweet confection. I open my mouth wider, lift the cannoli, and close my eyes as I wrap my lips around the crispy shell. A throaty moan of appreciation ripples from my chest as I savor my dessert.

My eyes pop open and lock on Max. His gaze is fire and scorches me. Brilliant greens deliver an unspoken promise. A promise no words can decipher. We sit like this—neither of us speaking, neither of us moving—for hour-long minutes.

Until his eyes drop to my lips. He swallows hard and his Adam's apple bobs heavy in his throat. And just before I add another dose of the sweetest pain and suffering, he speaks up. "I have something much more appetizing than the dessert between your lips."

"Is that so?" I singsong.

"It is. Keep that up" —he tips his head in my direction— "and I'll have to show you."

My insides swirl like a thermal tide pool. The heat slowly creeps up my neck. Rises and unfurls on my cheeks. Consumes me within seconds and has me parched.

Over the years, I have experienced a variety of men, every form of dirty talk, and an assortment of kink. But something about Max penetrates the barrier I keep in place. Sets me on fire. The deep baritone in his command. How he subtly inches closer. The way his gaze latches on my lips as his breath hitches. How his pulse noticeably throbs beneath his ear.

I swallow and remind myself this date is strictly casual.

Before long, I finish my dessert and Max pays the bill. When I scoop up my purse, Max bolts up from his seat and sidles up beside me, ready to withdraw my chair.

"Thank you."

"My pleasure." The two words hint at more, and I have no clue if it's another innuendo or a simple courtesy.

As we step away from the table, the back of his hand brushes mine before he takes it in his and twines our fingers. The small, bold touch sets off fireworks low in my belly. Emotions swirl and twist like a tornado beneath my ribcage. My breaths staccato.

Exiting the restaurant, I guide us toward my truck. Cars on the road almost drown out the cicadas. The lamp post lights above seem dimmer. More intimate. Hair lightly sweeps my cheek as I shiver in the warm summer night air. Perspiration dampens my skin with his hand in mine. The tornado in my chest spins violently and I lick my lips.

Why am I so nervous?

We reach my truck and pause next to the door. When his fingertips skim down the sides of my arms, a binary star explodes into a supernova across my skin. Slow and hot and intense the longer he caresses me. Lifting my hand to his lips, he peppers my knuckles with soft kisses as he holds my gaze. A fresh heatwave licks my skin. The gentle kisses are innocent in nature, but add kindling to the fire already burning inside me. Right now, Max could ask anything of me and I would cave.

Desire rolls off him and forms a bubble around us. His brilliant greens lock with my hazels as if he is ready to pounce. "Tami..." His chest expands and deflates almost imperceptibly.

"I had a really great time tonight. More than I thought I would. Thank you."

I study him for a beat and work to unearth the hidden meaning behind his words. Either he has mastered his poker face or his sentiment is genuine. I haven't decided which is true yet. Needless to say, he confounds me.

"I had a great time, too. Thank you for the date."

In that moment, something shifts between us. Not sure if it is the bottle of wine or the evident chemistry since I first laid eyes on him, but the attraction between us morphs. Takes on a life of its own. Takes us to a place where it isn't just a night out with a guy I like. But perhaps a slow evolution into something stronger. More powerful. Potent.

He leans into me and erases the last bit of vacancy. Eyes magnetized to my lips. I suck in a breath, close my eyes, and prepare for an incomparable kiss. A kiss I have lost sleep over.

And when his lips capture mine, the black skyline behind my lids is painted with stars. Energy and fervor and hunger pass from his lips to mine. The kiss deprives and consumes me. Awakens something deep inside me.

Lips crush. Hands grip. I inhale his spicy cedar scent and gasp at the sensory overload. Max licks my lower lip and I open up for him. His tongue tangles with mine and I taste the sweet basil and salty Parmigiano-Reggiano from minutes ago. I groan and he grips my hip with intensity. Slides a hand to my cheek. Anchors me against him.

Another moan echoes from my throat as his tongue sweeps over mine, returning stroke for stroke. Although I hold a secret of his hostage, in this moment, I don't care. I have met replicas of men like Max. Arrogant and egotistical and one-hundred-percent selfish.

But something about Max is different.

No matter how hard I try to pin down the difference, I end up empty-handed. Does that bother me? Not really. To be honest, I no longer care to fight the tide. I want him. Every part of him. Now. Desperately.

But a small part of me keeps saying no. *Don't do it. If you give it up now, that will be the end of the line.* And the reality of that snaps me from the lust-foggy moment.

I jerk back, break the kiss, and regard the heat of his stare. "I want to, but…"

"But what?" His eyes beseech me.

I want to, but I know you will bolt after I give you what you want.

I want to, but once I tell you about the other part of my world, you will jump ship.

I want to, but I know how it ends with every guy like you.

What can I say? "It's complicated."

"Can you be a little more specific?" Confusion bunches the midline of his forehead.

He isn't upset. Isn't angry. He just wants to understand the reason behind my decision.

"My life isn't so black and white, Max. There are so many shades in the spectrum in between. I want to. Believe me. But it's not that easy. For me, anyway."

He studies me with such intensity, I wonder if he is trying to read my mind. Or is deciding what to do next. Either way, his confusion is a novel written on the lines of his face. "That tells me nothing. Is it me? Did *I* do something?"

"No. It isn't you. Promise. Everything about tonight has been perfect. My life is just…" I need a different word. One that explains everything going on in my world, in one easy, compact word. And I am nowhere near ready to tell him the ins and outs of my life. We don't know each other well enough. How do I know if he will accept and comprehend *that* side of me? So, I opt for the same explanation. Again. And I mentally prepare myself to never see him after tonight. "Complicated."

A loud huff puffs from his lips as he faces away from me. No matter how many times I do this—reject a guy from taking things to the next level—it never gets easier. But tonight… tonight is different. Or so I believed.

Every other person who wines and dines me, they truly want nothing more than to have their way with me. Not saying that that isn't what Max wants too. I know he does. But there is more to the story.

I *feel* it.

The way he observes me; as if I were the only woman in the room. The way his body reacts to mine; like he can't control his behavior when near me. How his lips and tongue devour me; as if he only gets one last meal and I am his choice.

I want the charade to end and to scream yes at the top of my lungs. But I take no steps to end it. And I won't. If anything further happens between us, we need more time. Time to discover each other.

Sure, I have a few inside secrets about him, and he has zero on me. I should level the playing field by sharing something. But what? I only have one deep, dark secret. If I lay that spread on the table, I will be left holding no cards and he will gain a full house.

He faces me again and I wish I had a better vantage point of his expression. His eyes currently hidden in the dim, shadowed light. At a disadvantage, I can't read his mood. Defeat simmers in my chest and I prepare for the worst.

"Tami…" My name almost inaudible as it rolls off his tongue. "We all have complications. No one's life is perfect."

I swallow then take a deep breath. "True. It's just… every person I've shared a part of me with, it doesn't end well. For them or me. Before I expose that part of my world again, I have to know…" I hang my head as I twist and knot my fingers at my navel.

"Know what?"

With any other guy, I wouldn't explain myself. Or think twice about it. But Max has this forcefield around him. An energy that makes me want to open my mouth and tell him as much as possible without giving all my secrets away.

"That I'm not just some finish line you're trying to cross. That you're genuinely interested in having something more than a one-night stand with me. I deserve to know where things are or aren't heading with us. We both deserve to know, don't you think?"

Although I am unable to read his eyes in the darkness, I know the second he closes them. See the way his jaw tics. *Is he angry?* If that is the case, at least I found out now and not down the road. Not after I invested my heart.

"I am going to be completely honest with you. But fair warning, I may disappoint you." A void opens in my stomach as I patiently wait for him to continue. "When I asked you to go out with me tonight, I had my mind set on getting you in my bed. One way or another. Tami, I'm not the guy who *dates*. It's just not who I am." He pauses for three breaths then continues. "But I don't *want* to be that guy with you. There's something different about you. I don't know what it is and, if I'm completely honest, that scares the shit out of me. For the first time, I want more than just one evening with a woman. I want to savor you. Over and over again."

The void in my stomach fills and a flutter replaces it. Adrenaline spikes my bloodstream and I float in his confession. A thin sheen of sweat coats my skin. I didn't expect his admission and I mentally stumble back. My initial perception of him wasn't wrong—and a tiger doesn't change its stripes in one evening—but if what he just professed is true, it puts us in a whole new realm.

"I'd like that."

And although I still cannot see his eyes, I glimpse the outline of his lips as they curve up in a mischievous smile. "As would I. The night's still young," he teases.

I shake my head and laugh. "You're relentless."

"Can't fault a man for trying. It's in my DNA." He shrugs as if no better explanation exists.

"Wouldn't doubt that for a second."

"I really did have a great time tonight. And hope we can do this again sometime."

"Me too." I unlock my truck and Max opens the door for me. "See you during the week."

I step up and set my purse on the passenger side as I slide behind the wheel. Max shuts the door after I roll the window down. Leaning in the truck cab, he glances at the interior before returning his gaze to me. "Sweet dreams, beautiful."

With an incremental shift in his weight, his lips meet mine once more and I lose all train of thought. When he releases me from his intoxicating and addictive mouth, he steps back and grins at my stupefied expression. Pivoting on his heel, he saunters to his car, gets in and drives away.

Once his spell wears off and I am coherent enough to drive, I start up Tiff and drive home. The entire journey home is foggy as my brain swirls. Doubt bombards me. And I question the choice I made regarding Max. My brain wages war with my heart and hormones. But one thought continuously spins like a gyroscope in my head.

Should I, or shouldn't I?

My body screams yes, while my overactive imagination points a stern finger and says hell no.

Ugh! Sometimes I really hate my life.

CHAPTER 12

MAX

I have spent more time in the gym and jacking off this week than any other time in my life.

No other span of time, to my recollection, has been solely devoted to one woman. You name the distraction method and I guarantee I tried it. Every possible tactic to get her out of my head… I have done them all. And not one works.

Majority of my usual distraction techniques involve sex or naked women. But the thought of sex with another woman right now, amazing as it sounds, wrenches my stomach in knots. Not quite certain when my switch flipped and I became a pussy-whipped bitch, but it happened.

And I haven't even had the fucking pussy yet.

Motherfuckin' bullshit.

Four days have passed since our date. And even longer since I've had a fine piece of ass between the sheets. Since tasting her sweet perfection, it feels *wrong* to check out other women. Guilt smothers me the instant my thoughts stray.

God, if her mouth tastes that delectable, my imagination

runs wild with what the rest of her tastes like. The saltiness of her skin. The sweet tanginess between her magnificent thighs. Her body is a surefire guarantee to send me to heaven and hell simultaneously.

Fucked… that is what I am. Completely, utterly, royally fucked. My balls rest firmly in her clutches and she doesn't even know it yet.

Speaking of balls. Mine long surpassed the stage of blue. If I were to describe the level of deprivation that my balls have reached, I'd have to say they're bluer than Papa Smurf's balls while suffering a bout of hypothermia. If I don't rectify the problem soon, they may just shrivel up and go north to hibernate until further notice. No matter how many times I yank my dick, no matter how many times I get off, it does nothing to relieve the agony.

And I no longer care if I appear desperate, one way or another, this suffering has to end. A man can't fucking live like this. A man has fucking needs. Natural human functions that need to occur at regular intervals. And my functionality requires fulfillment. Like last week.

Tami strolls into the gym with a vivacious sway of her hips. Each day, I swear to the almighty she has every intention to torture me. Flaunting her full hourglass figure in my face. Taunting me with her body like the prize it obviously is. If she wasn't so damn reserved, I would have already thrown her on my bed and fucked her from dusk to dawn. Missionary, doggy-style, cowgirl, reverse cowgirl, against the wall, in the shower, my mouth on her, her mouth on me. Every motherfucking position possible.

Fuck.

The very idea of having my way with her has my cock screaming for release. I shift my weight in an attempt to stifle my growing erection. Nothing like having a boner in the gym. While instructing a class. And all eyes focus on your body. Fucking fantastic.

"Hey, how are you?" Her lips curve up into the smile I have become addicted to witnessing.

"Same old, same old. You?"

"Nothing new with me either. So many mouths, so little time." She chuckles as she walks off and heads for the locker room.

What the hell is that supposed to mean? Is she making a crack at our kiss the other night? Is she out in the world, kissing other guys? The last thought is probably far-fetched, but just the idea of Tami kissing some douchebag sends a red, stabby rage through my veins. Pressure compresses my chest as my breathing turns jagged and comes in short, rapid bursts.

Lost in thought, I don't see her when she approaches with a furrowed brow. "You okay?"

Not fucking really, but there is no way I plan on sharing that news with her. "Yeah. Fine."

"Are you sure? You're a little flushed."

"I said I'm fine," I snap, a bit harsher than necessary.

She holds her hands up in defeat and walks away from me, heading to her usual spot for warm-up.

Damnit all to hell. What the hell is wrong with me? Get your head in the game, Kingston. Things will go absolutely nowhere with this woman if you keep acting like an asshole.

Approaching the section of the mat where she makes yoga look like a new guide to sex, I begin doing stretches of my own. I swallow my pride and buck up the courage to say something I rarely do.

"Sorry." The word tastes bitter on my tongue. "Didn't mean to snap at you. Just having a shitty day."

Her eyes search my face and hunt for the truth in my words. And even though apologies are not something I speak often; this apology is one-hundred-percent genuine. And I spot the moment she reaches this conclusion. She faces away from me and transitions into warrior pose.

"You're forgiven. Don't let it happen again, though. I've dealt with enough bullshit in my life. I take strides to avoid it now."

I nod. "Noted."

Silence stretches between us as we both do our warm-up routines. Typically, I would try to fill silence with witty remarks or egotistical comments. But with Tami, silence is oddly comfortable.

"Sorry you had a shitty day. Want to talk about it?" Tami snaps me from my introspection.

She really is trying. Part of me jubilant at the notion, another part of me reserved. But if I want anything to happen with this woman, I can't be my normal, arrogant, asshole self. I, literally, have to man up.

"Work was pretty lackluster, but sometimes that comes with the territory. Don't get me wrong, I love coaching people into eating healthier and becoming the best version of themselves. But nowadays, so many people just want the quick fix. They don't want to put in the work or take pride in the effort taken."

Reaching down to touch her toes, a maneuver meant to stretch her hamstrings, but has me licking my lips, she nods. "Couldn't agree more. When I tell people all I do to maintain a healthy body, they scoff at me and try to tell me an easier way. I tell them I don't want a quick fix. That I enjoy the journey. That I love the process to reap the rewards. And how I want to feel good at the end of the day. Same goes for dental work.

People, too often, push off taking care of their teeth. In the long run, it just makes things worse for your body overall."

And now her joking comment about mouths makes sense. As usual, I am the fucking fool who jumps to conclusions out of pure jealousy. Dumb. Ass. Idiot. Why the hell would I automatically assume she is out kissing other guys? Because that assumption is a dick move and something I would probably do, that is why.

After I stretch in silence for too long, she brushes her hand atop my shoulder and garners my attention. "Sure you're okay? You just seem out of it."

"Yeah. I really am sorry about how I acted earlier. Took something you said out of context and obviously needed to realize I was being a dipshit. Now I know it, can mentally slap myself, and move on. Ready for class?"

She cocks her head, narrows her eyes, and studies me a moment. Unanswered questions flit between us. The biggest question of all is what exactly I misinterpreted and why. But the pinched skin between her brows softens, as do her eyes. Does she forgive me for being a jerk? Possibly, but she may not forgive me in the future if I continue acting foolish.

But something else resides in her expression. Something deeper, heavier, more emotional. Intuition is not a characteristic I possess, but I sense a thicker layer of emotion radiating off her. An energy that would normally have me running for the hills.

But I don't want to run. Not from Tami.

If anything, I crave to be closer to her. A prisoner in her atmosphere. Gravity engulfs me under her invisible shield and holds me captive. And with each interaction, the weight of that gravity becomes less detectable and more alluring. But how do I not get crushed under the pressure?

"Ready when you are."

Sixty minutes of blood, sweat, tears, and adrenaline pass by as if time is a figment of the imagination. Part of the group continues doing cool-down exercises while the rest grab their belongings and leave. Tami exits the locker room with the strap of her duffel across her chest, finishing her bottle of water as she walks in my direction.

When she steps close enough for me to see a line of sweat roll down her neck, she reaches forward and rests a hand on my bicep. "Glad we got to chat earlier. Thanks for a great class." Her eyes perk up at the corners when she smiles.

I may be reading into her body language a little too deep. Hell, wouldn't be the first time. But the way she brushes her fingers against my skin. The way she leans forward and bites her lower lip. Is she making an excuse to stay and talk? Feigning reasons to touch me? If so, I would venture to guess she is as equally hooked. And a level playing field is far more desirable than me alone in the corner pining for her.

"Me too and you're welcome." Here goes nothing. "I'd love to see you again. Outside of here."

"I'd love that, too." Her lips perk up as a genuine smile brightens her pinked cheeks. A smile bright enough to illuminate the darkest night.

"How about tomorrow night? I know this great phở restaurant downtown."

Her face scrunches as regret shades her eyes. "Parts of the weekend are tougher for me. Sunday would work for me again, if that works for you."

"Sunday would be great. We can sort out the details later, if you want."

"Perfect. I have to run. Text you later?"

"It's a date." I smile her way as she bolts for the parking lot.

The smile she returns triggers an electrical zap in my groin. I groan quietly and pray no one hears. Briefly, I close my eyes and tell my cock it won't be long before it gets relief. But until then, I traipse toward the familiar locker room and step into one of the shower stalls, crank the water high and drown out the sounds of a man who is desperate for relief.

CHAPTER 13

TAMI

Reaching for the foundation, I dab some on a makeup sponge and blend it over the skin beneath my eyes. Satisfied with the coverage and blending, I pat the soft, powder-coated poof on my face next. Earlier, I contemplated which color to paint above my eyes and on my lips tonight. There are only so many combinations with the color palette I own, but I don't like repeating styles time and again.

I opt for soft teal and brush it lightly along the outer half of each eyelid, adding a shimmery opaque to the whole lid after. Adding a dash of rouge to a large, soft-bristled brush, I paint my cheekbones with the subtle color. Just enough to make them pop in the light. After a hint of mascara, I smear the nude gloss wand over my lips, pucker, and gaze at myself in the brightly lit mirror.

Not too much. But enough to be noticeable. Perfect.

I unhang my outfit and dress in the blue I chose for tonight. The color matches closely with my eye makeup and gives it that extra pop. Once ready, I step in front of the full-length mirror and twist left and right to see everything is in place and comfortable. Satisfied, I walk down the hall—the linoleum cool under my bare feet—and wave to a few people that pass along the way.

At the end of the hall, I spot Indigo and stop to chat with her a moment. Her long, black hair brushes her lower back, while some tendrils mask some of her cleavage. The music booms around us and I lean into her to chat about her family. We talk until the song ends. Indigo shares her father's constant abhorrence for our job and I wish there was a way to erase the sadness etched in her brow. I squeeze her tight in my arms and we kiss cheeks as the hug lessens.

When she drops her hands, I take a deep breath. Indigo shakes her head and dons a naughty smile. "Go get 'em, girl."

I lift my chin. "Always do."

Walking to the right, I bounce in the dark space and wait. My nerves fire off in a domino effect as every cell in my body stirs to life and the swarm of bees buzzes in my chest. Adrenaline bleeds into each molecule. My pulse drums behind my ears. My mouth dries as my palms sweat. The high pierces my lucidity so much, I almost miss my name being called.

Not a second later, a loud, bass-driven beat vibrates across the floor and I glide from my position to a brighter space. When the same reverberation happens again, I pivot and face the crowd of men and women sitting in the darkened club. All of them silent. All of them waiting for me. Only me.

I stalk forward as my hands trace up the sides of my torso and curl around the curves of my breasts. When the beat shifts to a ticking, I tap my fingertips down my abdomen, stopping before I reach the cyan fabric someone dubbed a slingshot, and tease the multiple sets of eyes glued to every single move I make.

Losing myself in the music, I dance across the stage,

performing the routine I rehearsed enough times to know when I need to pivot or spin or sway my hips.

When I first started dancing, it wasn't at a place as sophisticated as P.I. The Honey Cave isn't at the bottom of the totem pole, but it is nowhere near the top either. The first time I stepped on the stage, my only motivation was to make loads of money to help get me through college. After a few months, it morphed into something else.

Something addicting. A libidinous compulsion to display myself to a room full of strangers.

I love being on stage. I love the power I wield over the hundreds of people who sit like ravenous voyeurs. And I love the rush pumping throughout my body before, during, and after each performance. And the money is, now, a side perk. Dancing may have been something I started to make ends meet, but now... the reason I grace this stage three times a week is because I love the control. The empowerment is incomparable. The exhilaration is beyond surreal. Dancing courses hot in my bloodstream and I cannot imagine not doing it in the foreseeable future.

When I clutch the cold, silver pole in the center of the stage, I twirl around it twice before sliding down into a split and crawling toward the front of the stage.

That is when I spot Max.

And he is not alone tonight.

At the table with him is a tall man with beautiful, rich brown skin. Stalkier than Max, a wicked grin permanently turns up his lips. His head is shaved bald, and shines when the light hits it. The second man is a little shorter in stature and sits on the opposite side of the taller man. A bit pudgy around his midsection, he has a head of thinning black hair with a hint of salt and pepper scattered throughout. And a pair of thick, black glasses rest on his nose.

Seeing the two men with Max doesn't bother me. I have danced in front of so many people over the years, I don't tend to focus on the crowd anymore. What *does* bother me, though, is the nude dancer grinding on the taller man's lap. Right beside Max. Trying to encourage the three of them to participate in the lap dance.

For the first time in my life, my vision goes red.

For the first time ever, I want the music to end.

For the first time ever, jealousy surges in my chest.

Every atom beneath my skin begs me to jump off the stage and head straight for Max. To yank him away from the temptation of another woman. My body heats and pulsates as the current of jealousy soars through me. I don't miss a beat in my choreography and, when I face the crowd again, I notice Max's eyes magnetized to my body.

There may be a naked female bumping and grinding on his friend, but he is none the wiser. Not for a second. His eyes roam every speck of my body, lick a flame across my skin, and scald me like lava. And without thinking, I dance as if Max is the only person in the club.

My eyes find his as I sway my hips to the beat. When I remove the skimpy fabric, which will never be deemed clothing, I don't shift my gaze. When I pinch my nipples and give them a slight tug, I part my lips. And when I slide my hands down my body and pause for a beat at my apex before moving to my thighs, I lick my lips. All while we eye fuck each other.

And when the song finally ends, I strut off the stage and head straight in his direction. Stan hands me a satin robe as I take the steps. He doesn't skip a beat when he sees me, and rises from the table to follow me. After a breath, I glance over my shoulder—a mischievous smile dancing on my lips—and hook my finger in a *come-hither* motion.

I have zero intention of letting him know *I* am Candy. What he doesn't know won't hurt him. All good things come to those who wait. But, in the meantime, I plan to enjoy toying with him. Perhaps even give him a taste of his own medicine.

CHAPTER 14

MAX

For the first time in years, I don't want my friends tagging along for the evening. I would rather ride solo to P.I., sit in the dark, and watch a real-life fantasy glide across the stage. Rocco was a smart man when he thought up and named this restaurant and club. He hadn't been lying when he said it would be my new, favorite private infatuation.

And I have zero shame owning my new found addiction.

Candy is pure perfection in every sense of the word. Honestly, I could watch her hours, daily, and still not tire of everything she has to offer. Absolute, pure opulence.

Nic and Jason sit on my left when we reach the table I choose—center stage. Each of us orders a drink and talks shit for a few minutes. A petite blonde darts across the stage; her dancing more vulgar than I prefer. Nic and Jason, though, fixate on her and ready themselves to hoot and holler when she finishes. Before the blonde's dance ends, Nic signals for the server, and pays for a dance from the woman on stage. I over-hear the server call her Nikki.

Note to self—Nikki is not my type.

When Nikki finishes whatever that is she did on the stage, Nic and Jason stand, cocks proud and noticeably tenting their pants, and clap like virgin juveniles. Me… I duck from view; in case anyone peers over at our table. As Nikki approaches the table, the emcee hollers over the speaker and announces Candy.

My friends may sit less than two feet from me with a woman rubbing her ass and tits all over them, but I miss every second of it. And I give zero fucks.

Candy cascades across the stage, her hair two tones of blue tonight. The patches of material covering her nipples and pussy match the darker color in her wig as thinner strands wrap around her torso. She twerks and gyrates to the music like waves crashing along the shoreline. Her body rolls fluidly with the beat. The exhibition more than hypnotic. More of a symbiotic relationship. As if born to grace the stage.

A minute into the song, her body rocks side to side as she slowly drifts down until she hovers mere inches off the stage floor in a widespread plank. She crawls forward on the stage— fingers splayed, an arch in her spine as if on the prowl—and captivates me, hunting me like a predator stalking prey. And I swear, without a doubt, she locks eyes with me.

A flash fire blazes in my groin. The look we share is intense and loaded. For a split-second, a sense of familiarity strikes me; her eyes almost recognizable. The familiarity intrigues me, but I push the notion aside and enjoy the remainder of her dance—which, in a sudden shift of events, appears to be solely for me.

The blue patches covering her nipples and apex fall to the floor. And just like that, I have returned to heaven. Her hands roam over her tan flesh, teasing her nipples and between her thighs for a blink of time. With each touch, each caress, my cock hardens further. Strains painfully against my zipper. When the song ends, her chin rests on her shoulder as she shakes her ass, walks off stage and winks. At me.

No longer in my line of sight, disappointment floods me when realization hits me head-on. I should have paid for more time with her while she danced. But I was so lost in her, outright enthralled by her display, and how tonight's show appeared to be for my eyes only.

But what do I know? Probable I imagined her focus was only on me. That my desperation for her has my mind playing tricks on me.

In my right periphery, I notice her walking across the room. Her body wrapped in a cotton candy pink robe. Is she headed in my direction? Hopeful, I stand and lock eyes with her. Her gaze fixes on mine as she passes our table. My legs take one step, then another, moving of their own accord and following her. She peeks over her shoulder and spots me behind her. She curls her finger and calls after me with a smirk on her lips.

Like a lost puppy, I fall in line. She stops when she reaches a large, black door with a brass knob. A tall, stalky bouncer stands guard at the door. Stepping up behind her, I stand a couple feet back and respect her boundaries. I have to consistently remind myself of where I am and how easily my privileges can be revoked by one idiotic move.

The sweet chime of her voice penetrates the air and tickles my balls. "Chucky, I'm taking this gentleman in the room. I'll come out when we're done. No time frame, okay?" Candy winks at him and he nods.

Candy twists the knob and opens the door, both of us stepping in the room. A sharp click echoes in the room as she closes the door behind us. Suddenly, every sense flips to hyperalert.

The room is long and narrow. The walls and floor a mix of black, white, and grays. A chair and chaise sit near one of the longer walls, both black leather with studs securing it to the frame. Thin gold stripes garnish the room sporadically and add marble effect and an air of luxury.

My fingertips brush over the cool leather as heat trickles up my limbs, spreads head to toes, and singes deep in my belly. The air smells of leather and sex and thickens with each passing second. My breath shallows and intensifies in rhythm.

When I spin to face her, her eyes remain partially hidden by her wig. The low lighting adds a different level of intimacy and kicks my nerves into high gear. She places her hand on my chest—the delicious burn sears me to the core—and shoves me back toward the chaise. My knees nudge the seat's edge and I stumble to sit. The cool leather a welcome relief and juxtaposition against my heated skin. I keep my gaze locked on hers as I drop down and my back rests against the studded cushion.

Candy stalks toward me. With every step she takes, a new molecule comes alive inside me. Inch by inch, my body blazes hotter and hotter. She is so close. Almost too close. Her fingers unfasten the sash securing her robe. And before I can blink, the satin robe falls open, slips off her shoulders, and ripples in a puddle at her feet. The vibrations of my rough swallow bounces off the walls. My dick throbs beneath my zipper and cries at being held hostage. Candy crawls atop the chaise and straddles me, rendering me immobile. Her perky nipples brush against my chest as she inches up my body and her cheek grazes mine as she positions her lips beneath my ear.

"In here, I'm in charge. Understand?" Her sweet as sin voice commands.

I swallow the wad of cotton lodged in my throat. My voice scratchy and embarrassing when I respond with a nod. "Yes, I understand."

"That means, if I want you to do something, you can. As long as I give you permission."

"I understand," I repeat.

"Good boy."

She licks the shell of my ear before taking the lobe between her lips and sucking. My eyes roll back at the feel of her lips on my skin. My cock twitches and the jolt doesn't go undetected by her. Her hand slides down my torso, between our bodies, and halts over my erection as she palms me.

"Is this for me?"

I lose the ability to speak, let alone function. My eyes drift shut and revel in the contact as a constant buzz courses through my bloodstream—an overly familiar and potent sensation. When I locate my voice, I peel my eyes open and stare at her sweet face.

"All for you."

She grinds her hips over my erection and the pressure encourages my arousal further. A guttural moan rips from my chest. "I love how hard you are for me." Her hips slowly rock forward and back again as my hips lift slightly in reaction. "I want to reward you."

My eyes startle wide in surprise. "And how would you reward me? I've been given the riot act about the rules."

A smirk gleams on her face. "In here, the rules are completely mine. Don't worry, sweetheart." The way she uses the word *sweetheart* has me pausing for a second. But then she continues speaking and my mind loses all sense of coherent thought. "I want you to suck my nipples. No hands, though."

Sweet baby Jesus. Is this happening? Really happening? Please don't let this be a dream. Even if this is a dream, I don't need to be told twice.

Her hips settle over mine as she leans forward and thrusts her luscious breasts closer to my lips. Inching up a bit, I pop my mouth open, tongue ready to dart out as she dips her perky flesh between my lips.

Sweet, warm, velvety smooth skin rests on my lips and tongue and I drift to heaven. Opening wider, I suction her nipple between my lips, sucking with a bit of teeth. A moan rumbles from her lips as she tips her head back and grinds her hips over my erection harder. Shifting my lips from the first breast to the second, I take full advantage of this moment. Her body picks up in tempo. The volume of her cries grows louder. Her hot pussy presses harder against my erection.

My teeth clamp down on her nipple and she shudders from head to toe. Her forearms rest on the back of the chaise behind me as her hooded eyes meet mine again.

"Good boy."

"I wouldn't dare disobey," I vow.

"Happy to hear that. And since you made me come all over your pants, I think you deserve another reward."

I have no clue what I did to get this woman to choose me, but I will do whatever the fuck she tells me. Call me a pussy-whipped bitch, I give no motherfucking fucks. Watching her come on top of me was the sweetest bliss.

"I am a slave to whatever you deem worthy."

A sneaky smile lights up her face. She leans forward, takes my ear in her mouth again, and sucks her way down my neck as her hand trails toward my pants. A rush of exultation over-whelms me as she undoes the button and slides down the zipper. Her hand slips underneath my briefs and caresses the length of my cock, skin-to-skin, and I hiss.

"So hot and silky smooth." Her words are raspy next to my ear. I suck in a deep breath as her hand glides up and down my length, stroking me firmly. "Can't decide if I want you in my hand or my mouth."

The thought of my cock in her mouth does unimaginable and unintelligible things to me. But I don't make the decisions in here, so I answer her as neutral as possible.

"Remember, beautiful, you're in charge in here."

She hums in delight and strokes my shaft with more vigor. "Maybe I'll have a little bit of both."

Before I realize what she is doing, she slides down my body and wraps her lips around my dick. Hot, wet desire skitters up and down my length. I gape down at her. My jaw slackens as my body begs for release. And that is when I notice her snake a hand between her legs.

Holy fucking hell! Swear to god I must be dreaming. How the hell is this real?

After stroking up and down my cock with her tongue seven delicious times, about to lose myself in her mouth, she retreats. She skirts back up my body as her right hand continues to play with her clit and occasionally dip a finger inside. She wraps her left arm around me and my eyes roam between her face, her tits, and where her hands work to get us both off. Never have I seen such a magnificent sight in my life.

Her eyes lock on mine. "Hope you're close, pretty boy. About to come" —she pants— "and I want you to at the same time." Her desire is so personal. So intimate. And still some-what familiar.

Pure, unadulterated lust rests in her parted lips and heavy breaths. The way she watches me, but wants to roll her eyes back in her head. It mirrors the exact level of ardor I hold. I desperately ache to grab hold of her, to touch her, to help her reach her climax with my mouth or my fingers. But I simply answer her, knowing it won't take much for me to explode.

"Ready when you are, beautiful."

Her hands stroke faster, on my cock and her pussy. The friction is delicious torture and the ultimate temptation. If not for the bass-riddled music outside this room, everyone within a one-mile radius would hear our moans. Her cries morph—a feverish groan one second, and high-pitched, ragged breathing the next. I *feel* how close she is. Ready to explode on me again.

"Come for me, beautiful," I grunt.

My words like an ignition switch as she convulses over me. Then she finishes me off, and I shoot cum up my chest. She presses her forehead to mine for a beat and catches her breath. Too quick, she rises off of me, picks up her robe, cinches the sash and heads for the door.

With her hand on the knob, she twists to face me. "I really had a good time tonight. Maybe we can do it again sometime." And then she waltzes out the door, leaving me to relish in what just happened.

Holy fucking shit.

Did that actually happen? It was only a hand job, but something else happened between us. On a much deeper level. A spark beyond the dancer/patron level. A chemistry I have only felt when I was with one other person. And that chemistry confuses me. Has me feeling guilty. Has me questioning what the hell is going on.

But right now, I refuse to let myself dwell on that. Because nothing else will compare to what just occurred. And I want to savor this moment for as long as possible.

CHAPTER 15

TAMI

Exiting the private room, the lights and sounds of the club come at me full force and I pause to take a breath. I glance over at Chucky, give him a quick smile, and head for the dancer's dressing rooms to clean up and change.

Once in the solitude of my dressing room, I slide the wig from my head and stare at the woman in the mirror, stunned.

Can't believe I just did that with Max.

Seeing the dancer at his table give his friends a lap dance… I just lost it. This atomic-sized ball of foreign emotions took over me, made me irrational. Possessed me. I have been teasing him for weeks at the gym. Leading him on here and there when we went on our date. The last thing I want is another naked woman shaking her ass inches from his hard-on.

I press the heel of my palm firmly to my chest as a sharp pain lances me. The sensation not completely new to me, but I have never experienced it to this degree.

Jealousy.

A wicked emotion that rips people to shreds. I ball my hand into a tight fist as the jealousy enters my bloodstream and infiltrates every chemical compound in my body like a potent drug.

I have zero claim to Max. Zero. But in that moment, all I thought was *mine.*

So, I lured him away the only way I know how. With my body.

All I had to do when I walked past him was give the proper look. A look that screams *follow me.* That, even though he hadn't paid for anything, I would give him something he will not soon forget. Something he will fantasize over for days and weeks to come.

Initially, my game plan was to bring him into one of the private rooms and give him the lap dance of a lifetime. But the idea went out the window the moment the door closed behind me.

The air in that tiny room shifted. Buzzed. Came alive. The magnetism I always feel around Max sparked and amplified the closer I got to him. Originally, my plan was to taunt and tease him. To drive him insane with need. But then my body reacted to the closed-door situation—skin fevered, the silk robe stuck to my damp skin, the ache between my thighs building, building, building—and I couldn't stop myself. A primal need deep in my bones wanted to witness his reaction when I fisted him and brought him to climax. And I wanted him to feel me too. Watch me come undone. Because Max turns me on more than any other man I have known.

But, in his eyes, what just happened wasn't with me.

It happened with someone else.

A fantasy.

Candy, not Tami.

I stare at my reflection in the mirror, the bright white bulbs light up every feature and facet of my skin, and I wonder how I will see him again. Whenever I look at him, I won't just see his face, his defined muscles, or his cocky attitude. I will see the way his eyes glazed over for me. How his body went rigid. The way his teeth clamped on his lip just before we orgasmed together. And, of course, I will know the intimate details while he remains completely oblivious.

Grabbing the package of cosmetic wipes, I clean the makeup off my face. Following the same routine I do every night I work at P.I., I finish cleaning myself up and dress in less than twenty minutes. But I don't leave. Not yet. Instead, I sit on the tall chair and get lost in the image of the woman in the mirror. I don't *want* to leave yet, seeing as the possibility of bumping into Max is higher tonight than any previous.

Will he try to wait for me outside? Fuck. Did I just screw this all up?

After a couple hours pass, along with some chitchat and catching up with Indigo, I gather my belongings and head for the employee exit. The club, and bar upstairs, have been closed thirty minutes, but I am still on edge about leaving and being caught by the one person I am not ready to let in on this little secret. Paused at the door, one of the bouncers spots me and asks if I am okay.

"Yeah, fine. Just feel a bit off tonight. That's all."

"Want me to walk you to your truck, Miss Tami."

Smiling at his kindness, I reply, "That would be nice, Troy. Thank you."

"You're welcome. We have to make sure you ladies feel safe. At all costs."

Not as if I don't feel safe. More like exposed, even though

my secret is still mine. When we reach my truck, he waits for me to get in and crank the engine, then wishes me a good night as he walks back to the club.

Once on the road, my mind travels like highways on a map.

I think back to last weekend, when Max was in the club and I gave him a lap dance in the lounge area. That night was the first time I realized just how much I wanted him, but wasn't quite ready to reveal Candy and I are one and the same. And although he couldn't touch me, I knew how bad he wanted me. How much he still wants me.

But in that place, on that stage, in that lounge, tucked away in that private room… I am Candy. The ravishing beauty with a killer body who wiggles her curves to make the crowd drool over her. Candy has an air of mystery. With her various colored wigs and pseudonym. A hidden gem. A black opal in a sea of diamonds. Rare. Alluring. Priceless.

And even though I am Candy… I am not her.

Over the years, I have managed to separate those parts of myself. Candy is Candy and Tami is Tami. There is no blending of the two. The few times I intermingled Candy into my reality, my day-to-day life, it always ended badly.

Once men knew Tami and Candy were the same person, there was always unspoken expectations. That I will stop dancing because they can't handle other men ogling my body. That I will dance for them in the privacy of our bedroom, as if I will always be Candy and never Tami. And that there is an unspoken rule—I must be Aphrodite in the sex department. I have never had reason to doubt how great I am in the bedroom, but once Candy pops into the limelight, men assume I perform mystical, magical positions between the sheets. As if I am some Kamasutra goddess.

But I just want to be *me*.

I have been this person—Candy as much a part of me as Tami—for six years. She is me. I am her. But, in the same respect, I am my own person. Candy is a side of me not everyone accepts or respects or understands.

I—Tami—am beautiful and intelligent and witty. And I like to laugh and cry and enjoy every emotion under the sun. I love sunrises, but am a sucker for sunsets. If time allowed, I would spend more with my mom. To be in the kitchen with her, slow cooking and jarring homemade marinara. Chitchatting while we crack eggs in wells of flour on the counter to make fresh pasta. To listen to her stories and learn all the recipes passed down to her from other generations.

As much as I love the excitement, the undiluted rush, that comes from being on stage, at times I wonder how my life would be if I were no longer Candy. She doesn't rule my world, but that part of my life has hindered me from having something I crave. Something standing in front of me and shouting to the heavens.

Normalcy.

I long for normalcy more than ever. More than my next breath. *But what is normal?* Normal for some people is waking up early, working nine-to-five, eating dinner while watching television, and going to bed. Wash, lather, rinse, repeat.

No sex.

No heat.

No passion.

As much as I love the concept of routine and a regimented schedule, that cannot be all my life is. I *need* passion. I *need* heat. And for fuck's sake, I *need* sex. And it has been far too long since I have had the latter. Tonight… I almost caved on that card. So close, I practically tasted it.

Pulling into my parking space at home, I sit in the truck cab a minute and stare at the front door of my apartment. More like zone out while my eyes face the door. The porch light is on and I hone in on the moths as they swarm the glowing bulb. But the inside of the apartment is shrouded in darkness. No real surprise there. The last time Amber stayed up until three in the morning, even when she didn't have to work the next day, was when we were in college. As nice as it is to come in after work and not be lectured on how I spend my nights, I would love to have a friend to talk to about how I feel right now.

I may not be perfect, but I am still human. A real woman with real emotions and real problems. Amber doesn't exactly love the fact I dance—not since she and David got together— but I am a woman nonetheless. And I miss her. Miss her friendship. Miss her warm hugs. And I definitely miss her insightful wisdom.

I get out of my truck, grab my bag, and mosey up the stairwell. As quiet as possible, I unlock the front door and tiptoe inside, closing and bolting the door. I tread softly to my room, careful to make as little noise as possible. Once in the comfort of my own space, I shut the door and sigh. Plopping on my bed, I stare at the ceiling and lose focus.

I like him. More than I ever thought possible, to be honest. Only I don't know what to do now.

He will never look at me the same. Tami or Candy. Not after tonight. Not after his fantasy girl gave him a taste of what he has been surely dreaming about. I screwed myself. Royally. The worst part is I have no one to blame except myself.

Way to go! Way to fuck it up.

No way I can face him tomorrow. No way I can walk in

that gym and pretend like nothing happened. And not a chance in hell I can look him in the eyes, plaster on an artificial smile, and make generic conversation about anything except the craziness floating around in my head.

I just can't.... Way to go, me!

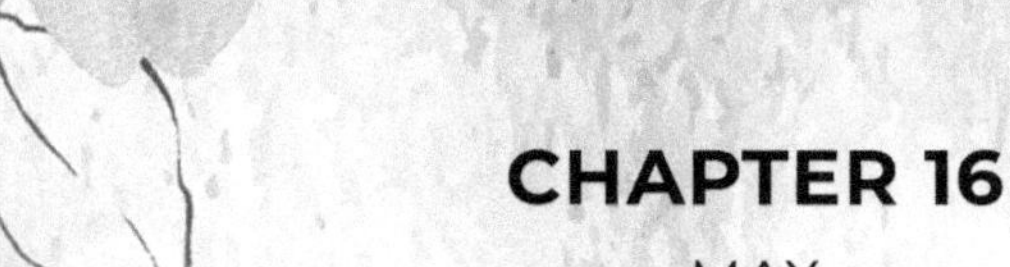

CHAPTER 16

MAX

Bright light streaks through my bedroom. The harsh beams wake me from a restless night of sleep. Rolling onto my right side, I check the clock on the bedside table and groan. Just after ten and it feels like I have already lost half the day. Besides the fact it is late morning, I got roughly four hours of sleep.

Ugh.

After everything at P.I. Friday night, I have had a knot in the pit of my stomach.

Not seeing Tami at the gym yesterday morning doesn't help. She hasn't missed a day yet and something just feels *off* about the whole situation. I sent her a text, asking if she was okay. And have gotten zero response.

For some reason, it doesn't feel as if she is blowing me off. But I don't know what to believe. The last time we spoke was Thursday. When I asked to see her again. Tonight.

Everything between us has been great. The same current still buzzes between us. The same current that has riddled me with guilt since I joined Candy in the private room Friday night.

God, I hope Tami doesn't learn about that. I know I can be an asshole from time to time, but the whole situation takes asshole to new heights.

I pick up my phone and toss the charging cord to the floor. Opening up our text history, I type out a quick message to her.

> Good morning beautiful. Wanted to see if we were still on for dinner tonight. Missed you yesterday.

> Morning handsome. Sorry I missed class. I'd love dinner tonight.

> Perfect. Can I pick you up?

> I'm a little out of the way, but sure.

> Send me your address. Are you good on motorcycles?

> Haven't been on one before, but I think I'll be good.

She sends me her address and I text back that I will pick her up around six and to dress casually. I do a quick run through of my emails and social media before leaving the bed. After getting my fill of sarcasm and memes, I head for the shower and get ready for the day.

After my usual Sunday routine—housework, time out by the pool, some televised sports—I dress for my date with Tami. Slipping on a pair of jeans and a short-sleeved, black shirt, I lace up my mid-calf black, leather boots. I ignore the small amount of stubble since I shaved this morning, grab an elastic band off the bathroom vanity and pull the little length of hair I have back, securing it loosely. Fetching my leather jacket, the spare jacket and helmets, I exit through the garage.

Once everything is secure, I open the garage, rev the bike to life and drive off. The route to Tami's place is roughly thirty minutes; the distance a perfect excuse to ride. Too much time has passed since my last ride and I remind myself I need to take her out for a spin more often.

There is an odd freedom associated with riding. The wind in your face. The speed and adrenaline. An exhilaration I compare to flying. An absolute rush and pure intoxication. And the solitude. Not the lonely kind, but the type where you think without interruption.

When I arrive at Tami's apartment, I park the bike near her truck and hop off, taking the extra jacket upstairs with me. Taking the stairs two at a time, a twinge erupts in my gut. Nausea rolls in my stomach and threatens to escape.

I pause on the second-floor landing a moment, suck in a deep breath and close my eyes. Over and over, I mentally repeat everything will be fine. I didn't do anything. I have nothing to feel guilty about. Deep breath in. Deep breath out. When I open my eyes, I continue up to the next flight and stop at her door. Another deep breath, then I lift my loose fist and knock.

When Tami opens the door, the air whooshes from my chest.

I have seen this woman in sports bras and yoga pants, a tight little red dress and fuck me heels, but this... this is my favorite look on her.

She wears skinny black jeans, tears at the knees and a little on her thighs, and a white V-neck that flaunts only a fraction of the cleavage I love to secretly admire. A silver key on a chain rests at the top of her sternum with the word *beauty* etched into the metal. Her hair is swept back in two Dutch braids, a style I have never seen on her.

"Hey. You ready to go?" The dry scratch of my voice surprises me, and I swallow.

"Let me grab my phone and keys." She collects what she needs, steps out on the small porch and locks the door. "Ready," she says. A brilliant smile lights up her face and warmth blooms in my chest.

Shaking off the odd sensation, I hand her the extra leather jacket and helmet. "These are for you while we're on the bike. Precautionary, of course."

We plod down the steps in silence and over to my bike. She studies me as I get on before zipping up her jacket. Before she asks anything, I tell her the helmets have mics inside and we can talk while riding. I also explain how to get on and where she should place her feet while we ride.

She slips the helmet over her head and I hold my arm out, giving her leverage to mount the back of the bike. She places her foot on the foot peg, takes hold of my hand, and swings her other leg over the rear like she has done it a hundred times. Once secure behind me, I start the bike and rev the engine a few times as I walk the bike backward.

Leaning forward, I kick it into first gear. "Hold on tight."

The bike accelerates and, although we haven't really picked up speed yet, the warmth of her embrace tight around my waist and her weight pressing lightly against me creates a new high. Tonight isn't the first time I've had a woman on the back of my bike, but tonight is the first time I *want* the same woman on the back of my bike again.

When we hit the street and I can drive how this bike is meant to be ridden, I shift gears and pick up speed. Her grasp tightens, leaving no space between her front and my back, and

I smile like a fool. Besides the fact that I love riding, the press of her body against mine like this takes riding to a whole new level. I will drive us around the city all night if it means I get to have her clinging to me like this.

"Where are we going?" Her voice breaks through my daydream on the helmet headset.

"You'll see. Shouldn't take long."

Her arms squeeze me a little harder and I wonder if it is because I left our destination a mystery or another reason. Either way, the warmth in my chest returns along with a newfound sense of contentment. Not sure what it is about this woman, but she has me thinking, feeling, and behaving in ways I never have in the past.

Hurricane Tami has me thrilled and terrified.

A couple of blocks from the restaurant, I spot the Santa Monica Pier in the distance. Her fingers skim the edge of my waist, grazing a slim line of skin that must be peeking out from under my shirt and jacket. The intimate gesture adds kindling to the warmth in my chest and a flash of heat surges to my cock for a reason other than physical beauty.

Something in her touch is different. Heavier. More wanton. Part of me wants to ask what changed, but I choose to keep my mouth shut and enjoy what happens. Honestly, I don't care. Whatever this is, whatever is happening between us, I want more. For it to bloom and evolve.

I locate a parking space on the street near the restaurant and feed the meter. I extend my hand, gaze into her ravishing hazel eyes, and wait for her to take it. Her fingers trace over my palm and weave between mine before a breathtaking smile illuminates every facet of her heart-shaped face.

I guide us toward the restaurant, a bright neon sign in the window flashes "Tacos" to passersby.

"We're having tacos?" she asks with a cute hesitation that makes me want to kiss her.

"Best beachside tacos in town," I tell her.

"When you said casual, I wasn't sure what to expect. This is perfect." Her eyes sparkle at the prospect of eating tacos. Who knew something so simple made a woman happy?

"Glad you approve." And I couldn't be more honest or sincere.

I tug open the large glass door amongst the wall of windows facing the beach. We step out of the summer heat and inside the cool, quaint Mexican restaurant. The door closes behind us and I inhale the delicious aromas in the air. Cumin and chili, cilantro, and freshly made tortillas. My mouth waters as my stomach grumbles.

The floor is decorated in ornate Spanish tiles. A dining bar runs along the wall opposite the entrance and down one side. Several tables sit between the bar and glass front of the restaurant. The chairs throughout made of a tanned leather with large stitching, attached to colorful, metal frames. Round wicker lanterns dangle from above. The atmosphere inside is airy and open, eclectic and cozy.

We get seated at a table near the windows and are handed menus as the server informs us of specials. The server steps away to give us a moment to look over the menu. Silence stretches between us as we figure out what to eat. When the server returns, she places a carafe of water on the table between two empty glasses and a small pail of napkins.

"What can I get you two this evening?"

Tami orders the salmon quinoa salad and a passion smash margarita. I order a half portion of guacamole and chips, the shrimp tacos, and Modelo especial. The server assures me the appetizer will be out soon then leaves us.

A sudden, primal need to hear Tami's voice again courses through my veins as I attempt to initiate conversation. "I missed seeing you at the gym yesterday. Everything okay?"

I swear, for the smallest blip, pain mars her beautiful face. But as quickly as it appears, it vanishes. "Yeah, everything's fine. Was just exhausted and felt like I needed more sleep. Sorry I didn't text back."

"It's fine. As long as you're good, that's what matters."

"Probably just overexerting myself, between work and the new workout routine and day-to-day life stuff. Not giving myself as much downtime. Guess my body needed to catch up."

Reaching across the table, I take one of her hands that had been resting within reach. Her eyes dart toward the gesture and her brows pinch together. If I didn't know better, I'd say she is conflicted. About what? I don't know. Maybe us. She said she wants us to go slow. That past relationships never panned out because of other parts of her life. Parts she hasn't explained yet. As crazy as it sounds, especially coming from me, I want more time with her. I *want* things to progress.

"Is this okay?" I ask as my eyes shift from hers to our joined hands and back.

She nods imperceptibly. "Yes." Her voice is so soft. Gentle. "It's just…" I sit quiet and patient, not interrupting her train of thought as I anticipate what she might say. "I don't want to make promises. Not when things may not work out between us."

Her eyes flood with pain. As if she wants more from this relationship too, but has been burned so many times that the idea frightens her. And I long to tell her I will never do anything to hurt her, but my mouth can't seem to form the words. Because I don't know if I will follow through with said promise.

"I don't want to make promises, either. I won't sit here and lie to you. This is the first time I've ever wanted to spend more time with anyone, other than my guys. And sometimes that's questionable, too." Her eyes search mine for honesty before they drop to my lips, my throat—the candor of our exchange fevers me and forms a jittery ball beneath my diaphragm. "I like you, Tami. More than I've liked any woman. But I don't know what to do with that. Honestly, I've never done more than hook up. Then say I'll see them again when I have zero intention of doing so."

Puzzlement rests on her face and it tempts me to ask what she is thinking. But the moment gets interrupted by the server as she sets our drinks and the appetizer on the table. I opt not to delve further, pick up my bottle and tip it her direction. She clinks her glass to my bottle as we bid cheers in unison.

After our meal and a stunning tableside sunset, we indulge in cheesecake and gelato. I pay the bill and we exit into the warm evening air. Tami turns to walk toward the bike, but I redirect us as we cross the road and head for the sand.

"Where are we going now?"

"Another surprise," I admit, loving the way her eyes light up.

We mosey down the sidewalk for a bit, hand in hand, before I steer us onto the sand. She takes in the scenery and tries to decipher what's next. But with the darkening sky, she is unable to fully see the setup. Fifty feet away, on the beach, a small crowd gathers on blankets. I tug her into my side and guide us toward an empty blanket.

Once situated and comfortable, I point to the front of the crowd where a large piece of cloth has been erected. "It's movie night. Heard about a group offering movies on the beach during summer and thought it would be fun."

A smile plumps her cheeks as her eyes sparkle with delight. Suddenly, a deafening gallop echoes beneath my sternum as my lungs beg for more oxygen. "How fantastic." Her excitement is palpable. "Do you know what's playing?"

"Haven't the slightest." Nor do I care.

We get cozy on the blanket as a gentle breeze licks our skin and brushes a few baby hairs across her face. I lift my hand and tuck away the small strands. Her face softens under my touch and, in that moment, I want to kiss her. Taste her.

I lean in and her body veers infinitesimally closer to mine. Our lips centimeters apart. I dip down to taste her lips and stumble back as the opening intro to *Jaws* blares from speakers.

Still inches apart, she giggles and it is the sweetest, cutest fucking sound. And before I stop myself, I join in and laugh alongside her while a few of the couples shush us. I place a small peck on her lips, then cheek, before turning my attention toward the screen.

After two hours of shark attacks, screams, and Tami bundled in my arms on the beach, we stroll back to the bike and drive off. But I am not ready to go back to her apartment. The night is still somewhat young and I don't want our date to end.

Rather than drive east toward her apartment, I jump on the PCH and travel north. Within minutes, the lights of the city fade away and we ride peacefully in the quiet, brisk night. Her arms tighten around me as she magnetizes herself to me. Everything about this—us—feels perfect. I will drive all night with her if it means I get to keep this fire burning inside me.

Hours later, we zip through neighborhoods, minutes from her apartment. Neither of us has spoken a word since we left the beach. The silence is neither awkward nor uncomfortable. I park the bike behind her truck, kick the stand down, and let her dismount before I do. We walk in silence to her apartment and stop once we reach her door.

I have no desire for tonight to end, but with Tami, I refuse to be the one to initiate more. We lock gazes as my knuckles trace her jawline. Her eyes close and a deep, shuddering breath leaves her lips as she soaks up my touch. She may not invite me in—yet—but she sure as hell silently begs me to kiss her. I don't make her wait. My lips brush hers and her sigh warms my skin as she sags against me.

And now I am hungry. Hungry for her.

CHAPTER 17

TAMI

After the movie ends, Max drives us along the coast. The chilled night air cools my heated skin slightly. A layer of guilt still blankets my conscience, knowing what I did with Max at P.I. and him unaware it was me. At least I don't think he knows it was me. His whole demeanor tonight has been different—sweet, gentle, soft, almost *romantic*.

The closer we get to my apartment, the bigger and thicker the guilt cloud grows. I don't care how late it is or that I have to be at work at seven in the morning. The most significant piece to this puzzle right now is the man whose body currently molds mine. And I pray our pieces still fit together.

He parks his motorcycle behind my truck and waits for me to hop off before he does. Our walk to the front door is occupied with more comfortable silence. The ease we have shared most of the evening. My silence spins circles around knowing what I did with him two nights ago. As for his silence… I have no clue.

We reach the front door and flounder like two teenagers who haven't the slightest idea what happens next. As I dig in my pocket for my key, I stop. Halted by the fire blazing off him as he reaches up and brushes his knuckles against my jawline. A thrill weaves an intricate web beneath my breastbone. The slow expansion spirals out and takes over every rational thought. I close my eyes, breathe deep and memorize how his skin feels against mine.

I want him. More than anyone. Oddly, the reason seems blanketed in oblivion. But I *feel* it. Deep in my bones, a part of me calls out to and for him.

I tremble under his touch. Lean into his touch more; the weight of his touch not enough to satiate the restlessness I have felt for days. Without preamble, his lips graze mine and the world around us fades. A light sheen of sweat slicks my skin. My heart a pair of hummingbird wings, beating viciously. Lungs undecided if I need more or less oxygen. Rapid-fire sensations overwhelm me and I sigh against his soft, warm lips. My breath sweeps over his lips in invitation and he doesn't miss a beat.

His palms frame my face as he devours me with ravenous hunger. A shiver rolls down my spine. We are all lips and tongues and teeth. I fist the cotton shirt under his unzipped jacket. A hand stays on my cheek while the other glides down my torso, rests on my hip and drags me into him. Without question, I *feel* what I do to him. The bulge beneath his zipper thick and solid.

He breaks the kiss. Renders me breathless, speechless. For a moment, my eyes shut to keep the world at bay. I relish how his tongue tangled with mine. The heat and weight and intensity of his kiss. Slowly, I open my eyes, peer up at him and stop breathing. The fire and intensity in his eyes swallows me whole. An intensity stronger than two nights ago.

"Tami..." My name gruff and wanton on his lips. It curls

around his tongue and I press my thighs together. "Please," he begs. "Can I come in?"

Under the glow of the porch light, we stand silent. I stare up at him, study the rigidity of his jaw, the pucker of his lips, the hungry glow of his irises.

Every cell inside me wants to unlock this door, drag him to my bedroom, and have my way with him. And vice versa. But part of me holds back. Part of me keeps flashing back to two nights ago, when I lured him into that private room and gave him a fantasy to remember for months—years—to come. A visual to get himself off to.

Although the woman in that room *was* me, it also was not. Not in his eyes. In his eyes, Candy is this striking bombshell with the body of a goddess and dance moves that make the world disappear. Yes, I am the same woman. But he doesn't know such things. And as much as I want to reveal this secret, I also need to protect myself. And my heart.

As if sensing my inner turmoil, he snakes his arms around my waist and tugs me as close to him as possible. His lips ghost over mine. "Please, Tami." Kissing me tender—more tender than any other kiss we have shared—his mouth skims my cheekbone, my ear, down the column of my throat. "*Please,*" he begs again.

Cracks form in my will to remain strong. The need to hold my ground starts to crumble beneath my feet. He pours gasoline on the flame when his lips graze my skin.

I tip my head back and gasp; lungs heaving to catch a breath. He senses my hesitation as if we have known each other years and not weeks. Max clamps down on my shoulder with his teeth and lightly bites my skin. The sting tosses any remaining uncertainty out the window as my lungs fight for air. I level my gaze, fist his shirt and crash my mouth to his.

A volcano erupts inside me and I forget the world exists. Because right now, Max and this kiss are my world.

Our tongues tangle in a web of greed, ravenous hunger fueled by weeks of deprivation. I break the kiss to nibble along his jawline before inching back to meet his gaze.

"Yes." One word has never said so much.

All thumbs as I unlock the door, I yank him inside and toward my room. I shut the door and we crash together. His lips on mine. Hands wage war with clothes. I shove his jacket down his arms and to the floor. Lift his shirt over his head and send it flying. Unbuckle his belt fast enough to illicit a fine. Just as I unbutton his jeans, he grabs my hands and stops me.

"The idea of you stripping me bare does crazy things to me. But… I'm not the only one who's wearing clothes." A smirk plays on his lips in the moonlight.

My lips part and he presses a finger to them. We stand still as stone and take each other in, in the darkness. He closes his eyes a beat. When he opens them, I don't breathe. His gaze locks with mine and penetrates deep in my marrow. So much swirls in his brilliant green irises. Passion and heat. Hunger and pain. Need and want. Greed and something I can't pinpoint.

He leans in closer with wide eyes, a hint of scrutiny below the surface. When his lips brush mine, gaze locked in place, it feels more potent. Powerful. Heady. A connection opens between us. One not previously there. He draws my lower lip between his teeth, sucking and nibbling. Part of me wants to close my eyes. To allow my other senses free rein over my body. But I don't. I let the lust invade me and spill from my eyes to his.

His fingertips skirt over the waistband of my jeans. A hiss escapes my lips as I gasp and suck in my belly. Max guides his hands up my torso, peels the jacket off my arms with slow precision, and lets it fall to the floor. Coasting his fingertips down either side of my abdomen, he hesitates when he reaches the bottom of my shirt.

"I've thought about this moment since the day I first saw you," he whispers into the darkness.

At a loss for what to say, I breathe heavier. Harsher. I want to tell him I have thought about him and us and this several times. And after what happened Friday night, I haven't slept much. But I say nothing. Instead, I lean closer, tip my head toward his chest and press my lips to his hot skin. He sucks in a deep, steadying breath as his hands clutch at my waist.

My lips dance along his clavicle, down his sternum, and over to his nipple. When I take the pert flesh between my lips, he hisses loudly, and strengthens his grip on me. Then, he yanks me back, rips my shirt over my head and unclasps my bra. He hauls me against his fevered skin and ravishes me with his mouth.

I lose focus as the room blurs. Get lost in the way his lips and tongue graze over the contours and angles of my body. Become a slave to his tongue as it tastes my skin. Forget embarrassment as I pant with need the more he worships me.

Yanking the band from his hair, I comb my fingers through his curls, make a fist and jerk back. Hard. He growls against my skin. The vibration ricochets out of his chest and strikes a chord between my thighs. Then his mouth encases my nipple before he clamps down.

He walks me backward until the edge of the bed bumps my legs. Before I get a word in, he captures my mouth again. His dexterous fingers unbutton and unzip my jeans. He shoves them down my legs before he lowers me to the mattress.

I scoot back; the moonlight dances on my skin. His eyes eat me alive as they scan me tip to top.

"No panties, huh? Glad I didn't know that earlier. Our date might have been much shorter."

He undoes his pants and shoves them down along with his briefs. His erection slaps against his abdomen, thick and proud. Wrapping one hand around his cock, he strokes up his shaft while he devours every inch of me with his fiery gaze.

Crawling up the bed, he sets condoms off to the side and kisses his way up until he reaches my lips. He consumes me as if he will never get the chance again. Then he begins his slow descent. Each lick stirs fire in my veins. Each suck has that fire bubbling to the surface. Every nibble toward my apex has me internally screaming for more.

And then he is there.

His hot breath on my clit. Short bursts of air heave from his lungs and dampen my flesh. His eyes bore into mine, fueling me with intensity and hunger and necessity. On the verge of whimpering, I open my mouth. Ready to tell him how desperate I am to have his mouth on me.

But I don't get the opportunity.

His mouth clamps over me and suckles before he licks me base to clit. I suck in a sharp breath. My back arches off the mattress. He latches on to my hips and pins me down as he grinds his mouth between my legs. Dizziness consumes me as I mentally stumble. A heatwave spreads over my skin. Sweat flares from every pore. I bite my lip as a fiery orgasm builds and scorches every molecule inside me.

His magical tongue stimulates and flicks and tastes me. He teases and builds me up. Has me on the cusp of begging for more. I fist his hair and drive him closer. I grind my hips into him and fuck his face with determination. His tongue swirls around my clit, again and again, before I shudder and release on his tongue.

Before I catch my breath or float down from my high, Max tears open a condom wrapper and sheaths himself. He plants his forearms beside my head, cages me in, and leans down to kiss me. Deep. I moan at my salty tang on his tongue. He breaks the kiss and hovers a breath from my lips.

"Fucking sexy as hell. I've dreamt how you might taste. Never expected I'd be insatiable. Don't think I'll ever have my fill of you."

His lips drop to mine and taste me again. And just as he breaks the kiss, he thrusts his hips forward and invades me. I tip my head back and smash my breasts to his pecs as I gasp. He doesn't move. Doesn't say a word. We remain in this limbo state as we both adjust to the heat and girth and stretch of each other. When he comes back into focus, I trail my hands down the planes of his back until I reach his ass and squeeze.

"Fuck me…" The words spill from my lips, but the wanton woman speaking them is foreign to my ears. Voice nothing but pure lust and insatiable hunger.

I just opened the floodgates. Max seizes one of my legs and hooks it over his shoulder. "As you wish."

He rocks his hips back ever so slowly, leaves just the crown of his cock inside me, then slams into me and bottoms out. This angle lets him in deeper. And he. Is. Everywhere.

I cry out. Loud enough to wake Amber and several neighbors. He rears back, drives forward and grunts as he hits that sweet spot inside me. And then he picks up speed. Hips thrusting faster. Harder. Our cries echo in the air and bleed through the walls.

Not usually one to be vocal in the bedroom, I don't fight what Max does to me. How he has woken something deep inside me. Emotions I generally suppress to do my job with a clear conscience. But something about Max has these concealed emotions rising to the surface. Has me edging closer. Has me craving more of him. His hands on my body, his heady scent in the air I breathe, his moans of pleasure echoing in my ears, his undeniable taste on my tongue.

My body climbs and tightens around him as he pistons in and out of me.

"Come for me, baby. Need to feel you let go," he pants.

He thrusts his hips forward and I roll my eyes back in my head. The one-two punch of his cock hitting that sweet spot deep inside me and his body slapping mine sets me off. My body shakes and grips him tight. His cock swells just before he grunts my name and releases inside me.

We lay there, his body half covering mine, drenched in sweat as we catch our breath and surf the postcoital wave. I comb my fingers through his hair as his fingers draw lazy shapes on my skin.

In this little blip of time, a sense of wholeness and peace washes over me. A peculiar sensation, but one I don't fight or deny. If anything, I wrap my mind around it and embrace it. Embrace the idea of having Max in my life. Embrace the idea of us.

The room grows quiet as our labored breaths settle and we melt into each other. Max has been still a while and I wonder if he fell asleep. I sigh into the dark as my eyes drift shut and I let my mind wander to a place of peace.

Just on the cusp of sleep, Max shifts off me. Goose bumps prickle my skin as cool air replaces his warmth.

Propping up on my elbows, I watch as he picks up his underwear and jeans and slips them on.

"What are you doing?"

A quizzical expression mars his face. "Have to go home, Tami. I work in the morning. Can't exactly show up like this," he bites out as he gestures the length of his body.

What's with the attitude? Why the blunt remark?

A pang stabs low in my belly and I can't help but voice my concern. "Did I do something wrong?"

He locates his shirt, forces his arms through the sleeves and yanks it over his head. He sits at the foot of the bed, puts his socks and boots back on, and makes every effort not to look in my direction. When he finishes the task, he rests his elbows on his knees, and drops his head in his hands as an audible sigh lingers in the air.

I almost don't hear him when he speaks, his mouth muffled by his palms. "You didn't do anything wrong. It's just that…" The room becomes eerily quiet a moment. As if someone clicked mute. "I don't know what I'm supposed to do here."

Tucking my feet under me, I scoot closer to him, run a hand from his shoulder to his waist while the other hand rests under my chin atop the opposite shoulder. I kiss the back of his neck then whisper in his ear.

"I don't either. This is new for me, too. Not sex, but the other stuff. We can do things at whatever pace is right for us."

He swivels his head and searches my gaze. "Honestly, I've never wanted to spend more time with a woman. Ever. So, this is foreign territory. Don't know which way is up, down, right or left. May never know. Not trying to make things weird. Just seems fair to tell you how I feel."

"I appreciate your honesty. The last *relationship* I had was before college. And do they really count at that age? My adult self would say no." Pausing a moment to take a breath, I continue. "I'm okay with us taking things a bit slower. And I'm just as out of my element as you are. We don't really know that much about each other, and I'd like that to change. We both have history; secrets. That won't all come out after a couple dates or one great night of sex. Takes time. And trust."

He nods, stares at his palms as he processes what I said. His eyes drift back to me again.

"I really do have to go. Not because I want to, but because I have to. Can't show up in a doctor's office in street clothes. They'd probably fire my ass." He laughs softly and his mood feels lighter a moment ago.

"I understand. Maybe next time you can stay. Or I can. Whichever."

A smirk tugs up the corner of his mouth. "Don't think we'd make it to work if I woke up next to you. I'd never want to leave the bed."

I laugh at the truth behind his words. He rises from the bed, bends over and snatches his jacket from the floor by the door. Crawling off the bed, I reach for my robe and tie the sash around my waist, prepared to walk him to the door. He studies me briefly and his brows bunch in the middle.

"What is it?"

He scrutinizes me a moment then shakes his head. "Nothing. Just felt like déjà vu."

And for a beat, I consider he may put two and two together and figure out who I am. If he does, he never mentions it as we walk from my room to the front door. I hand him the jacket I wore earlier, but he knocks my hand away, a radiant smile spreading across his face.

"Hold on to it. You'll need it the next time we ride."

How can such a simple group of words put me at ease?

He kisses me slow and sweet before he turns the knob and exits the apartment. I watch as he takes the steps two at a time. Hear him rev the motorcycle and drive away.

I shut the door and meander back to my room in a daze.

Plopping down on the bed, I wrap myself in the top sheet and inhale a long drag of his scent and mine mixed together. Rolling on my side, the sheet bunches in my arms as my mind whirls. Questions and uncertainty pop up like a digital marquee. What will happen when I tell him about *me*? Will he freak? Will he be open? Or will that be the end before we have a beginning?

Defeatism runs vicious laps in my head. I clutch the sheet closer to my chest. Beneath my sternum, a first-degree burn mars my pericardium. Tears pool my eyes. And the idea of losing Max overwhelms me.

In his arms, the apprehension fades away. But as soon as he leaves, anxiety swarms me like angry bees and punctures every ounce of optimism.

I just don't want to lose him… before he's even mine to have.

CHAPTER 18

MAX

I park in the shade, get out of my car and trek to the entrance of Wholly You. Walking through the front door, Tina greets me with the same overeager smile and hello she does every morning. *Thank god I never fuck women from work.* That woman has had a thing for me since day one. Sure, I am fine as fuck. But if I haven't given you the time of day yet, it isn't happening, sweetheart.

I sit down at my desk, fire up the slow as hell computer and check my emails. Same shit, new day. I answer the dozen or so emails sitting in my inbox then double-check my schedule. Today seems pretty light. A typical Monday involves several follow-up clients, but only half my usual fill the roster. More than likely, the others took vacation time with their family. Happens every summer.

Pulling client files for the day, I review those scheduled before lunch. As I peruse file one, my mind drifts back to last night. The folder rests in my hands, my elbows on the desk. I lose focus at the memory of Tami's silky skin against mine.

Her skin so warm. Curves so dangerous, you have to take

them slow. Sweet, succulent nipples. Her taste an unexpected addiction.

Although Tami is physical perfection, her body isn't the only part of her that attracts me.

She is smart as hell and has a vivacious spirit. A magnetism that hauls me closer; an unavoidable gravity. And she holds an air of mystery.

Her arms around my waist as we drove the PCH flipped a switch in me. Heated me more than the summer sun. Her body molded to mine as if she always belonged there. The way she curled up next to me on the beach blanket; my heart never hammered at the idea of embracing a woman. But my heart misbehaves when it comes to Tami. And when we were linked, every atom and fiber and molecule inside me sang. Sparked to life. Glowed with brilliance. Felt alive for the first time.

No woman beckons my soul like Tami.

For a brief second, an idea surfaces. But I don't know what to do with it.

Candy may be my private infatuation—I will never forget what happened in that small, private room. From the moment I laid eyes on Candy, I was balls deep in lust with her. Every line and curve of her body oozes sex and desire and primal need.

But she isn't Tami. Tami is my *personal addiction*.

A twinge beneath my sternum follows this self-proclamation and I press the heel of my hand to my chest. A sensation I familiarize myself with. One I imagine won't fade soon. But why?

Whenever Tami and I share the same space, everything becomes a conduit for the escalating energy between us. Last night, in her bedroom, that raw current had a life of its own. Heady. Fierce. Intoxicating. Addictive.

With every bow of her back, every rock of her hips, every stroke and claw and clench of her hands fisting the sheets, I matched her move for move. When I claimed her body, she begged for more. A symbiotic force ebbed and flowed around us. Every kiss and touch and thrust had a familiar synchronicity—as if we had known each other eons. I don't understand the familiarity. Honestly, it confuses the hell out of me. Not sure it will ever make sense. What I do know is I love how alive I feel with her. Side by side. Hand in hand. Front to back. Tongues entangled. Bodies connected.

Our bond is chemical. Pure energy. Lust.

I continue staring at everything and nothing. My phone startles me out of my daydream and alerts me my first client will arrive soon. I shake my head and try to focus on what's important now. My job. Scanning the file, I scold myself for not putting priorities first.

Forty-five minutes later, Sally leaves my office with a huge smile. As she should. Sally has seen me for two months now, has maintained healthy dietary habits, and started walking thirty plus minutes a day. Her reward? She lost almost half her weight loss goal and two dress sizes. Clients like Sally make me love my job and the impact I have on their lives. I may be a hard-ass at times, but the end result is always worth it. And the clients agree.

With fifteen minutes until my next client, my mind wanders again. Flashes of last night pop up and I close my eyes as my skin fevers. Solar waves heat me head to toe and I question why. Why does this heat, this fire, form near my solar plexus when I think of Tami? When she is nearby.

No idea... but it pisses me off.

Am I developing *feelings* for Tami? Is that what this is?

News flash… I don't do feelings. No emotions. No strings. No bullshit. How it has always been. Right?

So, why does no strings with Tami make me want to gut punch myself? Give myself a swift kick to the balls?

An angel sits on one shoulder and whispers sweet nothings. Reminds me how amazing it would be to have Tami in my daily life. Imagine the delicious possibilities of that life.

But a fiery little devil sits on the opposite shoulder. Horns, tail, and Blivet firmly in place. He taunts me with a wicked smirk. Reminds me if I settle down with one woman, I will miss out on the endless variety of pussy.

I rest my elbows on the desk, drop my head in my hands and tug at my hair.

Have I fallen into the world's biggest clusterfuck? What the fuck am I supposed to do? If I keep dating Tami—the most challenging task of my life—there is the potential for unlimited sex. Which sounds like a dream all its own. But if I call it off—chalk it up to having a great time and that's it—will I be able to handle the repercussions? Will I be able to see her publicly and act as if we are just friends? Be able to move forward?

Fuck. What the hell am I supposed to do?

When did I turn into a goddamn pussy? Maybe I should call one of the guys and ask their opinion. But what help will they be? If anything, they will preach about never being tied to one woman. What they taught me. So how do I expect to get advice from them?

The reminder on my phone chimes. I mentally slap myself for getting this distracted at work. I quickly scan Peter's file, review his last few visits and make note of what progress I will look for with him today.

Just as the door to my office cracks open, my phone pings

with an incoming text. I don't check who it is, flip it to vibrate, and drop it in my pocket.

"Thank you for everything, Mr. Kingston. I appreciate you helping me start my way back to healthier habits."

"You're welcome, Janna. And please, call me Max. My father is Mr. Kingston."

We laugh a moment before I walk around the desk and lead her to the door. Newer clients, generally, take more time because of the initial intake and learning more about their lifestyle. I check my watch and note how quick the first half of the day flew by.

Exiting the office, I walk to the health food store with an in-store café a few blocks away. Remembering the text notification from earlier, I pull my phone from my pocket. A text from Tami. I unlock my phone and open the message.

> Hey! I had a really great time last night. I'd love to do it again. See you at CF tomorrow.

My fingers hover over the keyboard as I contemplate replying. My brain and balls play on the teeter-totter and I don't know who to listen to. I don't want to come off as an asshole—which I will if I don't respond. But I also don't want to give her false ideas about where this *relationship* is or isn't going. Because I have no clue.

So, I ignore the message.

I sit in the store café, eat my lunch, and keep going back to the message she sent. Is she just being polite? Does she think something more will happen between us? Does she think she is my fucking *girlfriend*?

The last question pops in my head and scares the shit out of me. I clutch my chest and breathe rapidly. *Fuck.* I pinch my eyes shut. *Deep breaths, Max.*

I can't fucking do this. Can't have some female clinging to me. Dictating where I go, what I do, who I hang out with… blah, blah, blah. No fucking way.

And just like that, I revert back to the cocky son of a bitch I was on the day I first saw Tami.

I need to set boundaries and limits and enforce them the same way I always have. Max Kingston is not the kind of guy who settles down, has two-point-five kids, and slips a gold band on a woman's left hand, let alone my own.

The longer I sit in the café and stare at my lunch, the more determined I am about setting our *relationship* straight. At keeping my rules intact. Which is for the best.

I have no intention of answering her text; that will just open the floodgates to more texting, and possibly phone calls. As much as I like Tami, I don't want to be a dick and block her number.

Finishing my lunch, I place the dishes in the washtubs by the trash bin, exit the café, and head back to the office. I cover the distance in minutes. As I open the door and turn down the hall, I tell myself, for the umpteenth time, not getting attached to Tami is the right move. And for the umpteenth time, my stomach twists and I hate myself a little more.

I am so royally fucked.

CHAPTER 19

TAMI

couple days have passed since I last saw or heard from Max. After our date Sunday night, not to mention the life-altering sex, I sensed a shift between us. What I initially thought was a good shift. But now, I am not sure that is the case.

I try not to read into the whole situation too heavily. He said the only reason he couldn't stay Sunday night was work-related. And I get that. But it also feels like an easy excuse. I want to give him the benefit of the doubt. Want to believe he didn't up and leave because he got what he wanted all along. But giving him that benefit is really difficult when he won't communicate with me. At all.

"Hakes fa au ya do," Mrs. Benson mumbles as I move the ultrasonic tool over her teeth and her mouth fills with water.

Think she said *thanks for all you do*, so I answer with that in mind. "You're welcome, Mrs. Benson. Glad I've been able to help you get your teeth back to where they should be. Sometimes it takes a while, but it's worth it. How's Mr. Benson?"

Honestly, I don't know why I ask people questions when I

won't understand half of what they say. All in good fun, I suppose. See if I *can* figure out what they say. Like a crypto-quote, only different.

She proceeds to tell me he is doing well, how his law firm just landed a big case, and how excited she is for him and the other partners of the firm. Our conversation goes back and forth a little before I finish and get the dentist.

After Mrs. Benson's teeth get poked and prodded by the dentist, I add a quick coat of fluoride to her teeth and walk her to the check-out area, promising to see her in six months.

I clean up my station and complete a few other tasks before I leave for the day. The day has been chaotic and exhausting and endless, but I have been eager to hit the gym and release the pent-up energy.

The closer I get to seeing Max, the more my palms sweat. I press my palm to my sternum and breathe steadily, trying to settle my erratic heartbeat. For the first time, I feel lost. Not knowing what to do or think or feel.

I have no clue how much time has passed since I last dated. How does dating work nowadays? Max seems so aloof, distant. But I remind myself he was somewhat detached when we first met. And I don't want to read into his reactions or behaviors too much, but that is challenging when we don't talk.

But that all changes today.

Parking my truck, I stroll into the gym, go to the locker room and switch from my scrubs to a sports bra and leggings. Once my belongings are secured in a locker, I take a deep breath and make my way to the mat to stretch and warm up. I remind myself to stay calm and act the same as usual. Honestly, I love the constant flirting and banter.

Out on the floor for a solid ten minutes and I have yet to

see Max, which is odd. He always arrives well before class begins, doing his coach tasks and warming up. When class is a couple minutes from starting, I spot Max across the gym at one of the deadlift areas. I stare at him for a solid minute as he squats with a shit ton of weight on his shoulders. Snapping out of my Max-induced trance, I'm aware he sees me following his every move in the large mirror on the wall.

A smirk tugs up one side of his mouth as he stands to his full height and drops the bar behind him. The weights clang loudly as they smack the floor. He shoots the shit with a couple guys next to him before walking in my direction. Just as I stand to greet him, ready to ask how he is, he walks past me, shakes hands with another guy, and gives him a bro hug.

Seriously? Is this how he plans to behave? Like a fucking five-year-old?

Class starts and he barely glances my way. I spy him out of the corner of my eye as he helps a few of the newer people in the group. He is all hands with one woman, which pisses me the hell off.

The more I survey the situation, the more it seems his intention *is* to piss me off. To get under my skin. Well, Max can kiss my ass. If this is how he wants to play, he has no idea what I have in my arsenal.

Feigning the need for help, I walk over to Marquis. Marquis has a few inches on Max and is pure muscle. His rich, dark skin has me licking my lips. He keeps his hair and beard short and well-groomed—which would probably feel euphoric between my thighs. I ask him to help me with my form while I perform push-ups because my posture doesn't feel straight.

A bright smile lights up his face. "More than happy to help." His husky voice enough to make me melt.

"Thanks. I really appreciate it."

We step over to an open area and I get in plank position. I glance at where Max is and notice his eyes on us. The wicked vixen inside me glows brighter than the fluorescents above as I face the floor, ready to push-up like I have no idea what I am doing.

I begin the fake set of push-ups, sticking my butt up a smidge as I do. Knowing I am doing it wrong, intentionally. Marquis's hand presses lightly on my lower back, a hair above my ass, as he coaches me to lower my hips. I drop my hips a fraction, but know they are still not where they should be. He guides me again as my body moves closer to the floor and then back up. At one point, one of his hands rests on my lower back while the other braces my abs.

I keep up the charade another minute or two, allowing Marquis to believe he helps me improve. But I also observe Max as his face reddens more and more by the second.

Good. Two can play your damn games.

We work out another thirty-five minutes. Max pep talks the newer people at the end of the session. When he finishes his spiel, I walk in his direction, planning to ask what the hell his problem is. As fun as the whole cat-and-mouse game is, we are adults. And adults have conversations, even if the outcome is undesirable.

Ten feet away, he sees me. And for a split-second, I am caught in quicksand as he turns and bolts for the men's locker room.

What the actual fuck? So, this is it? You got what you wanted and you are done with me?

Well, I have news for you, pretty boy. Two can play this game and I play it so much better.

In the locker room, I snatch my duffel, skip the shower, and bolt for my truck. If he wants to be a dick, he won't see what I have in store coming.

"I hope you enjoyed the fun, pretty boy. Because soon, I'll blindside you. You'll wish you'd made a different choice. And I won't give a fuck."

CHAPTER 20

MAX

This is exactly what I need—a night out with the guys. I haven't been myself recently and that has leaked into other areas of my life.

Normally, I hang with them a few days a week, more on weekends, but we haven't seen each other in more than a week. Surprisingly, they aren't giving me shit over it.

When we enter The Sophisticate tonight, we scan the floor for Rocco, and ask to bring Tristan downstairs. Last time, Nic and I brought Jason along for the ride. We sold him within five minutes. Not really a challenge with all the beautiful women.

Rocco agrees to let us bring Tristan, but I have a feeling Tristan won't return. Not that he doesn't like clubs or beautiful women or nudity. More like he won't return because he has a gorgeous wife and a baby on the way. Since we picked him up, all he has done is talk about Renée and how excited he is to be a father.

We hit the bottom landing of the stairwell, walk down the dark corridor that leads to what I deem heaven; or one form of it. A week passed since I was last here. And a lot has happened in the last week.

I was lured into a private room, not far from where we sit, by a woman who is breathtakingly beautiful. In that room, she gave me something I wouldn't soon lose sight of or forget.

But also, in the last week, I went out with a woman who makes my heart pound painfully in my chest. We had a memorable evening together, did things I had never done with any other woman, and then I basically tossed her away. The way I have acted toward her since makes me nauseous.

Yesterday, I was tempted to reach out to her, shoot her a text and ask why she wasn't at the gym. But call me an asshole.

Had too much time passed to fix my mistake? For the first time in my life, I actually *feel* like the biggest piece of shit on planet Earth. I never thought I would feel this way about any woman. Hell, I have slept with countless women. Never once felt guilty for blowing them off.

So why do I feel like a douchebag now?

I snap out of my internal reverie and focus on Nic, Jason, and Tristan, and their conversation. Currently, they ramble on about the pretty, Native-American woman on the stage, who I believe is Indigo. Nic and Jason speak vulgarities; explicit with what they would do to her. Tristan sits on the sidelines, scans the place and takes it all in. He seems overwhelmed with it all. And for a second, I feel the same.

As Indigo's time on stage edges closer to an end, I suggest the guys pay for a lap dance. As selfish as it sounds, I don't want them ogling Candy and discussing all the various positions they hope to fuck her in. Call me possessive and territorial over her. Probably not the only one.

Indigo exits the stage as several people in the audience

hoot and holler their appreciation. Nic and Jason wave over a server, order another round of drinks and pay for a lap dance. They spend a moment trying to persuade Tristan to do the same, but he smiles politely and declines. I remain quiet in my chair, knowing it won't be long before Candy dances across the stage. I hope seeing her helps settle my head. She is the perfect distraction and exactly what I need right now.

The drinks arrive at the table, along with a petite Asian woman. She teases Nic and Jason, and their eyes get lost in her tiny physique. Tristan peers over at me with a *I'm ready to leave* expression on his face. I nod to him, giving him a look that says I understand and am okay with it. He only came out with us to get out of the house for a little bit and to appease me. But he really loves his wife and has moved past the stage of wanting to come to bars and clubs.

Tristan scoots his chair back, rises and gives me a quick nod before he wanders up the stairwell. I check Jason and Nic, and they are so focused on the woman in front of them, they don't even notice Tristan left. Hopefully, they focus on their lap dance a while longer, especially when I hear Candy is about to grace the stage.

The stage is dark as the curtains open. Candy's silhouette barely visible. A stage light pops on, and the glow is softer than usual. Her back faces the crowd. Her wig has long strands in pastel blue, purple, pink, and yellow that end in curls just above her wrists, which rest above her ass. And her body is painted in a light shimmer of glitter. As I study her body before the music starts, I spot something on her wrist. Something I can't quite make out, but rings familiar.

The music starts and my eyes scan up her body as her shoulders bounce up and down with the beat. The song is not the seductive melody I typically hear when she dances. It pops and bounces more. The song morphs and she gyrates her hips, her back still facing the audience. I ogle her waist as her hips circle again and again before transitioning into another move and spinning to face the audience.

And then I see her face. The absence of bangs on her wig makes her profile completely evident.

Fucking. Speechless.

I must be seeing shit. There is no fucking way in hell I am seeing things clearly. I lift my hands to my eyes, rub them and peer in her direction again. When my eyes focus, she has the biggest fuck you smile plastered on her face as she stares at me.

What. The. Actual. Fuck?

She glides across the stage, crawls close to several men, tugging on their ties and grinding her body on the stage. And when she does maneuvers to remove the skimpy attire covering her body, I see red. Every cell in my body wants to fuck up any man that comes within ten feet of her. Actually, I want to fuck up any man that checks out her body longer than I deem comfortable.

The song drags on as if it will never end and she appears to be enjoying every second of torturing me. We will see about that.

My eyes don't leave hers as I raise my hand and signal for a server. When the server arrives, my eyes still on Candy—or Tami, or whatever her name really is—I pay for time with her after she leaves the stage. More than one dance's worth of time. When the server walks off, I wait for her eyes to meet mine as I lift my glass to her.

Her lips flatten in a tight line for a brief second and I know I have her right where I want her.

CHAPTER 21
TAMI

Indigo exits the stage and pats my shoulder as she passes. For a second, I hesitate, walking leisurely to get in position behind the closed curtain. Part of me excited, part of me freaking the hell out.

Tonight, I chose a song outside of my norm. One which will have every set of eyes hypnotized. Usually, I prefer dancing to something more alluring and sultry, but tonight's song has more of a kicked-up tempo and a hidden innuendo. The beat is fun and I can't wait to dance to it.

Especially since I know Max sits center stage. Things will change after tonight. Not quite sure how, but we will never be the same.

Spreading my legs wider than normal, I stack my wrists behind me and rest them above my tailbone. I inhale deeply and ready for the stagehand to draw the curtain open. A draft brushes against my backside and I know the barrier between me and the audience has vanished. A softer light pops on, and focuses on me from the waist up as requested.

I count to five before the music plays. The intro bobs and I alternate raising and lowering my shoulders with the beat. A reference to my dancer name echoes in the lyrics before the tempo changes. I rock my hips and circle them with exaggeration as I noticeably pop my ass out.

As the song morphs, I spin and face the sea of men and women, spotting Max immediately. His jaw drops and I love the exhilaration in my veins. He gawks at me with wide eyes in disbelief. I smile deviously and relish in the fact I revealed my identity at the perfect moment.

That's right, motherfucker. I'm your fantasy girl.

I gyrate across the stage, performing the routine I created after leaving CrossFit Tuesday. I crawl across the stage and hunt my prey as I aim for two men at a table near one end of the stage. When they are within touching distance, I reach forward and grab one of their ties, tugging him up and close to me, our faces inches apart. The poor guy's eyes widen and he looks like he has never been dominated by a woman. His eyes sparkle with excitement as his breathing picks up. So, for good measure, I grind into the stage like a wave and enjoy it as he squirms.

I let him go and head for a table at the other end of the stage, bypassing the center section intentionally. I continue my act, hoping everything I do has an effect on Max. When I check in on him, his face is red. Livid. He grinds his teeth and flexes his jaw.

He raises his hand and a server sidles up to his table, where he sits with the same two guys I saw with him before. Trina grinds over the two of them while Max keeps his eyes on me. When the server leans closer to Max, my pulse whooshes behind my ears. He talks with her a moment before she waltzes off. When he peeks back up at me and our eyes lock, he lifts his glass and sends me a shit-eating grin.

Son. Of. A. Bitch.

I shake off my irritation at the fact Max probably just paid to have time with me. Something I cannot get out of. Not unless I tell Rocco falsities to have Max kicked out.

Damnit.

The song ends quickly after Max believes he has gained the upper hand. I storm off the stage, am handed my robe, and told by one of the floor girls I have been requested for a dance. And the person paid for extra time.

A low growl rumbles in my chest when she tells me the table number and provides a description of Max. I fight the urge to tell her I already know him, because that little tidbit will do nothing but start trash talk. And catty bitches are the last thing I need.

Deciding to stay in my robe, rather than change, I give myself a minute to catch my breath and drink some water. I also give myself a pep talk, telling myself I still hold all the control in this scenario. Unlike our night together Sunday, he can't do anything with me here if I don't allow it. One last deep breath, I steel myself and walk out from backstage.

Weaving through the tables, I walk the direct path to where Max and his two friends sit, noting Trina is no longer there. Max gleams at me as I approach. A stupid, fucking grin plastered to his face. So, instead of being the sweet version he has known, I go all business when I reach his table.

"You requested a dance, sir," I say, blunter and more statement-like, rather than asking.

Max's smile grows painfully big. His cheeks redden and plump. For the first time, his friends notice me. As they inspect me, a small part of me wonders if Max never wanted his friends to see me. When the taller man opens his mouth in appraisal first, my question is answered.

Yes, Max purposely kept me to himself.

"Shit, Max. You're a lucky fucking bastard." The man slaps him on the back as if they are playing sports and I am the end goal. *Asshole.*

The other man doesn't say a word, but simply stares at me. His observation has me more uncomfortable than any words would. The second man leans over and whispers something to the taller man. Both their expressions turn lewd and undesirable as they scrutinize and drool over me. My arms tighten over my chest as I cinch my robe firmer into place.

Max notices my discomfort, pushes his chair back, and rises. "I did. But not here."

This whole situation is beyond awkward, but thankfully I don't have to entertain him with these two creepsters ogling the entire time.

With an imperceptible nod, I acknowledge. "Follow me." And out of some tiny habit, from our last time together, I reach down and wrap his hand in mine as I guide us away from his friends.

For a moment, I contemplate whether to take him to the lounge or one of the private rooms.

Gah! Confusion doesn't even begin to cover the storm swirling in my head. In some respects, I want the privacy and option to talk with him, and that is easiest in one of the private rooms. But being alone, in a closed room, with him right now has me on edge.

Finally deciding, I guide us to one of the private rooms. In all honesty, it will work best. We approach the doors and I tell the bouncer the same pitch as last time. He agrees as Max and I enter the small space.

I close the door and spin to face him. Before I can stop him, his hands cup my face and he crushes his lips to mine.

My initial reaction is to shove him off me. To yell at him. Tell him to get his hands off me. To punish him for treating me like a piece of trash after we had sex. To kick and scream and call him an asshole loud enough for the entire club to hear. But I don't. I can't.

Instead, I melt into him and sync my lips with his, opening up and granting him access. His tongue tangles with mine as a growl emanates from my throat. Goose bumps erupt on my flesh as he skims his fingers along the outside of my abdomen. The energy in the room is liquid fire and undiluted passion and insatiable hunger.

I tug at the bottom of his shirt, slip my hands beneath the cotton and skim his flesh until I reach his shoulder blades, sinking my nails in before I drag them down his back. A growl booms from his chest as he clutches me tighter. The feral sound vibrates low in my belly and moisture pools between my thighs.

We grope and tease and grind against each other as we grant ourselves a temporary pass at talking. Then Max starts walking us across the room, to the chaise, where he lays me down. The second my body hits the cool leather, I snap out of the lusty trance, yank my mouth from his, and shove his chest.

"No."

His hands rest on either side of me and press into the leather while he catches his breath.

"What?"

"I said *no.*"

"Are you serious right now?"

My skin fevers as my blood pressure pounds in my veins. *Am I serious? Is he for real?*

"Are *you* serious? Since Sunday, you've given me the cold

shoulder. But as soon as you find out I'm your fucking fantasy girl, everything's suddenly all good? Don't fucking think so."

A light touch to my bicep; an attempt to calm me. "Tami…"

"Don't call me that here," I squeal, sending him a death glare. It says how serious this is. That I am not playing games.

"Sorry." He takes a deep breath. He still hovers over me. "Sorry about this week. I've been an asshole. It's just…"

I study his expression and try to read the thoughts spinning in his head. "What? What is it that you're dying to get off your chest?" My words are laced with well-deserved venom.

"Damnit! I'm trying to apologize."

"Well, just an FYI, you suck at it."

He propels off the chaise and away from me, then leans against the wall across from me. "Jesus, Ta… T. Give me a fucking break. I don't know what the fuck I'm doing here." He gestures between us. "As much as I don't want to admit it, I'm scared shitless."

I jerk my head back and furrow my brows. "You're scared?" I soften my voice and rise from the chaise. "Why are you scared?"

Max follows me with his gaze as I slowly stride across the small space and lessen the space between us. He closes his eyes as he tips his head back and rests it against the wall. His chest rises and falls rapidly. Eyes pinched tightly before they pop open and he stares at the ceiling.

"Scared of what I feel for you." His words are barely a whisper, but I hear them.

It would be easy to reach out and touch him. But I resist. "And what is it, exactly, that you feel for me?"

I step closer. Close enough to wrap an arm around his waist and melt into him, but I won't. Not until he confesses what holds him back.

He drops his chin and pins me with his striking green irises and an unfamiliar emotion.

"I've never said the *L* word to anyone other than family. Not sure if that's what I'm feeling. Really have no clue. But something is there. Something powerful. Stronger than anything I've felt. When we went out the other night, it was the first time I felt heat and desire that wasn't sexual. It scared the shit out of me. Still does. This—" he presses his hand to his chest "—is all new to me, and I don't know what the hell I'm supposed to do. This is uncharted territory."

Unable to handle the distance between us—albeit small—I step into him and snake my arms around his waist. He hugs me close and holds me tighter than anyone ever has.

"You know… I'm scared, too. Scared of losing who I am because of someone else. Scared of putting my heart out there and getting it crushed into a million pieces. Scared of falling for you and letting you in. What if it goes great for a while… until you find someone new."

Cupping my face, Max locks me in place as he tilts his mouth over mine. Our lips centimeters apart as my eyes drift closed. His hands on my skin and confession fresh on his lips sends a rush through me. I remind myself to breathe.

"I will never look at another woman the way I look at you." He paints my lips with his, the pace slow and methodical. "You're all I see when I close my eyes."

Our mouths mold together. A slow seduction of lips and tongues and sucking and licking as we memorize the softness of each other. When the kiss breaks, I freeze with my eyes closed as I relish the moment.

"What you said, I hope it's true."

"I'll prove it to you," he promises. "Last week, when you brought me in here, and I was none the wiser as to who you were, I thought I was finally getting the woman who had haunted my dreams for weeks. But then, we went out Sunday. That night… it changed everything and freaked me out. Dinner and the movie and the ride up the coast. Your body flush against mine on the bike. And then after, in your apartment. Not to sound like a man-slut, but I have slept with a lot of women and you… there is no one like you. *No one.*"

Is he saying he only likes me because of my skills in the bedroom? For his sake, I certainly hope not.

"That can be taken one of two ways. Maybe you should clarify before I go making assumptions."

He presses into my frame and walks us backward until I bump the chaise.

"What I mean is… T, you are one of a kind. Not just in the bedroom, but all of the time. When you're near me, I can't think straight. My heart skips. I forget how to breathe. You make me feel things that I've never felt a day in my life. You make me want to be someone I have never been, better than anyone I've ever been." Max's lips crush mine as he slowly lowers me on the chaise. His hands skim my abdomen and my body comes to life as the satin loosens and falls open. "You are magnificent, and not just your body. But that *is* an added bonus." He chuckles before he drops his mouth between my breasts and kisses his way to my navel.

Fire licks my skin in reaction to his words and mouth on me. Unexpectedly, Max professed so much tonight. And his confession turns me on more than his touch.

My back bows off the leather as he licks and nips and tempts me. And without question, I want him inside me. Nothing between us. *Fuck.* I just need to *feel* him. Squeeze him. Milk him.

"Max…" I croak, breathy and wanton. "Fuck me. *Please.*"

He lifts his head, brow cocked. "But I don't have anything with me."

"It's okay. I get a shot. And I assume you never go unprotected."

"Never." His eyes dead serious.

"I need you. Please, Max," I whimper.

Without further preamble, he fumbles above me and I hear his pants unzip before he shoves them to the floor. He skates two fingers down my slit to feel how slick and ready I am for him.

"Damn, baby. I don't know how long I'm going to be able to handle this."

"I. Don't. Care. Just fuck me," I groan.

We say nothing else. Then he is there. Pressure and heat and pure ecstasy. He thrusts into me and I moan like a feral wildling. He attempts a slower pace—wanting to savor the moment—but I need his power and potency and prowess. I scrape my nails down his back to his ass, clamp on and force him to fuck me harder as I meet him thrust for thrust. When his rhythm picks up, I hook my legs around his waist and lock my ankles.

A harsh growl rips from his throat as he sinks his teeth into my shoulder, his hips piston with precision. He thrusts harder as primal nature takes over, pumping in and out of me forcefully. I sink my nails into his back, claw at his flesh as I belt out his name, and he plows me like a wildebeest. Within seconds, our bodies slicken, overheat, and beg for more.

He adjusts my legs, securing them over his shoulders, before he slams deeper in me and hits the exact spot needed to send me over the edge. Our grunts and moans and body slapping bounce off the walls. Liquid fire burns deep in my marrow, spills into my veins, and spreads like wildfire as my orgasm edges.

"Almost there," I pant, nails clawing his neck.

"God, you feel so fucking good wrapped around me." He slides a hand up to my throat and chokes me.

His words and grip on my throat edges me closer. "Don't stop, Max. *Oh god…* Please. Don't. Stop." He squeezes harder and slams into me.

Slap, slap, slap. I quiver and crumble beneath him as my walls fist his cock and milk every inch of him.

"*Fuck!* I'm going to come. *Oh fuck, T! Jesus.*"

He jack-rabbits his hips as his cock pulses inside me. I frame his face and lower his mouth to mine, kissing him hard. After our bodies settle, I shift out from under him, snatch my robe and slip it back on.

"What are you doing?" he asks, voice scratchy and breath ragged.

"As weird as it is, I'm at work and we've been in here awhile. I have to go back out there."

"You're kidding me, right?"

This is why I didn't want to tell him. This exact reason.

"No, I'm not kidding. This is why I didn't say anything sooner. We can discuss this later, I promise. But for now, I have to go."

I bend over him, press a peck to his cheek and turn for the door.

"I'll call you later," he mumbles.

"Okay. Talk to you then."

I turn the knob, walk out the door without a glance back, and ponder how this can possibly work. Darting across the floor, I go straight to my dressing room and peel my wig off. I try not to give into my thoughts or let the enormity of what just happened hit me.

No, I will wait until I leave. Wait until no one else can walk in and pry. Wait until I am alone, when no one will question my tears. Because tears are inevitable. Happy tears. Sad tears. Tears of confusion. Wondering how Max and I can possibly have a future. Because I want a future with him.

But can he handle a future with me? With Tami *and* Candy?

CHAPTER 22

MAX

It has been the longest goddamn week of my fucking existence.

I have done nothing but give and haven't received a fucking thing in return. Not one goddamn thing. Not only have I handed my balls over several times, I have also lost my fucking mind. Wouldn't be surprised if my brain forgot its purpose.

Friday was the last time I saw or spoke with Tami. When I all but forced her into a secluded room after discovering her true identity. Learning she was not only a nine-to-five type, but also this stunning, fiery vixen, has kept me on a mental Tilt-A-Whirl for days.

Her two sides have me swimming in an endless loop of fantasies. Both sides of her persona appeal to me in different ways. Call out to different parts of me. The light and the dark.

Candy—a sexy siren with her plethora of pastel-colored wigs and glitter-painted curves. The way she glides across the stage, contours her body like art, performs such an erotic act with such finesse. She renders me speechless, immobile and hard as stone. Her sultry performances are a direct line to my libido. White hot heat.

On the other end of the spectrum, Tami is this sassy, intelligent temptress. She captivates me in ways Candy does not. I love how she challenges me. How she puts me in my place when I act like a dick. She teases and taunts and makes me crave a woman in ways I never have in the past. Makes me ache for something other than just fucking her brains out.

Since she revealed her secret identity, a continuous loop of questions swirl in my head. Make me dizzy. Have me in unfamiliar headspace. Sadly, they are questions only I can answer.

Can I separate the two? Candy and Tami. Although they are technically the same woman, they are opposites in many ways. I don't have all the details, but from my time spent with each, they are two different women.

Can I allow her to be both? On her terms, not mine. Although she didn't explicitly say those words, I took what she did say to this degree. Being both sides of herself is why she has resisted relationships. Because no guy has been able to handle both sides of her.

I had been a complete asshole. Behaving like a goddamn teenager early last week. But I suppose being a dipshit is how I handle my feelings for her.

I have never been hungry for a woman the way I am for Tami.

This scalding pressure beneath my sternum… how do I manage this? Every time Tami steps into my orbit, my chest feels as if it will explode.

And her body… *fuck.* A beacon in the darkness only I see. Not a sex beacon—although, her body plays a key role. But something more primal. A call of nature. Like the Earth needing the moon to sway the tides, to keep us in orbit, to stay in balance.

All my previous habits scream at me. Tell me I have fucked myself. But I ignore the outdated rules. I no longer believe the truths they hold.

Such an odd realization, an odd feeling. To wipe away everything you have known for years.

But finding Tami has changed me. She altered the path my life traveled. Before Tami, Max Kingston was the typical cocky prick. A man who had no concept of who he truly was or what he wanted from life. All I craved was promiscuity. A man content with never seeing the same faceless woman twice.

Then Tami appeared. She grabbed me by the balls and threw all my impulses out the window.

I dream of no one except Tami. At first, that scared the shit out of me. The repetition of her face, her smile, her laughter. The blotchy pink on her throat and cheeks when she came. No other woman has been the star of my dreams or fantasies for weeks.

And now, I have major sucking up to do. I pray, in the end, she forgives me for my past. No one but Tami has made me consider change. She is the only woman to make me crave something beyond sex. Hungry for the next touch or embrace or kiss.

Scrolling through my email, I read for the twentieth time that the flowers I sent her Wednesday were in fact delivered. A bouquet of thirty-six long-stem red roses. The image on the website shows sparse greenery and baby's breath between the petals. Beautiful, but not more than Tami.

The fact I hadn't heard from Tami regarding the delivery makes me second-guess if they were dropped on the correct doorstep. I also sent her several texts this week and received zero replies, which doesn't help.

Her silence guts me. Is this her version of pouting? Intentionally ignoring me. Or has something happened to her? The Sophisticate and P.I. have bouncers everywhere, but what if something happened to her outside of the club? The bar and club only allow selective people in the doors, but that doesn't mean they all have good intentions.

I shake off the latter, confident it must be the first reason after how we left things. But why can't she just tell me she needs time to think? To adjust to us. Whatever version of us this is.

No matter how many messages I send that go unanswered, compulsion makes me send more. To apologize for my dickish behavior. For being a cocky bastard. For not considering her feelings when all she has done is put hers on the line.

I pick up my phone, open our text history and start typing.

> I get you don't want to talk. I don't blame you. Saying sorry isn't enough for how I've treated you. The way I feel about you… it's new for me. You may not believe me, but it's true. Don't feel obligated to answer, but please let me know you're okay. I'm worried.

Tossing my phone onto the bed, I head for the shower, crank the hot water, and pray it will soothe my tension. My body aches in new places. A permanent fatigue in place from my lack of sleep all week.

Since the moment I realized Candy was Tami, my mind hasn't calmed. Thoughts play a vicious ping-pong match in my skull. Astonishment. Exhilaration. Confusion. Passion. Worry. Hunger. Apprehension. Greed. And then we were in that room again, the same room where—before I discovered who Candy was—she shifted the level of intimacy.

Strange enough, our first night in the private room, the one constant in my thoughts was Tami. Not sure if it was her vibe —the invisible, potent energy I only ever feel with Tami—or if a small part of my subconscious *knew* it was her. No way of knowing now.

I finish showering, towel off, and put on a pair of slacks and a button-down. Once dressed, I jump in my car and mindlessly drive to the one place where I may find answers. I drift through the lighter traffic with ease. Before long, I park my car and stare up at the place that changed it all.

Walking in The Sophisticate, I beeline for the stairwell at the back of the restaurant. I trek down the familiar, dark corridor. The walls pulse with lust and hunger and sex. The lights dim and secretive and inviting.

Weeks ago, I loved the vibration coursing through my body as I walked this path. Allowed it to fuel my bloodstream and consume me. Swallow me whole as I entered the one place I felt most myself.

But now, I only associate the music with Tami. How my heart bangs against my ribcage and rips each bone away to get to her. How my heart runs like a wild stampede at the mere thought of seeing her.

Sitting at my usual table, I order a drink. I drum my fingers on the table as my knee bobs below. I nurse my drink, intent on drinking just one.

When I reach the bottom of the glass, I check the time. My brows pinch together when I realize how long I have sat here. Over an hour. In that time, at least three women have danced the stage more than once.

The server steps up and rests a hand on my shoulder. "Another drink, sugar?"

Although part of the act, the pet name makes me shift in my chair uncomfortably. Weeks ago, I would have taken advantage of her calling me *sugar*. Now... it is on the tip of my tongue to tell her not to address me as such. But I remain tight-lipped and composed, and respond as if unfazed.

"No, thanks. Quick question."

"What's up, sweetie?"

Another chill.

"When will Candy be on stage?"

A fake smile plumps her cheeks, her teeth bright in the dim club, her eyes lifeless.

"She's not here tonight, sugar. Took this weekend and the next off. But I can get one of the other girls for you."

"No, that won't be necessary." I hand her a tip before rising from the chair and exiting the club.

In my car, I sit stoic a few minutes. My knuckles whiten as I fist the steering wheel and zone out.

There is no hiding it now. Tami is intentionally avoiding me. After the unanswered texts, the flower delivery and constant failed attempts to get her attention, Tami knew I would come to P.I. The one place she would have to see me. Possibly spend time with me.

I slam my fists against the steering wheel then death grip it before I hang my head. I hate myself right now. Somehow, with such ease, I wrecked the best woman I have ever met. Ruined my chances before really having one.

Fuck.

Pressing the ignition button, the engine roars as I back out and drive off. In this irrational headspace, I shouldn't be on the road. But hell if I was calling one of the guys to pick me up. No fucking way. I would never hear the end of their bullshit. How pussy-whipped I am. At some point, I will hear it. But it won't be tonight.

Mindlessly, I navigate the streets, stopping and going at the appropriate times. Keeping the proper distance between me and other drivers.

In a haze, my subconscious steers me near Tami's apartment. Instinct taking the helm. Knowing I need to see her. Need proof she is safe. And maybe wanting an opportunity to explain myself in person. To read how she really feels about it all. Read her body language, hear her inflection, see the truth in her eyes.

Parking my car in one of the visitor spaces, I leisurely stroll toward her door. Toward her.

What do I say? What if she slams the door in my face? What if she won't open the door?

Soon, I stand inches from her door, eyes fixed on the off-white paint, balled fist a breath from the wood. Closing my eyes, I suck in a deep breath and hold it a couple beats before I force myself to knock.

When feet shuffle on the other side, I open my eyes and eagerly await what may be my last opportunity to see her.

It all happens in slow motion—the door handle twists and the door opens with only a small gap until the security chain straightens. Her hazel eyes are a duller shade of green than I remember as they study me. But the second I lay eyes on her, my heart stops and plummets to the pit of my stomach.

I have never been this nervous in my life. But I have also never had so much to lose.

CHAPTER 23

TAMI

Lounged across my bed with my two best friends, Netflix and Ben & Jerry's, I continue my woe-is-me-marathon with *10 Things I Hate About You* for the fifth time since last weekend. Generally, I cut it off before the sappy ending. My life won't include a sappy ending, so why bother indulging in such fantasies.

I scoop a heaping spoonful of dairy-free Cherry Garcia in my mouth just before someone knocks on the front door. For a moment, I wonder if David is at the door for Amber, but soon remember he left not long ago.

Begrudgingly, I pause the movie and amble to the door, armed with my ice cream. My fuzzy bunny slippers scuff the hardwood and I make a mental note to buy more area rugs so I don't hear how much I drag my feet.

Looking through the peephole, I spy Max standing on the opposite side. *Shit.*

I never considered him coming here to check up on me. Although, can't say it surprises me, considering I have ignored him over the last week. Time to put on my big girl panties, suck it up, and talk with him. Things won't get resolved, nor will he leave me alone, until we talk.

Chain lock still engaged, I twist the knob and crack open the door, just enough to take him in and see he looks like shit. I close my eyes, take a breath, then open and lock eyes with him.

So much of him is different. Eyes dim with dark half-moons painted beneath them. Shoulders caved. Lips lax, as if he hasn't smiled in weeks. And although he towers half a foot over me, tonight he seems more on my level. Smaller.

"Hey," he mumbles then sighs. "Can we talk a minute? Please."

I study the weary lines of his face and say nothing. Has he aged years in the last week? His normal confidence is nowhere to be seen.

He only wants to talk.

I shut the door, disengage the chain, and reopen the door, stepping back to let him in. Once inside, he peers around and shoves his hands in his pockets, waiting for me to lead the way. I close the door and lead us to my bedroom, stopping when I hear Amber's door open.

"*Really*, Tami? Now you're bringing *work* home? What the heck?"

I step in her direction with a snarl on my lips and hold my ground. "Last I checked, *Amber*, this is *my* apartment. And I'm not bringing *work* home. Max, this is Amber, my former best friend and current roommate. Amber, this is Max, my… I don't know, potential boyfriend. All depends on how our conversation goes."

Amber narrows her eyes and curls her top lip like she has a shit stain under her nose. "Whatever. I'm going back to my room. And locking my door."

Accusation laces her tone as she bites out the last bit, as if Max is a criminal and she fears for her life. Not sure what the hell David has done to her, but I would really love to have my best friend back. But that is an argument for a different day.

Spinning to face Max, I scurry past him and assume he follows as I head to my room. Back in my safe space, I walk to the bed, kick off my slippers, and crawl up to the exact place I was before he interrupted me. Scraping the spoon over the ice cream, I pile it high before shoving it in my mouth. When it hits my tongue, I close my eyes and moan.

Eyes shut, I *feel* Max's stare on my face. Slowly, I peel my eyes open and stare at him. His observation heady and curious. His head cocked to the side as if trying to read my thoughts and sort out my behavior. Standing tall but not straight, eyes narrowed, he bites the inside of his cheek.

Part of me is tempted to torment him a while and not speak. Another part of me just wants to get this whole situation over with. The longer he occupies my space, the less we will accomplish.

Talking around the ice cream in my mouth, I slur, "So Max, what brings you here?"

He presses his palms to his temples before combing his fingers through his hair. An audible sigh parts his lips and swallows all the air in the room. "Well, first, I wanted to make sure you were still alive." He tips his head back and stares at the ceiling. "Second, I thought we should talk."

Leveling his gaze, he locks eyes with me. A long list of unanswered questions mar his face. But something else resides there, too. Sadness. An emotion I never pictured on Max.

"So, talk."

He runs a hand through his hair again before stuffing both hands in his pockets and rocking back on his heels. He stares at the floor for one, two, three breaths, then lifts his questioning gaze back to me.

"Why are you so mad? I've sent you several messages, wanting to talk. But you never answered."

Popping the spoon from my mouth, I recall all the texts he has sent since Friday. They initially started with him wondering why I didn't want to see him after work Friday. Then they transitioned into him wanting to see me Saturday or Sunday. Another date. By Monday, the messages held hints of worry because I hadn't responded to any prior messages. Tuesday evening, he asked why I wasn't at the gym and said he missed me.

The flowers sat on my doorstep when I arrived home from work Wednesday. I glance over at the huge vase packed tight with several gorgeous roses. The note on the card simple—*Yours, Max*. I didn't want to read into it too much, but it felt as if this was a declaration. His way of saying he belonged to me. But I didn't unearth validity in that train of thought, so I ignored it.

"Sorry I didn't answer. Just wanted time to mull things over. Process it all. *So much* has happened in such a short period. And dating really isn't my thing, so…"

He inches closer to me. "What did I do to make you so angry?"

I chuckle and wonder how he hasn't figured it out yet. Max has brains and brawn. "You really have no idea, do you?" I ask, my voice laced with condescension.

He huffs in obvious frustration. "Do you think I'd text you nonstop or drive all over town if I did? I don't know where your head is Tami. So please, do me a favor. Enlighten me." The more he speaks, the firmer and louder his voice gets.

I set the now empty ice cream container and spoon down

next to my bed. The spoon clinks loud in the sudden silence. Taking a deep breath, I mentally prepare myself for every possible result from this conversation.

"I know you, Max. More than you think. I've been a dancer for years. Seen thousands of guys exactly like you. Good-looking. Smart. Cocky. Sex personified. And I've even dated a couple men like you, when I first started dancing. But the relationships always end the same. With me hurt." I shake my head.

"By now, I've also seen every expectation come to life. Some guys expect me to be a dancer twenty-four seven. Wear skimpy clothes and grind against them whenever *they* please. Others have said '*If you cared about how I felt, you'd stop dancing.*' Guilt tripping me. Telling me if I didn't stop, I didn't care.

"And then there's the ones who say they'll care about you no matter what, but then change their tune as time passes. They suddenly don't want to have sex with you. They play twenty questions, swearing they trust you, when truly they don't. Most people can't handle being with someone in my position. They don't know how to be okay with other people aroused by what I do. It's a sad but true existence."

He takes two steps closer. Stands less than five feet from where I sit on the bed. For a moment, he hangs his head, slowly sways it side to side, before lifting to stare me in the eyes again.

"I understand everything you just said. Get how you feel we could never be more because of how other men treated you. If our roles were reversed, I'm sure I would feel the same." Pausing, he sucks in two deep breaths then continues. "Tami, I don't want to change who you are. I like who you are. I simply need time to digest it all, and talking about this with you would certainly help. Can't I enjoy the different aspects of who you are? There has to be a reason why you chose to continue dancing, even when you didn't necessarily *have* to anymore. You love it. For reasons that should only matter to you. I would never want to take away something that makes you happy."

He shuffles another step in my direction, standing at the foot of the bed while I sit cross-legged in the middle. A small piece of me wants to reach out, grab his shirt, and tug him to me. I haven't touched or been in the same space as him in days. My livelihood has berated me the loss.

As badly as every splinter of my soul craves him, I refuse to dive in headfirst without a life preserver. All it would do is set me up for pain and heartache. And I haven't met anyone who purposely wants that.

I stare up at him, tears pooling at the corners of my eyes, throat dry. "You say that now, but you can't know how you'll feel three days from now. Or three weeks. Or three months. And let's not even go into years. I can't have you resent or hate me. Can't have you disgusted with me. I've dealt with enough bullshit in my life. I don't need more."

He drops down to the mattress and scoots closer, his knee brushing mine. And when he reaches out to wipe the tear on my cheek, I lean into his touch. So warm and soft and perfect.

"Tami, I don't know what exactly is happening between us, but I won't ignore it. Tried to do that a couple weeks ago. Didn't stick. Still felt the same intensity, although now it feels more raw. More compelling. But I was afraid. I've never done this before." He gestures between us. "Relationships are an anomaly. Even in my teens. The guys I hung out with were pretty much the same type I still associate with. Guys with one mission. Fuck the girl. I've never known different. Not until my mid-twenties and women wanted another night out. When one-and-done is all you've ever known, and enjoyed, how does one change? It's ingrained in me. But with you…"

His words trail off and leave me hanging. *What isn't he saying?*

"With me, what?" *Please don't use the infamous cheesy line, 'You're the one.'*

"With you, I want more. When we're in the same room, the same space, I feel alive. Like you're an electrical current that shocks and resuscitates me. All the years before you, I was asleep. My life dormant. When you touch me, that current zaps in my chest" —he taps a hand over his heart— "followed by this radiating warmth. Like I've stood too close to the sun too long. But it isn't painful." He shakes his head. "Actually, it's the most wonderful and addictive sensation. Makes me feel whole and wanted and free. The night of the first lap dance, when I was still oblivious, I felt some of those same feelings and was confused. Confused at how I have never felt this way in thirty-one years and I suddenly felt it for two women. Didn't know how to process it. Two nights before our recent date, you took me in that room and put your hands all over me. Not going to lie, I loved every fucking second. But I also felt guilty. Because I wanted *you*."

He speaks the last four words so softly, I question if he said them. But he did. And I comprehend the energy between us. Because I feel the same magnetic pulse, too. A vigorous circadian rhythm. It thrums and weaves and surges through every molecule, limb and organ.

Over the years, I have been attracted to plenty of men. Never once have I felt anything close to the magnetism Max and I share. An all-consuming hypnosis.

I press a hand to his on my cheek and close my eyes. One by one, I run through scenarios of us in my head. But every avenue ends the same. With one or both of us on the losing end. Max has never been in a legit relationship and I avoid them like the bubonic blague.

I just don't see how this will work.

As if he hears my internal turmoil, he inches closer and presses his forehead to mine.

"I will do whatever you want, no questions asked. The only thing I cannot do is walk away. I don't know what it is that has me so anchored, but I'm rooted in place and want to stay. For as long as you'll have me, I want you."

He closes the remaining space between us and presses his lips to mine. Heat licks every inch of my skin, tension expands above my diaphragm, and I forget how to breathe. His other hand cups my other cheek and draws me closer. Envelops me in heat and hunger and a tenderness I don't expect from him.

Max tonight has taken me by surprise.

We kiss as if the world is crumbling around us. Seconds turn to minutes. Minutes into hours. When we finally break apart, we both gasp for breath, eyes locked. The pad of his thumb strokes my lower lip with devotion. And the world goes hazy as I absorb this new level of affection. His breath is hot on the shell of my ear. A whoosh-whoosh-whoosh thrums behind my ears.

Breathe, Tami. Remember to breathe.

"Please," he pleads.

And I can no longer resist.

With everything he confessed tonight, plus his relentless nature, I cave to his sweet demands. I lean back, add slightly more distance, pray for clarity, and read his expression. I need to *see* his reaction. Have to know his train of thought.

"I'm willing to give this a chance."

The way his expression transforms steals my breath.

From a desperate plea to an unimaginable buoyancy. His smile bright enough to light up all of Los Angeles. Triumph a brilliant glow in his bottle-green irises.

Before he gets too excited, I bite the bullet and continue. "But I have conditions."

His face drops a split-second, but recovers just as quickly. "Lay them on me. I will do my damnedest. Whatever it takes. If I'm able, I will."

I study him a beat, guarded and ready for his reaction.

"First, I'm not giving up dancing. Not yet, anyway. Originally, I danced for the money, to help pay for college. But now, I dance because I love it. The high of being on stage. I love how it feels."

He nods. "I figured that would be a stipulation. As challenging as it'll be for me to have other people ogle and drool over you, it's been something you've done years."

Well, he handled that better than expected. Not so sure how he will deal with the next.

"Speaking of ogling. May be a good idea if you don't come to the club as often. I don't respond well to jealousy and can't compromise my job because you don't like the way someone looks at or touches me. We have more bodyguards than I can count and they're good at their job."

And truly, there has never been a time at P.I. when I didn't feel safe. Rocco vets people well. Staff and patrons. He doesn't have time for bullshit or drama. Neither do I.

Max narrows his eyes then cocks his head. "I'd like to amend that condition. If I may?" I nod and gesture for him to continue. "If I promise to keep my cool and be on my best behavior, I'd like to still come in and watch you. I realize it's a job. And with how stubborn you've been from the beginning, you don't typically mingle work and pleasure. If, for whatever reason, I act like an ass or get possessive, you can ban me. But I have a paid membership and love watching you on stage."

He makes a valid point. So, I grant him flexibility on this condition as long as he stays true to his word.

"Lastly… I don't put up with bullshit. I know parts of your past and you know parts of mine. If you want us to be together, honesty is key. No skirting around the truth. No white lies. No lies of omission. Forgetfulness is forgiven up to a certain length of time and that timeframe is determined by the topic. I don't have time for games."

"Honesty. No problem," he promises.

"You have a lot of sucking up to do. And just so you know, gestures are more desirable than gifts. Not that I'll turn down a gift."

I bite my bottom lip and shake my head. How is this happening?

In some respects, Max is like most men in my past. But he is vastly different in other ways. More determined and stronger—not just physically—and goes after what he wants. And when Max wants something, he doesn't mess around. He goes full force; balls to the wall.

"Noted." He pecks my cheek. "Can I stay and finish the movie with you? Don't care what it is. We can just lay here. Not ready to leave yet."

"Sure, but don't know if you'll like it."

"As long as I get to lay next to you, I don't care."

"Okay."

I scoot up the bed and lay on my side then press play once he swaddles me. The movie plays and I sense his curiosity.

"What movie is this? Think I've seen it."

I snicker. "*10 Things I Hate About You*. Just the mood I was in."

He lays quiet behind me and I wonder if I upset him. Until he laughs. "I have seen this. Great movie. At least everything works out in the end." His arms tighten around me as he kisses my hair.

When the movie ends, I walk him to the door. We kiss briefly before he steps out and stands under the glow of the porch light. I want him to stay the night, but decide against it. Next time, perhaps.

"My friend, Cherry, is throwing a party tomorrow night. Promised her I'd go. Want to go?"

"I'd love to. Who is Cherry?"

"Someone from when I first started dancing. She's very outgoing and thinks the world is her stage. I take her in small doses, but love her all the same."

"Yeah, I'll go. Text me with the details and we'll go from there."

After one last kiss, he spins on his heel. I watch as he descends the stairs, strides to his car, and disappears inside. Once he leaves, I shuffle inside, lean against the door, and pray to whatever higher power listens.

Please, don't let him wreck me.

CHAPTER 24

MAX

Tami messages me early in the day and tells me the party starts at seven. Supposedly, there will be snacky foods and tons of booze, but I never rely on such things. Tami and I agree to meet up at six and grab a bite beforehand. Snacky foods generally equals shit food at large parties.

I park my bike behind her truck and jog up the stairs two at a time. Soon, we hop on the bike and navigate the city. We snag a quick bite to eat and chat about our days. It all feels so *normal*. Until now, I never sought normality. But Tami makes it effortless.

We finish dinner and Tami directs me to her friend's place. A quarter-mile away, cars pack every inch of on-street parking. Line both sides of the street. Loud music booms through my helmet. I wonder how many people are at this party and why no one complains about the noise. I throw parties, but I also respect my neighbors.

I park the bike—where some drunk idiot won't hit it—and

we hop off. Tami laces our fingers as we stroll toward the cacophony.

"Been a while since I've seen Cherry, but she knows how to party. By the looks of it, there's hundreds here."

"I'm all for a good party, but I may be glued to your side for the night. Considering I don't know anyone." Not as if new people intimidate me, but Tami is the only familiar face here. And this crowd is different.

"I'll keep you safe." She winks before opening the door and blasting us with the onslaught of the music. Feels like a concert. You have to shout and lean in close to hear. And once it ends, you still shout because everything sounds muffled.

We meander for a few songs. Scope out the party. Tami introduces me to people and we chat about random shit. Summer heat. Sports. Celebrity sightings. A little of this and that. Random, meaningless conversation to fill space.

Tami introduces me to two men—Chris and Jon. Bouncers from the club she worked at prior to P.I. I enjoy our conversation and am intrigued how they view their job. Both good guys, they feel like dancer secret service. Willing to do anything to ensure the dancer's safety. And never see them as eye candy or someone datable, but more as a sister or family member. A perspective I never considered. Surely, most men that work in clubs go through rigorous screenings to weed out creeps.

The whole concept provides me with relief I didn't know I needed.

We chat with a woman named Ginger. Instinct says it isn't her real name, but I don't ask. These women have anonymity for a reason. So, I ignore curiosity and listen as she and Tami catch up. Apparently, Tami worked with Ginger at the same place as Chris and Jon.

The three of them are nice to talk with, but I don't picture them at P.I. Nothing against them personally, just seems P.I. holds everyone—staff and clientele—to higher standards. Comparing them to those I met at P.I. is like comparing spastic and mellow toddlers. Complete opposites.

We wander into the kitchen to refill our drinks. I decide no more alcohol since I am driving and grab water. As we stroll back out, a woman with a bright red bob stops Tami.

"Hey, T! Glad you made it!" Her voice saccharine. She wraps her arms around Tami's neck and hugs her as if she never will again.

Tami breaks the hug, smiles and steps out of her reach. "Hey, Cherry! Me, too." Tami slides her hand down to mine. "Cherry, I'd like you to meet Max, my boyfriend. Max, this is Cherry."

Cherry's eyes sweep over my body and undress me. The visual assault gives me chills. I shiver enough for Tami to notice and she gives my hand a light squeeze. After Cherry finishes her head to toe examination, she extends a hand. Hesitant, I take it and make the exchange as brief as possible.

"Nice to meet you, Max. Did T tell you we worked together?"

"She may have mentioned it."

Cherry trails her fingers down Tami's bicep. "Yep. At the Honey Cave for a few years before she left us for that fancy gig."

Tami play-smacks Cherry's arm. "If someone offered you the job, you would've taken it in a heartbeat. Don't tell me otherwise. For what we do, it's a great place."

"Yeah, yeah, yeah. Miss All-Kinds-Of-Special." If I didn't know better, I would say Cherry has a green devil on her shoulder named jealousy. Not sure if it is the job or something else, but her animosity dangles like carrots. "Just because they handpicked you and you probably earn two to three times what I do..." She doesn't finish her thought, but confirms my suspicions. Cherry resents she wasn't chosen as one of the select few to dance at P.I.

As Tami and Cherry discuss things irrelevant to me, I take a moment to *really* look at Cherry.

She stands a couple inches shorter than Tami, but wears heels to make her taller. She wears next to zero clothing; a skimpy two-piece bathing suit—a top that barely covers her nipples and G-string bottoms with hardly any front fabric. The most notable observation... Cherry is grotesquely thin. Her ginormous breasts obviously not natural.

The conversation between Tami and Cherry tapers and I pray we walk away soon to hang with different people. Something about Cherry rubs me wrong. Can't quite put my finger on it. Just as we step away, Cherry shouts.

"Oh! Finally figured it out!"

Tami stares at her like she has two heads. "Figured what out, Cher?"

"Why your boyfriend looks so familiar." She shifts her eyes to me. "Think I've seen you in the Honey Cave. A couple months or so ago. I never forget a face, especially one like yours."

The blood drains from my face. I have never visited the Honey Cave. Not even with the guys. I wouldn't put it past Nic—he visits any establishment with women to ogle. Can't say the same.

Her obvious jealousy needs to be put in its place. Now.

"Must have me confused with someone else. Never been there. No offense, but it's not the atmosphere I prefer."

"You sure? Swear I gave the lap dance of a lifetime to you."

Now I know she is blowing smoke up my ass. Tami tenses at my side. Her body stiff as a board as she tightens her grip on my hand. Time to shut this bitch down.

"One-hundred-percent certain. Only gotten a lap dance from one woman. She's holding my hand." I hold up our joined hands. "Sorry for your loss."

In my periphery, a hint of a smile perks up Tami's lips. Cherry, on the other hand, looks as if someone killed her puppy and dumped it on her doorstep.

Don't fuck with me or my relationship, bitch. You will not hurt her.

Before either of us says another word, Cherry spins on her heel and storms off like a drama queen.

I glimpse Tami and press a soft kiss to her lips. "That was the complete truth. I may have been in several clubs before, but I've never been there. You're also the only woman from a strip club I've wanted close to my body."

"Thank you."

I cock my head. "For what?"

"For putting her in her place. She has had some hate-jealousy thing with me for years."

"Only because you're irresistible and have something she never will."

"Oh yeah. What?"

"Class."

CHAPTER 25

Cherry trying to pull that stunt with Max has me on edge.

She's worn her jealousy on her sleeve for years now. Since Rocco invited me to join the P.I. family and not her. But Rocco made his decision. On his own.

When Rocco visited the Honey Cave, P.I. was still in its infancy. He watched me and other dancers perform. Then asked if I was interested in doing the same job somewhere better. I didn't believe him at first. Not until he flaunted images of P.I.

He won me over in less than an hour.

From that moment forward, I have been on the receiving end of Cherry's animosity. She had been dancing years. And, to this day, insists I *stole* her only chance at earning *real* money as a dancer.

Working at P.I. definitely pads my bank account. But Rocco wants a specific look and caliber of women in his club. Not just someone who strips, jiggles their assets, and makes people horny. Yes, bodies are a factor—it is a strip club, after all—but Rocco also seeks elegance and professionalism and excellence.

Traits Cherry doesn't possess.

Years later and I do my best to bury the whole situation and remain friends with her. She makes it so damn difficult. Anytime she learns of something good in my life, she jumps on the vendetta train and pushes full steam ahead to ruin it.

Thank god, I have thick skin, strength and surround myself with like-minded individuals.

Taking a deep breath, I erase the whole conversation from my mind. I squeeze Max's hand and tell him I want to mingle a little more before we leave. We walk hand in hand around the room and chat with others—intentionally avoiding Cherry —until ready to go.

We spend the next half hour talking with a new couple— Shirley and Trevor. Needless to say, it shocks me when I learn neither of them works in clubs. They are Cherry's neighbors. Their motto—*the party's going to happen with or without us, might as well enjoy it too.*

Shirley and Trevor seem like nice people and I have a feeling they only know the fun side of Cherry.

Max sits in a chair pushed against the wall while I sit on the armrest. Comfortable with Shirley and Trevor here, I lean down and tell him I need to use the restroom, then we can leave. He nods as I excuse myself from the conversation and weave my way down the hallway.

I wait in the small bathroom line and pray no one pees or pukes on the toilet before I use it. After the people in front of me get their turn, I pop in, do my business, and wash up. When I step out of the bathroom, several people whistle, hoot, and holler from the other room. The raucousness doesn't surprise me, considering how many people are here and most of them work in clubs.

What I don't expect to see is the very thing I do as I round the corner.

Max is exactly where I left him, in the chair against the wall. But Cherry has somehow "lost" the minuscule fabric covering her body and rubs her ass and pussy on my boyfriend's lap. His hands rest awkwardly on her hips.

This right here. This is the tipping point. I have fucking had enough.

I storm forward as my vision flares red and rage swarms my bloodstream. I fist Cherry's choppy red hair and jerk her off Max. Hard. She falls to the floor and I shout loud enough to be heard over the music. "What the fuck are you doing?" Heat scorches my skin from bust to brows as I grind my molars.

She peeks up at me with a snide smirk on her lips. "Can't help it, *Candy*. He said he wanted me. You know I can't deny anyone."

Cherry is damn lucky I don't break her nose. I seethe at her words and restrain myself from beating the shit out of her. Her *game* went too far this time.

Max jumps up from the chair with his hands up and embarrassment on his face. "No fucking way, cunt. Not a fat chance in hell." I walk away and he grabs my arm. "Please, let me tell you what happened. There are more than enough people here who will vouch for me."

"I can't deal with this right now. Remember our conversation last night?" He nods. "This right here, it's just another reason to add to the list that will no doubt continue to grow."

As much as I want the truth, I also don't. Here is yet another reason why I can't be in a goddamn relationship. I can't deal with jealousy. From another person—Max—or myself. I don't have time to fit drama in my life. Drama always leads to accusations and insecurity. Drama throws doubt in the mix. It overwhelms and consumes and is far too much for me to handle.

Yanking my arm from his grip, I weave through the party-goers as they all stare. I shove past their unyielding bodies. And when I make it to the door, I step out and slam it behind me. I just need to get away from the whole situation. I need fresh air. And more than anything, I need time alone. My brain needs peace. Quiet to think all this through and come up with a viable solution.

Before Max bolts out after me, I jog down the path in front of Cherry's house and sprint down the sidewalk. Ready to easily run ten miles without a breather. I need to clear my head and get away from everyone.

What I really need is to sort out what my eyes saw versus what my heart felt versus what is true. The only way to do that is to get away from all of them.

CHAPTER 26

MAX

Tami and I have talked with another couple—Shirley and Trevor—for a while. They seem nice. We have talked careers and where we see ourselves down the road, but nothing heavy. Trevor and I gossip sports a few minutes while Tami and Shirley discuss non-sports.

Right here. Right now. My arm around Tami's waist, her on the armrest, is perfection. Everything about her, about us, is absolutely perfect. Never once have I imagined this for my future. A relationship. The same woman at my side, day in and out, providing solace and satisfaction. My hand on her, an innocent touch, grounds and rockets me sky-high simultaneously.

Trevor and I laugh over some joke a friend told him—something about blondes, phallic vegetables and different "recipes" they used. Corny as fuck, but I can't help but laugh.

Tami leans down and the air shifts. Heat radiates between us and stirs my dick to life beneath my fly. God, I fucking love the way this woman makes me ache.

"Before we head out, I need to use the bathroom." Her lips

brush the shell of my ear. Her hot breath paints my skin and wakes every desirous molecule inside me.

When she leans back, all I do is nod, not trusting my words with others so close. She rises from the chair and saunters down the hall. Shirley, Trevor, and I chat a couple minutes before I tell them we are leaving when Tami returns. When the current song ends, they stroll off and bid me goodnight.

I scan the room and wait for Tami. The music shifts to something from a porn movie. I grimace and shake my head, more than eager to leave. This party has been semi-enjoyable, but now several people are naked. Normally, nudity doesn't bother me. But a twisted knot in my gut has me on edge. Need to get out of here.

As I rise from the chair to search for Tami, someone shoves me down.

"What the fuck?"

I look up and spot a head of bright red hair. Cherry. *Fuck.*

"Where do you think you're going, gorgeous?" She trails her fingers over my chest. Bile coats my throat as I shrink away. I shiver as a chill slithers up my spine.

"Get your fucking hands off me and get the hell out of my way." This bitch has one second to follow through or things are about to get real fucking nasty.

"Sure thing, sugar." She removes her hand from my chest and I breathe easier. Until she spins around and thrusts her ass in my groin. Rotating to see me, she says, "I know this is what you really want."

I grip her hips and try to force her off me. She doesn't budge. Her scrawny frame much stronger than expected. Everyone within ten feet catcalls or wolf whistles and I get more irritated with each passing second.

This is not okay. This trashy female needs to get her ass off me. Now.

"Get. The. Fuck. Off. Me. Now."

Out of nowhere, Cherry flies off my lap and relief floods me. Briefly. Until I realize who flung her off me. Tami. *Damnit.* I hoped to rectify the situation before she returned from the bathroom.

Tami grabs a fistful of Cherry's hair as she flings her to the floor as if weightless. I peer up at Tami, her cheeks are almost as red as Cherry's hair. Jesus, she is fucking pissed.

"What the fuck are you doing?" she screams, her tone violent and thunderous and directed at the woman on the floor.

Cherry slowly twists her face to stare up at Tami. A sinister smile spreads wide on her lips. As if this isn't her first rodeo. "Can't help it, *Candy*," she says with venom. "He said he wanted me. You know I can't deny anyone."

What. The. Fuck.

Hell no.

I jump out of the chair, ready to leave. Anger and fear swirl in my veins with the look Tami gives me. Eyes locked, I work to puzzle out her thoughts. I glance down at the bitch on the floor and shake my head vehemently.

"No fucking way, cunt. Not a fat chance in hell."

Tami starts walking away from the whole situation and I reach out for her, needing to touch her. Needing her to know what Cherry said is utter bullshit.

"Please, let me tell you what happened. There are more than enough people here who will vouch for me," I plead with her.

She stares at me momentarily as she battles over what to

say or do next. "I can't deal with this right now. Remember our conversation last night?" I nod. "This right here, it's just another reason to add to the list that will no doubt continue to grow."

Her words pierce my heart with a dull knife, slowly gutting and tearing me open, leaving me raw. *No.*

I didn't do a damn thing wrong and *I am* the one being punished. How is this happening right now? How can she choose to believe that bitch's word over mine? I have done nothing but put myself out there for Tami, willingly became vulnerable for her, and this is what I get in return.

In a fog, I don't register when Tami withdraws from my grip. Stunned, I stand motionless as my brain comprehends what I *should* do versus what I *am* doing. Just as my fog-coated thoughts clear, I chase after Tami, who vanished. I assume she bolted out the door.

How much time has passed since she tugged out of my grip? Not sure, but I have to fix this.

Feet from the door, someone yanks me backward. When I spin around, a head of bright red hair and a face I hope to never see again stands inches from me.

"If you know what's good for you, you'll take your fucking hand off of me. *Now.*"

Beyond done with this bitch's games, I snap. She may be jealous of Tami—I give no fucks why—but I refuse to be a pawn in whatever game she's playing.

She thrusts her way-too-big, bare tits in my face as she grinds against me. "Oh, come on, sugar. She's gone now. You don't have to pretend anymore. You know you want a round with Cherry on top."

This bitch is seriously fucked-up. I glare at where her hand still rests on my arm and peel it from my flesh. Her desperation for attention disgusts me.

"If you ever touch me again, you'll wish you never existed. Don't push your luck." I place my hands on her shoulders and shove her away. "And if I ever see you near Tami again, I'll make your life a living hell. *Now get the FUCK out of my way.*"

Fearless, she steps aside with a villainous smirk. "It'll never work with her. She'd rather die alone than deal with reality. When you realize that, come and see me. You know where I live." She stalks off and doesn't give me a second to rebut her comment.

I shake my head, try to clear the nightmare that just occurred, and walk out the front door. At first glance, all I see are cars. A few people loiter in the yard and I approach them, hoping they saw Tami.

"Hey, did you see a brunette leave in the last five minutes?"

I guess the timeframe because I have no idea how much time has passed since Tami left and Cherry held me hostage.

The glossy-eyed couple give me blank stares. "Dude, we haven't seen anyone. We're a little busy, if you know what I mean," the man says. The woman flushes and smacks him on the chest as she ogles him.

"Thanks anyway." I walk off.

At the sidewalk, I look left and right and see nothing except cars. No people. No Tami. *Shit.*

Jogging down the sidewalk, I pass several houses before it dawns on me she got a decent head start. I turn back and run to the bike, determined to find her. With a five- to ten-minute lead, she probably didn't get far on foot.

I jump on the bike and it roars to life. A few revs of the engine, then I drive off. I roam the neighborhood streets, but don't find her.

Where the hell did she go? How far did she get? Fuck, I need to find her. Not just to fix this, but to also tell her the truth.

Tami may be upset, but I refuse to let this bullshit wreck us. This isn't the end.

CHAPTER 27

TAMI

I run miles before spotting an open grocery store.

The doors whoosh open as I enter and pause to catch my breath. I amble to an open register and purchase a bottled water. I unscrew the cap and guzzle it down. My throat a little less dry, I unlock my phone, tap on the Uber app and request a ride. The driver's picture, car make and model, and tag number pop up on the screen.

The driver arrives quickly and I hop in the back seat then verify my destination. He steers us from the store and drives out of the city toward my apartment. The older gentleman behind the wheel tries sparking conversation and I politely tell him I would like silence. With a gentle smile, he obliges.

The old man weaves through the city as soft jazz plays in muted tones in the background. The streets grow quieter the closer we get to my apartment. I welcome the peacefulness the quiet brings and replay everything that happened at Cherry's tonight.

The night started out perfect. Max picked me up, looking fine as hell with his never-ending smile. We got on the motorcycle and I flashed back to the night we drove along the Pacific Coast Highway—my arms wrapped around his waist, the heat between us nothing to do with the summer weather, and our bodies molding together easily.

Things were good for a blip of time while at Cherry's, too. She didn't find us for about an hour. And if completely honest with myself, I would have been okay not seeing her at all.

That line of thinking now has me questioning why I ever suggested we go in the first place.

From the moment she laid eyes on Max, it all went downhill. Every time Cherry caught wind of my happiness, she tried to sabotage it. Tonight, I walked irresistible bait right in her front door.

What the hell was I thinking?

But then she was gone, preoccupied by someone else for a while. Max and I enjoyed our time with Trevor and Shirley. Good conversation flowing between the four of us. It felt... normal. I like normal. I want normal. And I thought I had it for an inkling of time. Everything fit into place and felt quintessential.

Then... hell broke loose. *Fucking Cherry and her bullshit.*

I stepped away to use the goddamn bathroom. Gone less than five minutes and Cherry pounced. She took advantage of me and the moment.

I don't foresee it in the near future, but if she quits sabotaging everyone else's life, she may actually find someone to be happy with. Someone to share her life with. And though her jealousy stems from me being asked to work at an elite club, she could have the same opportunity if she stopped acting the petty bitch.

The second I saw her grinding on Max, his hands at her hips, arms locked, muscles tense, I knew he was shoving her away. But I lost it. So sick of her conniving bitch ways. Sick of her unrelenting determination to ruin my happiness.

Somehow, I restrained myself. Somehow, I didn't beat the shit out of her. I am bigger than that. At least I tell myself I am.

But Cherry needs to know I am done. Done with the bullshit and done with her. As soon as I walked out her door, relief washed over me. Dead weight lifted off my shoulders. I felt free of her bullshit.

Although I shouldn't have left Max inside, I needed away. From Cherry and the situation. I needed air. Once I've had time to mull it over, once I've had time to settle the rage boiling in my veins, I will call Max. Clear the air and fix us.

But I need clarity first. I need to think without the Cherry fog around me. To remind myself I trust Max, especially with my heart.

The car pulls up in front of my apartment building. "Thank you," I tell the driver. I take the stairs at a leisurely pace as my head swims with the events of the evening. *After I'm inside, I'll call Max.* I don't want him to worry.

Inserting my key in the lock, I open the door and step into my dark apartment. I toe off my shoes, a noise startles me from behind.

A figure trudges through the darkness in my direction. Hundreds of defense techniques run through my head as the shadow gets closer. A cell phone lights up in the person's hands and I spot a familiar face. David. *Thank god.* I was ready to go into full panic/combat mode. Lucky him, I haven't used the kicks I learned yet.

I clutch my chest and take a deep breath. "Jesus, David. You scared the shit out of me."

He peers up at me with an undecipherable expression in the muted light. "Watch your mouth, Tami." His tone a slap to the face. "Don't you dare use His name and then profanity. Bad enough you sin regularly and don't go to church to ask for forgiveness. You disgust me."

For some odd reason, this is the most David has said directly to me in one conversation. And he scolds me like a child. Reprimands me for cussing after saying Jesus. I fix my gaze with his and refuse to back down.

"I wasn't trying to be disrespectful, you just scared me and it was the first thought that came to mind."

"Well maybe you need to change the way you think," he spits back.

What the hell is his problem? What the hell makes this man think he is righteous and mighty? David is far from perfect. Since he and Amber have been together, David has done nothing except brainwash her. She doesn't think for herself anymore. Always relies on him to make decisions—from dinner to what she should wear outside the apartment.

Amber has lost herself and it saddens me.

"What does *that* mean? I'm a good person. Wish no ill will on anyone. Not even people I dislike." That includes him and Cherry. Although, David officially takes the lead.

"If you were such a *good* person, I'd see you in church with Amber and me every week. Maybe if you actually learned a thing or two, you'd be a bit more respectful and respectable."

Seriously? Who the hell does he think he is?

"Sorry, what did you just say to me? You've got to be kidding me. Since when are you the dictator of all things mighty." My rhetoric thick with sarcasm.

"You best watch how you speak to me," he states with a level of authority he doesn't own. My inability to bend to his will obviously pisses him off. But I am not Amber. And this asshole will not belittle me.

"Actually, I think you have that backward. You'd best remember where you are. You are in *my* home and if you don't watch what you say and how you speak to *me*, you won't be returning." Piece of shit. How dare he disrespect me.

"You know what, little girl. You don't scare me. Maybe you'd get more respect if you weren't a whore."

Done. More than fucking done with this pompous ass.

He has been on my last nerve since Amber introduced him. Such a grandiose, overweight, degrading lowlife. And who is he to stand in front of another person and judge their life and the way they live? Church may not be a place I frequent, but that doesn't make me a bad person.

Being a nasty human makes you a bad person.

Pointing my finger at the door, I snap. "Get the *fuck* out! Do not step foot in this apartment ever again. If I see you here, or hear you've been here, I'll file a restraining order and a no-trespass order."

He starts toward the door as I go in the direction of my bedroom. His hand reaches for the knob as he mumbles something under his breath I don't make out. He opens the door and I turn my back to him, not wanting to acknowledge him. When the latch clicks shut, I exhale the breath I had been holding.

I comb my fingers through my hair and wonder how I will explain this to Amber in the morning. Hope this is the wake-up call she needs to hear. Fingers crossed.

David is as sick and twisted as a serial killer. Maybe worse. He parades around high and mighty, but I have always seen him. Always felt *something* off. Not that I wished for things to come to this, but I am glad it happened. And as unfortunate as it is, I am glad his true colors made an appearance and I finally saw him for who he is. Who I always thought he was. Somehow, Amber will see too.

Just as I turn to lock and chain the front door, a sharp pain thwacks the back of my head. The room spins. Too fast. I stumble forward and try to maintain my footing when another stabbing pain collides with the side of my head.

And then the world turns black.

CHAPTER 28

MAX

I have driven circles too long. And I have looped up and down every street surrounding Cherry's neighborhood. No sign of Tammy. Even scoured every parking lot. Peeked through every window and door of the storefronts. Hours have passed since I last saw her. And not knowing where she is freaks me the fuck out.

Hope she found a way home. God, I hope like hell she found a *safe* ride and didn't ask some random person from the party.

Pulling over to breathe a moment, I check my watch and realize two hours have passed. I give up on randomly roaming the streets. Maybe she called a cab or requested an Uber and went home.

Parked in an empty lot, I close my eyes and take a few deep, cleansing breaths. I take my phone from my back pocket and unlock it. I just need to hear her voice. If anything, just to know she made it home safely.

In my contacts, I tap the phone icon under her name and lift the phone to my ear. The phone rings and rings and rings, then goes to voicemail. I leave a message. "Tami, I know you're upset. Just want to make sure you're okay. Please call me back. Let me know you're safe."

Hanging up, I open up our text history and type a quick message.

> Please let me know you're safe. I'm sorry.

I sit on my bike in the vacant lot and stare at the screen, waiting for a response. Ten minutes pass and still no reply. Her phone isn't dead, otherwise my call would have gone straight to voicemail. She hasn't opened my message, unless she turned off the read-receipt option.

Something doesn't sit right. She didn't answer any of my texts or calls during the week, when she was upset with me. But this is different. After our talk, I don't feel she would intentionally ignore me. Especially if all I ask is to know she is safe.

A black hole forms in my chest and expands with every passing second. It sucks away every positive thought and leaves anxiety in its wake. The void swells as more time passes without word from Tami.

"Something's wrong," I mutter to myself.

Sliding my phone in my pocket, I secure my helmet and get back on the road. Not sure what the hell is happening, but it can't be good.

I speed down the highway—the speedometer bars past the posted limit—and pray no cops pull me over. With the late hour, traffic is minimal. Thank fuck.

I take the highway as long as possible, enjoying the lack of interruption. As soon as I exit, I hit every fucking red light. Seems every person under the sun roams the smaller streets the closer I get to Tami's apartment. I growl when I hit another red light, rev the bike and stow the urge to run the light.

The traffic gods continue to torture me. And my anxiety hits an all-time high.

Stopped at a light, I pull out my phone and check for any response from her. Nothing. *Fuck.*

Slipping my phone in my pocket, I rev the bike and garner attention. A car full of women glance over eye-fuck me. I roll my eyes and look away. Weeks ago, old me would have flirted back. Old me would have asked to follow them home.

Weeks ago, I was a different man. An asshole and a manwhore. Now... now I am new Max. Better Max. Max two-point-oh. Thanks to one woman.

I turn away from the women trying to flash their tits at me and shake my head, laughing. The fact I no longer want another woman's body or attention amazes me. No woman compares to Tami, the only woman worthy of my attention.

The light turns green and I speed like my ass is on fire, leaving other drivers in a smoke cloud. The next two lights stay green and I wonder if fate tested me at the last signal. Seeing if I would bend or break when faced with temptation. I smile, knowing I passed with flying colors. Not a challenge when you only have eyes for one woman.

Tami isn't just a pretty package I want to flaunt on my arm.

Aside from physical beauty, Tami hosts several admiral qualities. Traits I never found attractive in other women. Intelligence, ingenuity, humor. She has an incredible, addictive laugh. And when she smiles, everyone stops and stares. She has a tough exterior, but the gentlest heart. And she has a vibrancy that lures you in and doesn't let go.

I weave through the complex, quiet as possible. I park the bike behind her truck when I notice a tan sedan in the guest parking for her building. The car unfamiliar from my previous visits. Kickstand down, I dismount the bike and study the car suspiciously.

I approach the car and peer in the passenger window. On the seat sits a briefcase with papers scattered over the closed lid. The floorboard is littered with empty cups, food wrappers, and fast food bags. A white lab coat with *David Cameron, M.D.* stitched in the fabric hangs on the passenger headrest.

If memory serves, Tami said her roommate is engaged to a David. She also said he never stayed late because of his and her roommate's beliefs.

Something snaps inside me. Not sure if it is anger or jealousy.

If he never stays the night with his fiancée, why is he here now? He certainly wouldn't be sleeping in her bed.

Tami has opened herself to me. Told me how she feels about me. Yet, my instinct is to assume deceit. After what she saw at her friend's house tonight, would she stoop so low? My irrational thoughts lean closer to yes than no. And I hate the dull knife piercing between my ribs.

Storming up the stairs two at a time, I stop at her door and rap my knuckles against the painted grain. Seconds pass with no response or sound from the opposite side. So, I knock again, this time louder and longer. I give a minute and still nothing. Heat and fire fuel my internal rage and I pound harder on the door, not caring if the other tenants hear.

Just as I go to beat the door again, it swings open. A petite blonde with a few colorful streaks in her hair stands with her hands on her hips.

"*What the heck.* Who are you? And why are you beating on my door? Do you know what time it is? It's late and you're waking up the whole complex."

"Uh, sorry." My rage dwindles a fraction with the way she stares daggers at me. "Is Tami here? We went out tonight and she left without me. Tried texting and calling, but she won't answer." I huff and swallow down how desperate I sound. "Just want to make sure she made it home safe."

She rolls her eyes. "Well, you didn't need to bang on the door like that. The first knock woke me up, I just had to get to the door. Hang on a minute, I'll see if she's home."

She closes the door and I hear the lock and slide chain reengage.

Two minutes. If she doesn't return in two minutes, I will take matters into my own hands.

CHAPTER 29

AMBER

ang, bang, bang.

Ugh. I roll to my side, yank the pillow out from under my head and press it over my exposed ear. I make the banging disappear by smothering myself as I drift back to sleep.

Bang, bang, bang.

My eyes pop open under the pillow. *What is going on out there? What the heck is that incessant banging?* Is Tami hammering nails in the wall?

I glance at the clock on my nightstand. Just after eleven. I know things have been off between us for a while, but I don't picture her being so rude. Don't imagine her being so disruptive this late at night. We disagree on several things, more now than when we met, but we never act childish.

Bang, bang, bang, bang, bang, bang.

Bolting upright, I hear the bangs more clearly. Coming from the front door. With quiet, methodical moves, I crawl out of bed, reach under the bed skirt and pick up the wooden bat. My knuckles sting as I grip the grain and walk toward the door. Step by step, I scan the apartment for anything out of place.

Bang, bang, bang, bang, bang, bang.

Everything looks as it did before bed. Except near the door, I spot Tami's cell and keys on the foyer table.

I don't remember her coming in. Maybe she had too much to drink and crashed hard. Probably why she hasn't come to see who's banging on the door.

Don't know if I should thank her for being so quiet when she came in or be upset. Wouldn't surprise me if she is the reason someone is banging on the door.

I peer through the peephole and see a guy with brown skin, curly hair, and a leather jacket. *Thanks for bringing work home, Tami. Thought we agreed this kind of stuff wouldn't happen.*

I step back, leave the chain in place, unlock the deadbolt and crack the door open. Pinning my hands to my hips, I snarl at the guy standing on the porch.

"*What the heck.* Who are you? And why are you beating on my door? Do you know what time it is? It's late and you're waking the whole complex up."

He looks taken aback as concern etches his face. "Uh, sorry," he states. I don't really give a darn. I would never be so disrespectful as to go to another person's home and bang on their door like a buffoon. "Is Tami home? We went out tonight and she left without me. Tried texting and calling, but she won't answer. Just want to make sure she made it home safe."

You have got to be freaking kidding me. Seriously?

I roll my eyes at the idea of this guy wanting to be Tami's knight. *Better get your sword ready because with her job, you will have more battles.*

"Well, you didn't need to bang on the door like that. The

first knock woke me up, I just had to get to the door. Hang on a minute, I'll see if she's home."

I shut the door, re-bolt the lock and reach for the slide lock, grazing the track to make sure it's still in place. Standing the bat against the wall behind the door, I pad across the foyer and head for Tami's room. As I get closer, I hear strange noises. With each step, the noise grows louder, but remains indiscernible.

What the heck is that? I have heard enough crazy noises for one evening.

A random thought pops in my head.

If the guy at the door is who Tami went with, but didn't *leave* with... who did she leave with?

True, we have grown apart the last two years, but I know Tami well enough. She wouldn't go somewhere with one person and leave with someone else. She isn't that type of person.

Maybe she is watching a movie.

I inch closer to the door, cup my hands around my ear and press against the door. Still strange noises, but nothing discernable.

Perhaps she got mad at the guy, came home, and is sulking on her bed with a pint of ice cream and a sappy movie. That has to be it. I will just peek my head in and let her know about the guy at the door. Let her decide whether or not to send him away.

I slide my hand around the cool metal knob and crank it right slowly, trying to be quiet in case she fell asleep. The latch slides all the way back and the door swings inward steadily. Her room mostly dark. The small Himalayan salt lamp in the corner glows softly. And it is all the light I need to see the horror before me.

Nausea roils in my stomach. Bile rises in my throat as I clutch my stomach, ready to vomit. Because this... this is... deplorable.

I stand frozen in the doorway. The door swings the rest of the way open. In the dimly lit room, Tami lies on her bed, asleep or drugged or unconscious—not sure which, but her eyes are closed. Hands bound with her robe sash. The remaining length tied off to the side of her bed on a curtain catch. A balled pair of socks shoved in her mouth. Her body stripped bare and limp.

She is not *asleep. Oh, god.*

Frightening as it is to see my roommate—my friend—in this state, it isn't the most disturbing part of this whole scenario. Not by a long shot.

Acid hits the back of my tongue and I get the first taste of revulsion.

No, the most disturbing part would be my fiancé. Completely naked. Thrusting himself inside Tami.

He hasn't noticed the open door. Or my presence. Or the fact I am watching him assault my friend.

Another dose of acid rises and singes another layer of my throat. I slap a hand over my mouth as I stand suspended in time and witness this atrocity. At the hands of a man I thought I knew. At the hands of a man I thought I loved.

Her body limply jerks toward the head of the bed with every forward thrust. Her hands dangle in the binds. Her body ripples under the movement.

This cannot be real. This cannot be happening.

I close my eyes briefly and pray that when I open them Tami will be sound asleep in her bed. That this whole horrific scene is some barbaric nightmare. *Deep breaths, Amber.* I open my eyes as David grunts. And there is no way I can resist vomiting any longer. The contents of my stomach hit my mouth, but I swallow it down.

What do I do?

Before I overthink it, I scream at the top of my lungs. An ear-piercing pitch. Scream as if someone has a knife to my neck. My lungs deflate as my vocal cords belt incredible decibels. My throat harsh as steel wool as I belt more cries. Unable to scream anymore, I brace myself on the doorframe as my world morphs into a slow motion video.

David whips his head in my direction. His hands forcefully grip Tami's lifeless torso, his dick still inside her. Shock registers on his face as he scrambles to withdraw from Tami and put his clothes back on. He drops her body to the bed with a harsh thump and her face rolls into the pillows.

I want to run to her, cover her, try to wake her. But the man fumbling to get his clothes on stands between us. I thought I knew him well. Now, I have no idea what to expect from David. And that scares the hell out of me.

Just as David steps one foot into his briefs, a loud bang ricochets behind me. I jump and press my back flush to the wall. Time speeds up and slows down simultaneously. I veer my attention toward Tami. How I need to get to Tami. How I need to help her.

And call the police.

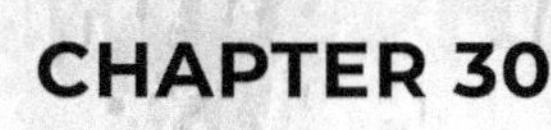

CHAPTER 30

MAX

Ugh. What the fuck is taking so long?

I check my watch and realize only seconds have passed since Tami's roommate closed the door. But fuck if it doesn't feel like an eternity. I lean against the frame, leg bouncing as I tap the outside of my thigh. God, I hope the roommate actually went to check on her and didn't go back to bed.

Pushing off the doorframe, I ball my fingers in a tight fist and prepare to pound on the door again. Before I get the chance, a deafening scream rips from inside the apartment and I instantly flip to panic mode. I beat the door repeatedly in the hopes the roommate will let me in. But the screams just continue as if unheard.

Panic switches to anxiety and something deep in my gut tells me I need to get inside. Now. Get to Tami. Because the scream isn't hers. Because the scream turns my blood ice cold.

Stepping back from the door, I throw my body weight into my left leg before I shift and kick in the door with my right. Upon impact, the grain splinters under the pressure, but doesn't budge an inch. So, I kick again. This time, the door opens, but not completely with the chain in place. I inhale deeply, rear back and, on the exhale, kick the door with all my weight. The frame gives and the door dangles catawampus.

I run the short distance to Tami's room and spot her room-mate flush against the wall. The terror on her face freaks me the fuck out. But what I see next has me murderous. Everything goes red.

Don't care about the repercussions because I plan to kill this motherfucker.

Some fat ass, motherfucking piece of shit stands inches away from Tami—who appears unconscious, no less—and has the audacity to redress himself. I curl my fingers into my palms and swear I break the skin.

This goddamn motherfucker raped my girlfriend. Dead. FUCK-ING. DEAD.

I launch forward and tackle the disgusting piece of shit as he fumbles to pull his briefs up. If memory serves, this lump of garbage is the roommate's fiancé. The man whose car is parked outside. Who claims saintly behavior.

I tackle him to the ground, ball my fists and pummel his face over and over. He jerks to block each punch I land on his face and makes a sad attempt to wriggle out from under me.

You aren't going anywhere, you fucking disgusting excuse for a human.

Thwack, thwack, thwack.

My fists connect with his face again and again. Bones crunch and skin splits. I lose feeling in my knuckles as blood smears his face. Not sure if it is his blood or mine. Don't give a fuck. He tries to get a blow in here and there, but I hammer him in the gut and he stops.

On the cusp of consciousness, I rise off him and step back. I plant one foot firmly on the floor, swing the other back and drive forward, nailing him in the balls. Hard. He curls in on himself and whimpers like the fucking cowardice, piece of shit he is. I have zero remorse for beating the shit out of him. At all. He deserves much worse.

I don't feel done with him. So, I rear back again, kick him hard near the kidneys and watch as he releases the semi-fetal position he'd curled into. Beating him to a pulp brings no satisfaction. But the moment he blacks out, I stop.

Since I don't need to worry about him fleeing, I crawl up the bed to Tami. Her roommate sits beside her, strokes her hair, repeatedly tells her to wake up and how terribly sorry she is.

I wave a hand in her face and she peeks up with tear-stained cheeks. "Have you called the police?"

She shakes her head as tears flood her eyes and spill down her cheeks. "I'll call," she croaks out before rising from the bed. She steps over dickhead on the floor and stumbles out of the room.

The second I hear her speaking in the other room—voice frail, words a mess of stutters—to the 911 operator, my body relaxes slightly. I pick up the blanket at the foot of Tami's bed and drape it over her body, wanting to keep her warm and preserve her dignity. She may take her clothes off as a job, but that doesn't mean she wants her body exposed and vulnerable to every person in a ten-mile radius. Or her privacy violated.

"The police sh-should be here soon," the roommate states when she comes back in the room. She resumes her place beside Tami. "Sorry to ask, but what is your name?" She cringes at having to ask.

"Max." I extend a scraped-knuckles, bloody hand in her direction. "My name is Max. Wish we met under better circumstances."

She shakes my hand and nods. "In case Tami hasn't told you, I'm Amber. We met in college, we were roommates then too, and became great friends. Over the last year or so, things changed between us. I think he had something to do with us growing apart." She points her chin to where her asshole fiancé lays passed out on the floor.

We fall silent. Time moves forward as we stare at Tami, dazed by what happened. At some point, Amber loosens the binds around Tami's wrists. I take one of her hands in mine while Amber continuously runs her fingers through Tami's hair. Lost in thought, I don't immediately register shoe taps against the hardwood. I jerk my head up in time to see two officers entering the living room with guns drawn.

"We're in here," Amber calls out.

"Is anyone armed?" an officer shouts.

"We have no weapons. Please hurry." I don't recognize the sound of my own voice as I speak. Squeaky and raspy and desperate. But I stash my ego. Tami needs medical attention.

The officers enter the room. One steps close to the bloody man on the floor while the other sidles up to the bed. "Can you explain what happened here?"

I proceed to tell them about my evening with Tami, from when I picked her up until she left the party and I couldn't find her. Inevitably, ending up here and what happened once I kicked in the door. When I finish, Amber shares her side of the evening, how David came over for dinner, and after they watched a movie. That is the last she remembers—assuming she fell asleep and David put her to bed.

Amber shares everything she witnessed as she opened Tami's door. How she almost threw up, but stopped herself and just screamed.

I fill in gaps after I heard Amber yelling. I won't deny

beating David to a bloody pulp. He deserves every single strike to his battered face. Each brutal blow. And when his face split and blood seeped from open wounds, I pummeled him again. Harder. I give no fucks about possibly doing life-damaging harm to this pathetic excuse of a human. If that gets me arrested or put in jail, I'll gladly accept the cuffs. As long as Tami is safe, I give two shits about anything else. Her safety matters most.

EMTs rush into the room with duffel bags slung over their shoulders. Amber and I step away from Tami as they move closer. They wrap her with an emergency thermal blanket and check her vitals. One of the medics states her breathing is shallow and blood pressure low.

A fresh wave of panic swallows me when a stretcher rolls in the room. They hoist her body on to a hard, plastic back-board. Velcro straps wrap around and lock her body in place. *One, two, three.* They lift her simultaneously, set her on the gurney, connect additional straps and wheel her out of the room.

"Where are they taking her?" I ask, frantic. After every-thing, I don't want Tami out of my sight.

An officer relays which hospital they are transporting her to and says to follow the ambulance. "Someone should also pack some of her belongings, so she has clothes to wear once discharged."

I peer over at Amber and she nods. "I know where all her stuff is, I'll pack then come find you at the hospital."

"Thanks, Amber." I give a polite smile then fall in line behind the EMTs.

Carefully, they wheel Tami out of the apartment to the stairwell. Before now, I never considered they would need to take her downstairs.

I fidget, eager to ask if they need help. Just as I open my mouth, the two men collapse the legs and tilt the gurney vertical. I stop breathing. As if they'd done it countless times, they lift her off the ground and creep down the steps with precision. It takes them longer, but they move her safely.

At the base of the stairs, they flip her horizontal, extend the legs, and wheel her to the ambulance. As they load her in, I verify which hospital, in case we get separated. The EMT reiterates before stepping in the ambulance and slamming the doors.

I jog to my bike, gear up, and rev the engine. Staying less than a car length back, I watch them work on Tami. One EMT adds an IV drip as the other sticks pads to her chest and clamps on wires. I assume this is routine. I don't know medical protocols. Have never *been* in a situation like this; neither has anyone close.

Tami better survive this.

If she doesn't, no one will like the beast I become. No one will be able to stop the beast I become. No one.

CHAPTER 31

TAMI

Whispers echo around me in foggy tones. The person talking off in the distance. The person talking speaks with such gentleness. I beg my eyes to open. To break me free from the darkness. An encapsulating darkness.

My eyes feel so heavy. Weighted. The muscles unyielding and weak and exhausted.

The voices drift farther away.

I breathe in cool air and relax my body on the exhale. The darkness blankets sight and sound, but it doesn't scare me. And slowly, I drift to where nothing but comfort and happiness and freedom exist.

The voices fade as I drift to the world of fairy tales and dreams and silence. Back to where peace lives.

My mind startles awake, but my body didn't get the memo.

I lay helpless in the bed. Fight to clench my fingers. Strain to wiggle my toes. But each attempt ends in failure. My body rigid and immobile.

I mentally yell at my muscles to move. For my eyes to open. But they don't. Refusing to give up, I try again. This time to lift my hand. Scrunch my brow. Anything. Still… nothing. As if I have lost motor function.

Then I give a go at saying something. A simple hello. A groan. Anything. But not a word, let alone a sound, spills from my lips.

What is happening? What a big, scary question. But how the hell will I get answers if I can't speak? *Why can't I move or speak or see?*

Dread is a sensory deprivation chamber as I ponder the worst. Am I dead?

Is this what it's like? When you die, is it just some endless torture chamber? A game where you hear voices, but can't see or feel or speak. A vicious cycle of unknown—where you are, what will happen next, if there is anything beyond this.

But the relentless thought spiral stops when I hear a voice. Volume loud enough to determine who is in the room.

I breathe a sigh of relief. Hope soars and rips away the fear blanketing me moments ago.

"Do you think she'll wake soon?" the voice asks. A voice so intimately familiar, but my mind can't quite decipher *who* the voice belongs to. Close. So close.

"I'd like to believe so. Her stats look normal. Same with the scans and bloodwork. When she wakes is up to her. Her body will tell her when it's ready. She's been through a lot. Have patience. She'll need a lot of patience and support when she wakes. You should prepare for that."

The second voice stops speaking. Then I hear nothing.

Wish I could sit up and wave. Maybe yell at the top of my

lungs. But neither happens. No matter the effort, no matter how hard I will myself to move or speak, my body lies limp and silent.

The first voice starts speaking again. I strain to listen. But a thick fog settles around my mind. The voices continue their conversation, but I no longer understand them. The fog thickens and the voices fade into the void.

A place so dark, yet soothing and peaceful. So very peaceful. Temptation. Soon, I slip back under the warm blanket of bliss. The voices nowhere to be heard.

A cacophony of beeps rings in my ears. The volume deafening.

I tilt my head away from the sound. I cringe, not just from the shrill piercing my eardrums, but also because every inch of me feels broken. A plowed pedestrian in a hit and run.

Slowly, my body wakes up. Bones and muscles and nerves stir back to life. With each noisy beep, the pain grows more unbearable. From head to toe, the pain is everywhere.

A constant thrum whooshes through my head as my pulse pounds behind my eyes. A sharp sting on the back of my head is an ice pick twisting in my skull. I open my mouth to speak, but can't form words.

My face not my own. Cheekbones, jaw, and eyes swollen and sore. With each inhalation, my breasts ache. Some weird, incomparable pain. Have they been torn from my body?

I attempt to lift an arm—the muscles weak—as fire shoots down my bicep, along my forearm, and encases my wrist.

Of all the aches and pains and tenderness in my body, none compare to the branding iron between my thighs. What the hell is happening?

My skin raw and ripped and screaming for salvation. Have I body swapped with someone? Agreed to some freakish experiment? Am I living someone else's nightmare of constant pain and agony?

I slowly peel my eyes open. My breathing spikes when I don't recognize the room. The space dark and foreign with sounds that won't quit.

I twist my head left, groan after minimal rotation, and notice a bright display of numbers and colors. The machine beeps with each contraction of my heart. *That explains the beeping.* I stare at the digital display and get lost in the rhythm of my own heart.

Th-thump. Th-thump. Th-thump. The tempo mesmerizes me briefly.

I blink and slowly turn my head, scan the room, and discern I must be in a medical facility. Not sure where, but I assume it's a hospital. As I scan the room, my eyes trace the silhouette outline of a man. He lounges in a chair near the foot of the bed. Farther, I spy a woman in a different chair.

Both asleep, I sigh heavily into the darkness as I fight to remember what happened to land me here.

As if he senses my state of consciousness, the man stirs and peers up at me. When realization dawns, he bolts up in the chair with wide eyes. Three erratic beats beep in the silence as fear creeps into my veins. I jerk back with a groan as pain lances my lower back.

I don't remember what happened or who is responsible. Anxiety jumpstarts my heart and fists my lungs. The unidentified man frightens me and makes me second-guess where I am. Whether or not I am safe.

The man rises from the chair inch by inch. As he

straightens his legs, he raises his hands in surrender and pads closer. "You're okay, Tami. You're safe now."

Closer to the bed, the dim light above the bed highlights his profile. I study his features—light brown skin, a mess of tight curls secured at the crown, face etched with worry and confidence. I tilt my head and stare up at him, masking the sharp pain from the base of my skull down my spine.

He doesn't say another word and I appreciate the time he grants to sort this out on my own.

Another small step closer and he lowers his hands. I narrow my eyes. Stare into his glass bottle-green irises. Drop down to his full lips. So familiar.

I breathe heavier and the monitor beeps faster. Louder. Recognition weaves its web in my mind and I squint as memories flood back in.

"Max? Is that you?"

His shoulders sag as he exhales. Tears pool at the corners of his eyes. "Yeah, beautiful. It's me." He speaks whisper soft as he sits on the edge of the bed and leans into me. "How do you feel?"

A tear rolls down his cheek. He reaches up and quickly wipes it away with the back of his hand. I have no idea what would make Max cry, especially since he doesn't seem the type. To cry or be vulnerable.

"I hurt. *Everywhere.*" I lick my cracked lips. "And I need water."

I lift a hand and grab at my throat. The IV line tugs the skin of my hand and I wince. *Another pain to add to the list.*

"I'll get you some water, and a nurse. Hold on a second." He twists toward a rolling tray table at the foot of the bed, pours a small amount of water into a cup and pops a straw in it. As he hands it to me, he presses a gentle kiss to my forehead then stands from the bed and exits the room.

Max returns with a petite, older woman in scrubs. She sidles up beside the bed, gives a soft smile, reads the monitor, checks the IV line, then faces me.

"Hi there, sweetheart. My name is Lyla. Do you know where you are?"

I stare back into her sweet, sympathetic eyes that crinkle at the corners. She makes me feel safe and at ease. "Guessing a hospital, but I don't know which."

She nods. "You're in the hospital recovery wing. You've been here three days." She studies the fluid level in the IV drip bag. "It's okay for you to drink water, just take small sips. I'll go page the doctor, but she may not arrive for an hour or more."

I nod and it hurts. "Thank you," I rasp then reach for my throat.

"You're welcome, sweetie. Just keep resting. We'll get you taken care of and better." She points a finger at Max, then to the woman lying in the chair, which I surmise to be Amber. "One of these two has always been here with you. We practically forced him to leave your side, just to get some food from the cafeteria." A gentle smile plumps her cheeks and a hint of adoration colors her thin skin.

Nurse Lyla exits the room and silence floats in the space between my consistent heartbeat on the monitor. I peek up at Max and read a swirl of emotions in the lines on his face. They speak his thoughts without him uttering a word. Fear. Concern. Loss. Pain. Anger. Panic. And, surprisingly, happiness.

I reach for his hand and feel immediate warmth when his fingers wrap around mine.

Through years of schooling, I learned several interesting facts about the human body. But one in particular stands out in this very moment. One I never believed because I had never experienced it. When the brain locks away trauma. Experiences it wants you to forget for a time, so you can physically recuperate before your mind heals.

Max knows what happened to me. Anguish etches his brow line. Pain paints shadows beneath his eyes. Heartache spills down his cheeks. But love radiates from his warm touch as he strokes my hand with his thumb.

He may not want to share what happened to me.

Bad enough to see or hear what happened firsthand, but then to relive it. Again, and possibly again. He has had days to simmer over what happened. Whereas with me, I have absolutely no idea. Right now, it is all speculation.

I stare at our joined hands a moment and relish in the warmth and strength, passion and energy I receive from his touch. I take a deep breath, peer into his eyes and ask him the one question I know he doesn't want to answer.

"Max, what happened?"

CHAPTER 32

MAX

The nurse turns and exits the room. Silence is a dark cloud hovering over us. My inability to speak says more than words ever will. But what the hell do I say?

Somehow, Amber sleeps through everything—my and Tami's conversation and the nurse visit. Amber has gotten as much sleep as me—next to none. So, for now, I let her sleep. One of us will fill her in later.

Tami's eyes dart between mine in search of answers. I *feel* the trail her eyes take as she searches my face. *Feel* the tremble in her touch as she feebly clutches my hand. I want to tell her everything, at least the parts I know. But in the same breath, I want to shelter and shield her from the horror. Don't want to rehash the nightmare that will haunt us all, especially her. But I don't want her to learn what happened from an outsider. There is no *easy* way to tell her.

Is it so bad that I want to protect her from the pain?

Protect her sanity.

Protect her heart.

Protect her soul.

I want her to have a sense of security. To feel loved and safe and carefree. Above all, I don't want her life to change. To be consumed by what happened to her. Or to give any power to the person who did this.

Her eyes drop to our joined hands. The second hand on the clock above the door ticks loud and slow. Love and heat radiate from her, settling in my bones. I pray Tami senses how much I care for her. Feels how deep our connection is rooted. Registers I will do anything for her. With her. That I want more.

Most of all, I hope she reciprocates.

She sits quietly, pensive. After a deep breath, her eyes meet mine and I see it. The questions. So many questions in need of answers. Answers that wring my insides and make me nauseous. I don't want to speak the words aloud, but know I shouldn't leave her in the dark. For three days, I have known this moment would come. What I didn't realize was how I would feel when it actually did.

"Max, what happened?"

I close my eyes, pinch them tight, cringe internally, and beg for the ice pick between my ribs to dislodge. Her ignorance of what happened is cruel and painful and unbearable. And breaking the news may shatter her. I squeeze her hand tighter and open my eyes. How do I go about this? First things first.

"What do you remember?"

Tami narrows her eyes at me as if I have two heads. Then she relaxes and tips her head back to stare at the ceiling. Taciturn a minute, her eyes shoot back to me as her cheeks redden with anger. I shift foot to foot, suddenly uncomfortable.

What the hell did she remember? Her gaze as murderous as mine was three days ago.

Her voice drips acid and hatred. "Walking out of Cherry's bathroom. The crowd going ballistic. Turning the corner to see her, butt-ass naked, rubbing all over you."

Her rage a ticking time bomb. Her skin blistering red in seconds. The heart monitor beeps angrily as her pulse and blood pressure shoot up.

I squeeze her hand and stroke her tangled tresses. Kiss her hair in an attempt to soothe and settle her.

"Calm down, baby. Please, try to calm down. Nothing else happened with Cherry. I will explain in better detail later. Is that the last thing you remember?"

Relief lightens my strained heart when she doesn't pull her hand away. Has to be a good sign, right?

Tami inhales deep through her nose then exhales slowly through her lips. She does this over and over. Her breathing quiets to a slow, steady rhythm. The monitor resumes the beat I memorized her first night here. And her body sags into the stiff, rumpled sheets.

"It's not *the* last thing I remember, but I definitely remember that." She pauses to study me and my solemn demeanor. Instinct tells me my calm helps her channel her calm. If true, I need to keep up the pretense as long as possible. "I also remember you trying to get away from her. Then I ran down the street." She pins me with her hazels. "Promise, I wasn't running from you. More like I wanted to escape her and the chaos she brings."

This lifts a burden I didn't know weighed me down.

"I remember being pissed that she wanted to ruin the good in my life. Again. I stopped at a store, bought water, and ordered an Uber."

She stops talking and I open my mouth to ask if that is the last thing she remembers, but she cuts me off. Yanking her hand free, she covers her mouth. A slow burn spreads through my chest. Gnaws and claws my heart before spreading throughout my body.

Does she remember? Did she glimpse the horrendous things inflicted upon her? Does she know what that piece of shit did to her?

A knife stabs and twists in my gut. I will never forgive myself for not getting there quick enough to stop him. To beat the piss out of him before he did the unthinkable.

What has her gasping? What memories have resurfaced? I need to know before I flip her world upside down.

"What? What did you remember?"

"It's… it's just… I-I can't remember anything after. Not the car ride or getting home. Did I make it home?" Anxiety cripples her voice. Her eyes dart between mine and beg for answers.

"Yes, you made it home."

Her shoulders sag. The lines above her brow smooth out. Eyes on me, I become acutely aware the second she realizes something happened at home. Her previously relieved tension amps up.

"If I made it home, why am I in the hospital, Max?"

Her gaze drops to scan her arms and exposed skin. Sucks to admit I am grateful her legs and back are hidden. Both of which are littered with bruises and lacerations.

Tami meets my wilting expression. Dread pales her complexion. This won't be a walk in the park, but I can't *not* tell her. She deserves to know. She deserves the right to decide what happens next. Personally, I hope the asshole rots in prison and gets what he gave. Daily. And that is me being kind.

"When you got home, David was still there—"

"David? That can't be right. He's never there past nine. His whole rule with Amber about staying pure, or whatever, until they're married." Her brows pinch together.

Hesitant, I close my eyes, suck in a breath, open them and proceed with caution.

"David was still there, sweetheart. Not certain as to the details of what happened between when you walked in the front door and a short span of time after, but…" I pause as the ice pick twists deeper between my ribs. Tears spill down my cheeks as I look her in the eyes.

This will change everything. Possibly even us.

God, I pray it doesn't.

"He attacked you." A soft-spoken voice startles me.

Amber walks to the other side of the bed and takes Tami's other hand in both of hers. Our conversation must have woken her. She nods to Tami.

"I didn't want to believe it at first either, but he attacked you," Amber repeats. "The doctor said he must've hit you on the back of the head with something hard and heavy."

Tami looks between us as Amber and I cry with the confession out in the open.

"Well that explains why my head hurts so much." Tami smiles for a second before looking between us again. "But that's not the whole story, is it? Because if that was it, only my head would hurt and not the rest of me."

With that, Amber relays her side of the evening and I mentally brace for what happens after.

"David came over for dinner that night. After, we watched a movie. At some point, I must've fallen asleep and he put me in bed. I don't remember. But then I heard banging at the door. When it didn't stop, I got out of bed to see who was at the door." She shoots me an irritated look, but it fades quickly.

"Max was so worried. He told me you left the party upset and he hadn't found you. And you didn't answer his calls or texts. He wanted to know you made it home safe."

Tears pool in Tami's eyes as she looks up at me. I give her a gentle, half-smile and squeeze her hand.

"You got it bad for me, don't you?" Her smirk lightens the heavy around us a moment.

I want to lighten the situation, flirt and banter with her, but now is not the time.

"You have no idea." I swallow hard and glance at Amber. Her head dips in shame and guilt. Amber takes partial blame for what David did, even after I told her not to. "So, Amber went to go check on you. She heard noises coming from your room and thought maybe you had fallen asleep with the TV on. She opened the door and saw something completely different."

Stabbing fire brands my heart. An unbearable pain I don't want to share, but must. Nothing in my measly life compares to this atrocity, but it would be wrong not to tell her. Excruciating as it is, it is worse to keep this secret.

An endless list of questions is written across Tami's face. Her eyes dart between us, etched with concern. "What?! What did you see?"

Amber closes her eyes. Her chest expands and stills a moment while she braces herself. "He was raping you," Amber mutters, breath above a whisper. The ice pick in my heart digs deeper. I sympathize with Amber. She thought she knew the man she intended to marry. Now, she has to live with who he really is.

"He what?!" Tami's shrill voice impales the air.

What happened to Tami has hit Amber hard. Seeing David as a monster hasn't been easy. I give her reprieve and take over. Squeezing Tami's hand, she snaps her head in my direction.

"This isn't easy for any of us, but I have to ask… how much do you want to hear?"

With laser precision, Tami's eyes bore into mine. "All of it."

I swallow and swear both of them hear the lodged rock scrape my throat. I hesitate and second-guess my reasons for telling her. But I remind myself of the injustice in not telling her.

So, I continue on, rehashing everything Amber and I shared with the police. I lay it all on the line and pray she recovers from this. Surviving horrific events is hard enough. Not remembering is worse. Having chunks of time stolen against your will is harrowing. Other people regaling a brutal act you don't remember must be frightening.

But I hope by us sharing, when her memory returns, she will cope easier.

I wrap up with David in police custody, and unfortunately breathing. I keep my voice calm, but an enraged beast consumes me. His violation… he best count his lucky stars he isn't six feet under. My composed demeanor, my soothing tone, is the result of Tami's doctor. Yesterday, she had a proactive talk with me and Amber.

The doctor said it is likely Tami won't remember much. Most trauma victims' brains shut out the initial start of what happened. A form of protection. It gives them time to heal. The doctor wasn't sure what Tami would remember or forget, but we had to prepare to share our side of the story. To help fill in the gaps.

Tami sits immobile, tears pooling in her eyes as they dart between us. She doesn't *want* to believe us. Her mouth opens, but she says nothing. Eventually, she mashes her lips in a tight line. She does this a few times.

The pools in her eyes well further. Tears spill down her cheeks and her shoulders shake as she sobs uncontrollably. My rage burns hotter as I watch the woman I care about fall apart. Amber reaches forward, strokes Tami's hair and brushes back wayward strands. She leans forward, presses her cheek to the top of Tami's head, shushes her and promises everything will be alright.

Please let her get through this.

My thumb brushes her cheekbone and wipes at the trail of tears. She peers up at me and pinches her eyes tight as she shakes her head. Does she think she won't recover from this? That *we* won't recover from this?

"Amber," I whisper, my eyes still on Tami. "Can you please give us a moment alone?" I glance at Amber and she nods. She kisses Tami atop her head and says she will wait in the hall.

Amber steps out and closes the door behind her. The heart rate monitor beeps loud and fast as Tami's sobs fill the room. Minutes pass and her cries taper down. Her pulse edges closer to normal. I want to scoop her up and cradle her in my arms. Tell her how much she means to me, even if it seems incomprehensible right now.

"Tami, this is a lot to take in. Can't imagine what you must be thinking or feeling. But I want you to know one thing. No matter what, I am here. I will be here. To sit with you all night while you cry. Or to give you space, if that's what you need, as long as Amber is with you. Last we spoke or saw each other was at the party, which ended in shitty circumstances. But I need you to know nothing happened with Cherry. I did not want or ask, for her attention. Now may not be the best time, but I need you to know you're the only woman I want."

A fresh wave of tears rolls down her cheeks. Her eyes bloodshot and nose runny. I sit silently as she tries to reign in her emotions, which is damn near impossible after everything.

She wrings her hands in her lap as she stares down. "How do you still want me?" she asks with frailty. Her chin wobbles as she bites her lip and refuses to look up.

No amount of planning prepares me for this moment. Although I knew it would come, I had no idea how it would feel.

The doctor said to be ready. Told me if I wanted to stay with Tami, she would need reassurances. Often. Feeling 'tainted' after acts of personal violation isn't uncommon. No two people cope the same, and some don't feel themselves for months or years. Not without support from the people who care most.

"Is that a legitimate question? How can I not?" I ask, voice soft and even. "Tami, you're not just some woman I want to hook up with. From the moment I laid eyes on you, I knew you were different. Unique. And not just your looks, but how you make me feel." I pat my chest.

"No woman lights my blood on fire like you. No woman makes my heart hammer like you. No woman draws me in and holds me close like you. No woman makes me want more from life except you. And no other woman makes me *not* want anyone else but you. Tami… you are all I see. You are all I will ever want. Even if you feel you aren't good enough, that you are damaged goods now, I beg to differ. You are exactly what and who I want. And you are perfect. For me."

Tears roll down her cheeks in parallel streams. She gasps and hiccups as she talks with emotion choking her. "You can have any woman you want. Why would you still want me?" She sobs and lifts her palms to cover her eyes.

"I don't want other women. Only you." I gently caress her bicep with my knuckles.

"Why?" she chokes out and swipes the back of her hand under her nose.

"Because…" I wipe tears from her cheeks, lift her chin with two fingers and bring her veiny, red eyes to mine. "I'm in love with you."

I fought my love for Tami initially. Played it off as an obsession or school-boy crush. But these last few days have shifted my focus. Made me see what matters and what I stood to lose. My love for Tami swam to the surface and I haven't been able to suppress it since. Nor do I want to.

The thought of losing her… my heart has shattered several times in the last three days. Scattered like millions of glass chards. Plummeted to the darkest sea caverns. Sprayed like ash in the wind.

I ache for the pain and suffering she will endure. But I refuse to not be by her side. To help her slowly erase this from her past.

She shakes her head. "How?" Her weary eyes read the truth written on my face.

"How do you explain love? You can't really. It's just… there. This fiery need that takes over and holds your heart hostage. You can fight it, but it will win. Always. I never knew love because I hadn't found you." The corner of my mouth kicks up. "A friend, Tristan, has been love-struck with a woman—now his wife—since the day they met. Watching and listening to him confused me. I couldn't grasp how he wanted her around so much. How they never tired of being together. Until I met you…

"The only thing I've wanted since meeting you is more of you. To see you, spend time with you. Talk about your life and mine. Hear about your goals and aspirations. The feeling never gets old. Never fades. If anything, it grows stronger each day."

Her tears flow without abandon. I frame her face and kiss her hair, her temples, her cheeks, the tip of her nose.

Between what happened with David and me confessing my love, she must be overwhelmed. I would be.

Minutes tick by and her tears slow, her eyes puffy and tired. Any minute, the doctor will waltz in and add a new layer of concern.

Her face in my hands, I lift her gaze to mine. I gravitate closer and press an impossibly gentle kiss on her lips. When I lean back, I rest my forehead on hers.

"I love you," I whisper. Three words I never imagined telling a woman.

"I love you, too," she chokes out and melts in my hands.

CHAPTER 33

TAMI

Max parks in the employee lot at The Sophisticate, cuts the engine and allows me a moment of silence before we go inside.

A week and a half ago, I left the hospital. Almost two weeks ago, my life changed in ways I never imagined. And now, my life will change again.

Discharged from the hospital, I went back to my apartment. But no matter how much Amber or I sanitized and straightened my room, or the rest of the apartment, I couldn't stay.

The first night, Max stayed. I laid awake all night. Stared at the ceiling. Tossed and turned as my imagination ran wild. Conjuring images of when I was unconscious. Conceptualizing what happened to me. But none of the images were real. But they did help, in a way.

During that first night, I remembered the exchange David and I shared before he hit me. Although he said cruel things to me, I never thought he would harm me. Or violate me.

The following morning, I told Max I no longer wanted to sleep in my bed. Even with me secure in his arms. He suggested buying a new bed or sleeping in the living room. They were great alternatives, but I dismissed them immediately. Told him I no longer felt comfortable or safe in the apartment. That I wanted to look for somewhere new to live.

Yes, it is a spontaneous decision. But I would never feel safe in that apartment, alone or not.

Reluctantly, Max offered the spare bedroom in his house. His hesitancy not because he didn't want me living in the same space. But more because of my recent trauma, which isn't the best time to make life-altering choices.

I respected him more then. Knowing he didn't want me to make irrational, spur of the moment decisions. But moving is the best option.

Since moving into Max's guest room, sleep has been better but nowhere near enough. Most nights, I sleep alone in an oversized bed. But on occasion, I go to Max and curl up beside him. He doesn't say a word. He just wraps me in his warm arms and presses a sweet kiss to my neck. It tempts me to snuggle with Max every night, but I need our relationship to slow down. For now. And he has been more gentlemanly than imaginable.

I take a deep breath, open the passenger door and step out. The warm summer air licks my skin and makes it tacky. Strands of my ponytail tickle my cheek. Max gets out and glances across the roof, a slow smile curving his lips up.

"Are you sure you want to do this?"

Max wants to be sure *I* make this decision—more life-altering—with a clear head. Deep down, Max is a great man. He may have been a pig for years, but it was a life he had been comfortable living. Not anymore.

"Yeah." I purse my lips. "I love dancing. The exhilaration

of being on stage. But I can't do it anymore. Be that vulnerable. That exposed." I shudder.

He steps around the back of the car, sidles up beside me, weaves his fingers with mine and injects warmth straight to my heart.

Damn, I love him.

He waits for me to lead. Giving me strength with his touch. We trek across the lot and enter through the employee entrance.

Still early, The Sophisticate and P.I. don't open for another two hours. The busy staff prepares for the evening ahead. Bartenders bustle behind tall countertops, checking and restocking liquor bottles. They clean glassware and wipe down the bar. Cut and refill fruit for drinks. Servers double-check the table linens are crisp and spotless. They straighten chairs and vacuum floors, roll silverware and light candles. Only half the employees are here, but the place is alive and hustling.

I lead us to the bar and smile at the bartender. "Hey, Sam."

"Hey, sweetie. Haven't seen ya in a few weeks. Doing alright?" A genuine smile dons his face. The crinkles I love so much pop up at the corners of his eyes. Sam is the sweetest man I have had the pleasure of knowing. He assumes a fatherly role, if not grandfatherly, toward most of the employees. He always lends his time and an ear to anyone in need. Lovable and one of a kind.

"Doing better. Need to speak to Rocco, though. Is he in his office?"

"Should be. Saw him head that way not long ago. You sure everything's okay?" He eyes Max suspiciously, and his protective nature makes my heart swell. I will really miss him.

"Yeah. Just need to talk to him. Promise to see you before I leave." I wink at Sam then lead us toward Rocco's office.

We stop in front of the closed office door and I freeze.

I know what I need to do, but facing Rocco makes the situation more real. Again. But I have to do this. I need to close this chapter in my life. I fear if I don't, I won't be able to forget what happened. Because I know myself. Know the horror will replay over and over every time I dress to go on stage. Every time the curtains part and hundreds of males visually grope me. Every time I remove the scanty clothing and expose myself physically. I will see myself assaulted by someone else.

And right now, I haven't found strength to forget it all. I just need more time.

Lifting my hand, I knock softly on the wood. A moment passes before a deep, familiar baritone says to come in. Glancing at Max, I take in his confident stance. The upward curve of his lips as he nods for me to enter the office. I give his hand a slight squeeze, lean in, and press a quick kiss to his cheek.

"Do you want me to come in?" His words the epitome of strength and courage. His body language a fortress of protection and solace.

I love having Max at my side, but this should be something I do alone. Rocco needs to believe this is my decision. That Max isn't pressuring me. That he isn't the reason behind what happened. If Max comes in, Rocco won't believe.

"No. I really need to do this on my own. Shouldn't be long, though. Maybe ten minutes, at most."

"I understand. I'll go back to the bar and talk with Sam. Come find me when you're done."

He plants a soft kiss on my forehead, releases my hand, and walks back toward the bar.

I inhale, twist the knob and exhale as I push the door open. *Here goes nothing*. I step into Rocco's office and spot him behind a colossal wood desk. He types rapidly on the keyboard. Papers scattered on the desk beside him.

He peers up and pauses when he sees me. A genuine smile lights up his face and my heart melts. I will miss Rocco the most. He has been the best boss, good ones are hard to come by in this industry.

"Hey, Tami. How are you?"

I haven't spoken with Rocco since I requested time off almost three weeks ago. I wanted to let him know what happened sooner, but couldn't bring myself to tell him over the phone. And I wasn't brave enough to visit here yet. I wasn't brave enough to share what happened, even if what I share isn't the entire story.

"I'm... doing better." Rocco studies me a moment then pushes his chair back and faces me head-on, giving his undivided attention. I swallow the wad of cotton in my throat. "A couple weeks ago, something happened. To me. I... I..." *Come on Tami, you can do this. You have to do this. This is Rocco. He's family.* "I was hurt."

Silently, he rises from the chair, rounds the desk, and leans on the edge. "Are you okay? What can I do? How can I help?"

Rocco has always been kindhearted toward the women he employs. And protective. His caring nature is one of his best traits and makes me smile. "Yeah, for now. Honestly, there isn't much you can do. But there's something I need to do."

"Whatever you need, say the word."

I clench and unclench my jittery hands in my lap. Steel my spine as I peer up at him. "I need to resign. Unfortunately, I need to make it effective immediately." My eyes drop to my hands as I breathe jaggedly.

"Tami." My name soft and sympathetic on his tongue. "I have no issues with granting you this, but I need to ask you something first." *Please don't ask. Please don't ask.* "Was it something someone here did to you?"

I release my captive breath and prepare to answer. Although he didn't ask directly, he still asked. And I have to learn how to talk about this. At least, that's what the therapist tells me. I shake my head, slow at first. After a sobbing inhale, the shake grows more frantic. "No. No one from here. But it was someone I knew."

His eyes redden and pool. Sorrow crinkles at the corners. Not because he will lose one of his best dancers, but because he actually cares about us. Everyone here is family. More family than most blood-related families. We have a bond that isn't so easily explained to outsiders.

"Are you safe?"

Rising from my seat, I hug him tightly. Hug him like I may never again. "I am now," I whisper in his ear. Releasing my grip, I step back. "I have a safe place to stay and someone looking after me. Every day gets a little better."

We walk to the door, and Rocco pulls me in for a side-hug. "If you need anything, even just to talk, I'm here. We all are. Remember that."

A snake coils around my heart and constricts. I can't breathe. Tears pool in my eyes and threaten to spill. I swallow past the emotional lump in my throat and drag in a ragged breath. "I'll remember. Thank you, Rocco. For everything."

He hugs me tighter. "No, thank you. For being a part of this family. I expect to hear from you, and see you, every now and again. Don't be a stranger. Okay? Once family, always family."

The oddest sensation resonates between my lungs. A hollow tremor. Like a ticking void. A quake that consumes and overwhelms me. A mixture of relief and loss.

Do people feel relief after loss? I feel inclined to say something comforting, to express my gratitude, but come up empty. The section of my brain—Broca's area—that translates thought to speech is on the fritz. So, I just nod and do my best to calm the ache strangling my heart.

"I won't be. Promise I'll stop by. Might be a little while, though."

"I understand." He hugs me hard one last time and says he will see me soon. Holding back tears, I walk out, close the door, wipe at my cheeks and go find Max.

I park in the driveway, cut the engine, and sit idle behind the wheel.

A little more than three weeks has passed since the incident at the apartment. Today also happens to be the first day I returned to work at the dental office. The whole day bizarre, especially since I hadn't been in the office in so long. But everyone treated me the same.

How did I explain my absence? Emergency appendectomy plus more rest and recovery than normal. I just hope my appendix doesn't actually burst while still working here.

Exhaling the day's stress, I exit the truck and go into the house. Inside, garlic and herbs float through the air. I inhale and close my eyes as my body lolls.

Just outside the kitchen, I halt when I see Max. He glides around the kitchen with ease, stirs the contents in a pan on the stove before returning to the cutting board where he chops vegetables for salads. Completely focused, Max hasn't noticed I am home yet.

Home.

The word rolls around in my head and locates a cozy nook

in the corner. It feels natural to call this place home. Without hesitation or trepidation.

I ogle him a moment longer, drool at how his muscles flex as he darts between the counter and stove. Bite the inside of my cheek as his biceps and forearms tighten; when the black cotton stretches taut across his broad shoulders.

Watching Max makes me hungry for something other than food. His patience and understanding as we trek this steep slope in our relationship is unparalleled. Physically, intimacy may be possible. Mentally? I don't think I am ready. The possibility of rejecting Max because of what happened depresses and irritates me.

"You'll know when it's time." My therapist's words ring in my head.

Rattling my keys, I drop them in my purse and alert Max I am home. He doesn't need to know I have made eyes at him the last five minutes. He sets the knife down, spins to face me with a smile the size of California and I instantly return the sentiment.

I love how easily we do that. Smile. How just seeing each other lifts us up.

More recently, we have spent all our free time together. And time with Max never gets old. Neither does the butterfly tornado beneath my breastbone. I feel each of them as their wings flap violently with excitement. Feel the buzz they create. How their storm builds exponentially with each passing second. A storm of undiluted heat.

Nothing dulls it. Ever.

His words, his touch, his lips on my skin… Max revives my soul.

Some say it is just a phase. The honeymoon stage of the relationship. I disagree.

Our relationship may still be young, but we have endured so much already. The fact Max hasn't run for the hills says more about his character than I imagined possible.

"Hey, didn't hear you come in. How was work?"

I set my purse on the counter, sidle up to him, and kiss him chastely on the lips. "Good. Smoother than expected. Thankfully, my schedule wasn't packed."

He picks up the knife and finishes chopping the onion. I stare after him as he goes back to the stove. He stirs the contents in the pan and another wave of garlic wafts up my nose. This man knows all the ways to my heart.

"Glad it went better than expected. Dinner should be ready in a few. Why don't you go change into something more comfortable and I'll finish here."

I step closer and kiss him, pressing my lips to his a little longer. When we break apart, I sigh then grab my purse and walk toward my room.

Although I moved in with Max almost a month ago, we still sleep in separate rooms. Mostly. In some respects, the separation makes me feel safe and protected; puts me more at ease. But the whole dynamic also feels awkward and uncomfortable and downright odd. Our relationship has evolved and shifted so much in the last five to six weeks.

Opening the bedroom door, a sweet perfume hits me like a wall of humidity. I flip the light switch and stumble back a step when I see the massive display in my room.

Sitting on practically every surface are dozens upon dozens of roses. On the dresser, a bundle of at least two dozen garnet roses in a vase with baby's breath and thin pieces of greenery. Peppered across the floor, a rainbow of pastel petals, the hues remind me of the beautiful colored wigs I wore. But the most eye-catching arrangement covers the bed.

Countless garnet roses are strewn over the heather gray comforter. Stems strategically placed. Petals scattered at random. A large bundle held together with a strip of canvas and a length of twine.

I shuffle through the floor petals in a daze, bump the bed with my knees and pick up one of the single roses. I lift it to my nose, the soft petals tickle my skin, and deeply inhale the exquisite perfume. The scent heavenly.

The display, the sentiment… fireflies whirl beneath my breastbone. Encompass my heart.

Warm arms snake around my waist and press my back to his front. Max kisses me sweet and seductive below the ear and whispers, "Hope you love them as much as I love you."

And right there, I melt in a puddle at his feet.

CHAPTER 34

MAX

Trying to woo a woman when you know absolutely nothing about wooing is the hardest fucking thing on the planet. I have no point of reference. Internet searches are scaring the shit out of me. Some points so obvious I want to slap whatever guy doesn't know the basics. I may have played the field before Tami, but my parents taught me how to be a gentleman. I just need to practice those lessons more now.

The last two weeks, I cooked us dinner—with the exception of Tami's days off, when she wanted to be in the kitchen. I took two months off from instructing at the gym, told them I needed personal time. Freeing my evenings and having more time with Tami has been life-changing.

In such a small increment of time, we have learned so much about each other and ourselves. Smaller tidbits and deeper details.

Details such as Tami's name—Tamara D'Amore. That her mother, Valentina, makes extraordinary, authentic Italian food. That she only knows her father's first name—Thomas—and he was a young, scrawny boy. Tami's mother met him at a high school party. They had a one-night stand. And shortly thereafter, Valentina discovered she was pregnant. Her family disowned them, but they made it work. Tami's upbringing wasn't easy by any means. She learned hard work at a young age and how to be frugal.

In some respects, that makes me the snobby rich kid. My youth the polar opposite of hers.

My mother, Beverly, came from a higher, middle-class family. Knew who she wanted to be and had her life mapped out before she met my father. Needless to say, he made her dreams a reality. My father, Grant, a local politician, was introduced to my mother through their parents at a social gathering. What was intended as a semi-arranged marriage became love at first sight. Both families approved, but made it abundantly clear certain aspirations needed fulfilling before they married.

My father was to attend law school and my mother needed to learn the ins and outs of being a proper housewife. To tend to the home, her husband and future children. The whole concept feels peculiar and unnatural to me, but it works for them. Married forty years, they have three children (me, my younger brother, Christopher, and my baby sister, Amelia) and have never been happier.

Years ago, I asked my mother if she feels she missed out on life, on a career, because she was home with us. She said, *"I still get to paint and create. Would it have been wonderful to see my art in a gallery? Yes. But I don't regret any of my choices. I may not have you if I'd chosen differently."* Back then, I didn't absorb our talks. Now, I circle back to them and compare them to my own life. To the choices I have made and continue to make for the future.

Conversations with Tami flow without effort. We discuss everything. Are one-hundred-percent honest with each other. Eager to learn more each day. A new and refreshing concept for me.

Since the incident in her apartment, I have been a perfect gentleman. Giving her the space and time she needs to recover. I pray what happened to her doesn't haunt her. It will never fully vanish, but I hope it doesn't restrain her from living life.

And my feelings for her? Fiercer than ever.

Her strength and courage make Tami that much more incredible. I constantly commend her bravery, in my thoughts, and am in awe of her resilience. Tami is a much stronger person than I will ever be. And I need to tell her just how awe-inspiring she is.

I open the door and a small bell screwed at the top jingles as the sweet fragrance of a million flowers invades my nasal cavities. To state the floral shop has an abundant selection would be an understatement. The only woman I have bought flowers for is my mother. And even then, I purchased them online and had them delivered. Physically entering a florist shop is a wholly new experience.

Wandering the store, my eyes glaze over at the various pre-made arrangements and loose stems. *Fuck. What did I get myself into? Why did I think this was a good idea?* Seriously, what *am* I doing? The enormity of how much thought goes into purchasing flowers has me nauseous as I wipe my clammy palms down my pants.

"Can I help you, sir?" A petite, older woman comes to my rescue. *Thank fuck.*

"Yes, ma'am. I want to purchase flowers for my girlfriend, but I've never done this before, so…" I shrug and give her a sheepish look.

My nervousness simmers down when a smile highlights her frail features. She claps her hands in front of her lips and rubs them together. "Oh, my favorite," she exclaims with obvious joy. I should hug her. "Do you happen to know her favorite flower?"

Of all our recent conversations, learning each other's favorites hasn't been one of them. Need to rectify that soon. "Unfortunately, no." I purse my lips.

"No worries, honey. There are plenty of flowers all women love. Follow me." She spins on her heel and quickly hobbles toward the back of the store, a woman with a mission.

I follow closely, but have trouble keeping up. It surprises me how quickly she zips through the store considering she stands a foot shorter than me. We stop in front of a walk-in cooler and she faces me. "Before I get carried away, can I ask your budget? Just so I have a ballpark."

"Not concerned about the cost. Just want to show her how much she means to me."

Her face lights up like Christmas morning. "Wonderful. We're going in here." She gestures to the walk-in. "It's a bit cold, but it helps keep the flowers fresh longer."

We enter the chilled room and the sweet scent of roses hits me instantly. With the number of roses in this cooler, I assumed the smell would be overbearing. But it isn't. I close my eyes and inhale, and it amazes me how I consider a smell beautiful. When I open my eyes, I notice the store owner watching me with a knowing smile.

"Before I just start grabbing roses for you, did you have an idea in mind? Do you want them in a vase? Loose? Wrapped in paper? Loose petals?"

Questions spill from her one after another, and it takes me a moment to register all the options. *I have no idea.* That's what I want to tell her. I have no expertise with flowers or romance or gift-giving. So, I shrug.

"All of the above?" My mouth stretches in a flat line as I cringe from the neck up.

Her singsong chuckle lightens the tension building inside me. "How about this… I'll pick out some flowers and ask your opinion. After we know which you want, we'll sort out how to present them. Sound good?"

"You're a lifesaver!" I say with sincerity. Seriously, can I hug this woman?

If left to me, I would have picked the first flowers I stumbled across and been done with it. But as she strolls through the cooler, she tells me the meanings behind each color and points them out.

"Red represents love, passion, beauty, courage, respect. The darker the red, the more passionately you feel. White represents purity and innocence. Dark pink—appreciation and gratitude. Light pink—sweetness, admiration, or sympathy. Yellow is for new beginnings, friendship, or joy. Orange—fascination, desire, and enthusiasm. Peach—appreciation and sincerity. Coral for desire. Lavender represents love at first sight and enchantment. A mix of colors—the person means everything to you."

My jaw drops. Who the hell knew flowers held such significance? Certainly not me.

"Uh…" She laughs and takes in my stunned, speechless expression. "I guess the darker red roses. And some loose petals as well."

"Before we go further, tell me the meaning behind your purchase. Helps guide me in the right direction."

"Well, I've been seeing this woman for almost two months, although we've flirted longer. Something happened to her recently and changed her life quite dramatically. But not how I feel about her. Actually, I feel more for her and it's gaining momentum. The change has thrown her and I want her to know I don't love her any less."

"Well, now. I know exactly what you need."

The woman darts around the space, plucking flowers from bins and placing them in a basket on the floor. The basket grows fuller by the minute. Satisfied, we exit the walk-in. She bundles a group of flowers, puts more in a vase with small, white buds and greenery, then loosely gathers the remaining and secures them in paper. Before cashing me out, she suggests different placements to guarantee a successful presentation.

After settling the bill, I haul half the flower shop to the car and drive home. Still early, I hope Tami worked all day her first day back and I have time to set everything up.

I park in the driveway and exhale a held breath when I don't see her truck. Quickly, I lug the flowers inside and bolt straight to her room. I arrange them per the instructions of the most amazing florist ever. That woman will definitely get more business from me in future.

After the flowers are in place, I exit the room and head for my in-home office. I pluck a pen from the cup, stationary from the box I purchased the other day, and roll out my chair. Once seated, I put pen to paper.

My dearest Tamara,

Nothing could have prepared me for this. For the way I feel about you. We haven't known each other long, but it feels I've known you all my life. The moment I saw you, I knew you were different. Not going to lie... my initial thoughts were about your body. How could they not be? You're stunning.

But then you stepped closer and my body felt something different. It confused and confounded me. Before you, women had one meaning. Sex.

But you aren't like other women.

No other woman makes my heart combust. But you do.

No other woman makes me breathless. But you do.

No other woman incinerates and drives me wild. But you do.

No other woman calls to me and makes my blood sing. But you do.

From the moment we met, I've seen no one but you. Before I learned your secret identity, even your counterpart stood in your shadow. I didn't want her the way I wanted you. You, Tamara, are enough for me. More than enough. Your beauty, integrity, and strength. Your courage and tenacity. You are one of a kind. And someone I can't live without.

All that said...

We have been a couple a short time now, but haven't told anyone as much. But I want to shout from the rooftops you belong to me. That you are mine and no one will replace you.

And... I'd love to share the same space with you. Sleep in the same bed. Hopefully I'm not premature in asking... I'd also love you to stay, in my home, and make it yours. Permanently. You moving in was temporary, but I don't want a single day without you here.

This place is only home with you here.

Never thought I'd tell a woman I love her, but my world would crumble if I didn't tell you daily. I have never been so madly in love and I hope you keep me.

I love you like the stars love the night.

Yours Always,

Maxwell

I read over the handwritten proclamation, then fold it into quarters. Returning to Tami's room, I place the note on the bed amongst the roses, scatter pale petals on the floor, then shut the door. I stare at the door a moment, my lungs tight and begging for air, and hope everything goes according to plan.

I snatch the florist shop bag and ditch the evidence in the outside garage. In the kitchen, I retrieve the ingredients to make dinner and get to work. I marinate salmon filets and start a pan of risotto. I add vegetables and spinach to bowls for salad. Then pop the salmon in the oven.

I swear the front door opens, but nothing follows, so I brush it off and focus on dinner. I stir the risotto then dart back to chop the remaining vegetables. As I add avocado to both salads, jingling keys garner my attention.

She is home.

The sight of her evokes the biggest, toothiest grin. Since meeting Tami, I smile more often than not.

I set the knife down and face her. She stands in the open area between the kitchen and living space, a soft glow on her face radiates warmth and happiness as she smiles back. My heart stutters to a sop. My breath hiccups then kick-starts and rattles my ribcage.

Tamara D'Amore—the only woman to steal my breath, stop my heart, then revive me.

"Hey, didn't hear you come in. How was work?"

She sets her purse on the counter, saunters over to me, and kisses me softly on the lips. "Good. Smoother than expected. Thankfully, my schedule wasn't packed." She sags, obviously relieved.

I briefly turn my attention back to dinner. Cut and toss thin onion slices in the bowls, then give the risotto another stir. The risotto has maybe five to ten minutes and the salmon will be ready around the same time. Perfect.

"Glad it went better than expected. Dinner should be ready in a few. Why don't you go change into something more comfortable and I'll finish here." No doubt her scrubs are pretty comfortable, but she needs a reason to visit her room and see my surprise.

She leans in and kisses me, lips lingering a beat. The

familiar and addictive euphoria we share passes from her lips to mine. A shiver rolls up my spine and I forget to breathe a moment.

She snags her purse and treks toward her room. I stir the risotto once, lower the heat, then tiptoe behind Tami.

Distanced enough for her to not realize I followed, I lean against the wall and witness her reaction. She opens the door and inhales deeply. Her hand reaches for the light switch and flips it. When the room lights, she stumbles back a step. Her head shakes as she lifts a hand to rest over her heart.

She ambles forward and takes in the display. Without hurry, she reaches the foot of the bed. A large rose bundle lies beside the folded letter. Tami plucks a single stem, brings it to her nose and inhales the perfume.

Her entire frame loosens. I step up behind her and envelop her in my arms.

There is nothing better than this. Tami in my arms. Nothing compares to our bond. And nothing can break it.

I drop my lips to the spot below her ear, the one that makes her shiver, and scorch her tender skin with a kiss. She tastes like paradise. Sweet and fruity. I stop myself from kissing farther down her neck. Then whisper in her ear. "Hope you love them as much as I love you."

Her head tips back and drops on my shoulder as she circles her hips over my groin. A soft hum rumbles in her throat. Those simple gestures speak louder than words. Tami speaks with her body more than her voice. Tells me where her head and heart and needs lie.

She turns her head, brings a hand to the back of my neck, presses her lips to mine and kisses me hard.

She parts her lips and I deepen the kiss. The room disappears as our lips and tongues and moans familiarize once again. She spins in my arms, presses her front to mine, and I lose myself in the feel of her.

Until the stove timer buzzes and snaps me out of my lust-drunk fog.

Groaning, I nibble at her lips before reluctantly retreating. "Take your time. I'll get dinner ready."

Jogging back to the kitchen, I turn off the risotto and give it a quick stir. I pull the salmon from the oven and let it cool before I slice it for the salads. I fetch wine from the bottle fridge, pop the cork and set it on the counter to breathe. Once I cut the fish and divide it between the salads, I carry them to the table. Then portion out two small bowls of risotto and set them by our salads. Lastly, I cut crusty bread, arrange it in a basket and grab fresh herbs, olive oil and balsamic to dip.

I pour wine into our glasses, take my seat at the table, and wait for Tami to join.

Minutes tick by and I wonder if the whole evening— flowers and dinner—is too much too soon. I swipe my hands down my thighs as my knee bounces under the table.

She must be reading the letter. Did she finish it? Did I overwhelm her? Say too much? *Is it too soon*? I slam my eyes shut. *Fuck*.

Lightly, she pads across the room and my eyes snap open. I glance her way and follow the lines of her body, from her bare feet to her loose, wavy espresso locks. And when our eyes meet, I stop breathing. Her eyes are red and puffy and flooded with tears. Tears stain her cheeks and drip from her chin. But she doesn't look away.

No. I didn't mean to cause her pain. Didn't mean to make her cry.

I fly out of the chair and step to her, not sure whether or not I should touch her. She stares at the base of my throat. Is she purposely avoiding eye contact? No, I won't have it. Not now. Not in this moment. Not after I spilled my heart to her on paper.

I lift a hand to her cheek. Cup the tender angle of her jaw and swipe my thumb across the line of tears. I tuck my fingers under her chin and lift her eyes to mine. When her hazels lock on me, I absorb her tears in a whole new light. The corners of her lips curve up at the edges and her eyes mimic the action. I raise my other hand and frame her face, lean down and kiss the two trails on her cheeks.

"Glad these are happy tears. For a moment there, you had me worried."

Her smile widens and knocks me breathless. My heart expands in ways I never dreamt possible. "Only tears of happiness. Your note… it just took me by surprise, is all. Wasn't expecting what you wrote."

I swallow down my nerves. "And how do you feel since reading my letter?"

Her gaze latches on mine and doesn't let go. "Think I'm ready to go on the back patio and yell at the top of my lungs that you belong to me. And I belong to you." She pushes up on her toes and gives me the sweetest, most tender kiss. "I love you, too, Maxwell."

And I have never loved hearing my full name as much as I do in this moment.

"Love you, too, baby."

EPILOGUE

TAMI

I finish cleaning Mrs. Blake's teeth, then tell her I will return with Dr. Talbott. I hop up, press a button on the wall, and go in search of the doctor.

Dr. Marie Talbott—one of the top dentists in the state of California. An inspiration to many in the dental community, she gives several informative and innovative lectures about the current setting of the dental industry and where she sees it heading in the future. I am just thrilled to be given the opportunity to work alongside her every day.

A little more than two years ago, things with my previous employer went downhill fast. The doctor began to care more about his wallet rather than his patients and employees. The evidence easier to see with each passing day. When I voiced my concerns to Max, he suggested maybe it was finally time to seek new employment.

When I interviewed with Dr. Talbott's office, I fidgeted and squirmed worse than a five-year-old. She sensed my anxiety, told me to relax and just be myself. Two days after the interview, I received a job offer. Couldn't have been more thankful I landed a new job when I did. Because shortly thereafter, the other office was audited and some not so great things were happening behind the scenes with It's A Bright Day Dental.

Dr. Talbott visits with Mrs. Blake, performing her routine final examination of my work and telling Mrs. Blake her findings and suggestions for future treatment. As Dr. Talbott stands to leave, she glances my way. "Fantastic work, Tami. Keep up your brushing habits, Mrs. Blake. See you in six months."

I walk Mrs. Blake to reception and wish her well until I see her in six months. Back at my workstation, I slip into full throttle mode as I rapidly clean and sanitize every surface. Eager to get home to Max and help prep for our party tonight.

Six months after I officially moved in with Max, a new comfort developed between us. One I never thought would pan out, but ended up being one of our most pivotal moments.

It had been challenging, after a few months, to not have the outlet and adrenaline rush dancing provided. I didn't want to go back to dancing, but needed something to replace that piece of me. When I mentioned it to Max, he made suggestions and we chose parties. We invite select people of like mind or that share a similar lifestyle.

One thing led to another and the parties evolved into what they are today. Private, intimate, and the perfect fix we both need.

I exit through the employee door, wave goodbye to everyone, and hop in my truck to drive home. Soon, I park in the driveway next to Max's car. A loony smile pushes up my cheeks with Max already home. I walk in the house and sigh as music bounces off the walls and vibrates my bones. Balanced perfectly and not too loud, the beat settles me the way only music does.

In the kitchen, Max organizes dishware for the food and drinks we serve once everyone arrives. He glances up as I approach, picks up the remote and mutes the music. "Hey, baby. Sorry about that. Was in the zone and lost track of the time."

I saunter to him, snake my arms around his neck and give him a proper kiss. His arms wind around my waist and haul me closer. When the kiss breaks, I press a chaste kiss to his cheek.

"No need to apologize. Just walked in. Need help?"

"Pretty much done. Just need to pull stuff out of the fridge before everyone arrives."

"Perfect. Well, if my assistance isn't needed, I'll go jump in the shower and get cleaned up."

He bends down and kisses me breathless. "Go shower. I'll be there in a minute. Just need to make sure I have everything in place." A hand glides down my ass and smacks before I walk off.

In the bedroom, I peel off my scrubs and toss them in the hamper. Then go to the en suite bathroom and crank the shower. While the water heats, I tug the elastic band from my hair and brush out any knots.

I step under the hot spray and drop my chin to my chest to let the heat soothe my aching muscles. As I rinse out the shampoo, Max slips his arms around my waist. Suds gone, he joins me under the spray, kisses me feverishly and roams my skin as if the first time.

The fire and intensity between us haven't waned. If anything, the potency of our relationship magnifies daily. I never get my fill of Max. And he never gets enough of me.

Our love has evolved into a living, breathing life force. One I refuse to live without.

MAX

Tami saunters off to shower with a sway in her hips that beckons my cock. Without trying, she makes me instantly hard. I wrap up the final party prep fast and in a hurry, so I can join her and satiate the pulsing appendage between my legs. I take out the last liquor bottles, set them in the drinks area and jog to the bedroom.

The water from the shower hits the tile light then heavy. *Must be washing her hair.* Stripping my clothes, I tiptoe toward the shower and stop when she comes into view through the glass. I watch her a moment—head under the water, eyes closed as she rinses her hair—palm my dick, and remind myself I am the luckiest son of a bitch. Lucky I have such a gorgeous woman in my life every day.

My cock throbs for relief. I step into the shower, wrap my arms around her, and wait for her to finish rinsing. Done, I step under the water and kiss her senseless. The chemistry between us hasn't faded, but ignited to exponential levels. The bond we share—incomprehensible and incomparable. Near each other, the rest of the world no longer exists.

Breaking the kiss, I trail my lips down her neck and sink teeth where her neck and shoulder meet. Her breath hitches. She thrusts her hips forward and grinds against my cock. When we are like this, completely absorbed with one another, no verbal exchange is needed. Our bodies do all the talking. And right now, she wants me as much as I want her.

I lift her from the floor, her legs wrap around my waist. Slamming her against the tile, I cover her mouth with mine. Lick her lower lip and invade her when she gasps. She tastes of sweet mint and a flavor one-hundred-percent Tami. I line the head of my cock with her entrance and rock my hips forward. She moans as we connect in the most intimate way. I don't move. Give her a moment to adjust to the position. Wait for her signal to continue.

Her nails sink in my flesh. Game on.

In a blink, we are all lips and tongues and hands and moans. I grip her ass harder and hold her firmly in place as I plunge into her with animalistic intensity. She breaks our kiss, tips her head back and cries out as I piston my hips.

I lick a trail from shoulder to ear and bite her fleshy skin. A growl roars in my chest. "You like it when I fuck you hard, baby?"

"*God, yes…* Fuck me harder. Harder." Pleasure ripples up my spine.

I brace my legs and slam her weight down as I thrust my hips up. She moans louder. Hungrier. More wanton. Fists my hair. Mewls in my ear. Slams her head against the tile. Edges closer—her walls tighten around my cock.

"*Fucking hell. Don't. You. Dare. Stop.*"

"You're wish" —I pant against her neck— "is my command." I thrust forward once, twice, three times. She constricts and ravages me like a serpent. And I follow her down the path to ecstasy.

The rest of our shower is spent washing each other and me taking advantage while touching her. Finished, we towel off and dress for the party. Our guests should arrive in the next thirty minutes.

We head out to the main part of the house. Double-check the house is set up how we like. We finish last minute tasks with food and drinks.

The doorbell chimes and we glance at each other. Smiles in place, ready to greet our guests.

One by one, our friends arrive and the party slowly takes shape. We host parties once a month and invite roughly a dozen people. The guests hand-selected by us. Specific rules laid out and implemented. Rules every attendee must agree and adhere to. We have hosted more than a dozen parties now and they get better with time.

I perk up when a group of familiar faces enter. "Hey Rick, good to see you, man." We embrace and slap each other on the back before breaking apart. "Christy. Thomas. Ella." We all exchange hugs as Tami sidles up beside me and greets them. Tami and I have kept in touch with Rocco and the whole Sophisticate/P.I. family, which now includes this group.

Shortly after Tami left P.I., we learned Rocco was opening a new restaurant and club. Opulence and Boundless. Opulence is similar in nature to The Sophisticate, but with a new palette of colors and different menus. But Boundless was nothing like P.I. Where P.I. is an upscale strip club, Boundless is literally a sex club. Tami and I joined on opening night, but don't visit often. Rocco introduced us to Rick as part of the family and the relationship between the six of us has blossomed ever since. Having friends of like mind is hard to find and irreplaceable.

Once everyone arrives, the front door locks and the music cranks up. Most of our guests are familiar with each other, as we tend to invite several of the same people. There is food aplenty and the alcohol flows. Everyone has a great time catching up with each other and splitting off into pairs or small groups—some in the living room, others on the back patio by the pool. Party night is the one night a month where we see more than just our own flesh.

Tami and I meander out to the patio, passing a ménage—

two men, one woman. We both trail a hand down the woman's back as she rests on all fours and each man fills her. Her back arches at our touch and she hisses. We pass another couple, two women, enjoying each other immensely—all mouths and tongues and fingers.

Reaching a double lounger on the far side of the pool, I lay Tami down. Her bare flesh begs for my touch as I trace my fingers down her breasts, over her abdomen, and between her thighs. *Fuck.* Her folds slick and eager and hungry.

This is us. Tami and I are sexual creatures by nature.

Rather than extinguish who we are, we discovered an alternative way to express it. Our monthly parties let us get off watching others. For our guests, the party is an organized, safe orgy. A place for sexual creatures such as ourselves to be free. For us, the party is a form of liberation. We are bound to each other—I desire no one else and neither does Tami—but we still have fantasies. Fantasies we get to fulfill through voyeurism.

The first party rule—Tami and I are with each other. No one else. Just her and I. No one else touches us, in any capacity, or they get banned.

Without the parties, our sex life is incomprehensible. With the parties, it connects us to pasts we no longer partake in. For Tami, it satiates the need she has to be on stage. Delivers the adrenaline rush of being watched. For me, it provides me a sample of my past self without involving anyone other than Tami.

I glide my fingers between her folds and peek up to see her looking off. Follow her line of sight and notice her watching the two women we passed. I hover over her. Her pebbled nipples harsh against my pecs as I pump my fingers in and out of her.

"Do you like watching them, beautiful?"

"Yes..."

"Does it make you wetter for me?"

"God, yes..."

"Do you want me to fuck you while you watch them?"

"Please..." Her begging is so soft and desperate.

I withdraw my fingers, trace up her slit, circle her clit once, twice, three times. Then, I rock my hips forward and plunge inside her. She moans my name. Her eyes drift from the women to me. *Fuck, she drives me wild.* I thrust forward and rock back, vigorously drive into her.

Rolling us, she straddles and rides me. *God, I love the way she rides my cock.*

I fist her hips, rock her as I piston forward and meet her thrust for thrust. She pinches her nipples and rolls them between her fingers. Her cries come faster, grow louder. Her hips jerk feverishly as her walls tighten around my dick. Just as her release comes, I sit up and fuck the air from her lungs.

When her pussy pulses around me, I crush her to me and bring my lips to her ear. "Marry me, Tami. Fuck! I love you so goddamn much. Will you marry me?" My own release consumes me and the world goes black a second.

She freezes above me. Breath still ragged. Hair a wild mess. She inches back to look me in the eye. "Was that a serious question? Or something in the heat of the moment?"

My eyes deadlock on hers, face never more serious. "Not the heat of the moment. Marry me, Tami. You, me, us. Our life is never something I imagined. The fire between us never fades, it only gets stronger. God, I love you so fucking much. Can't imagine life without you. Make me the happiest man in the world. Say yes. Marry me. Say you want to keep me forever. Be my wife."

Her eyes flood with tears. One escapes and spills down her cheek. I wipe it with my thumb and mouth *I love you*.

"I love you, too." Another tear rolls down her cheek. "And, yes, I would love to be your forever. Your wife. I'll marry you."

Ready to jump up, I remember I am still inside her. I help her off me. Laughter erupts from us both as we rise from the lounger. When I catch my breath, I shout loud enough for everyone to hear.

"She said yes!"

Hoots and hollers reverberate from the back porch throughout the house. Yells of *congratulations* and *way to go, man*. Cheers from all our guests. She stares back at me with questions in her eyes.

"Everyone knew you were proposing?"

I beam with pride. "Yep. They've known the last week. Surprise!" She smacks my chest before I haul her into my arms and envelop her with warmth. Her body molded to mine, the party fades away and I stare into her brilliant hazel eyes. "I love you so much, future Mrs. Tamara Kingston."

"I love you, too, future husband."

Nothing has ever sounded so perfect in all my life. *Husband*. And I can't wait to see what the future holds with Tamara Kingston by my side. *My wife*.

SWEET TOOTH PLAYLIST

Here are some of the songs from the *Sweet Tooth* playlist. You can listen to the entire playlist on Spotify!

The Hills | The Weeknd
Laffy Taffy | D4L
Fantasy | Black Atlass
Professional | The Weeknd
Work | Iggy Azalea
Get On Your Knees | Nicki Minaj, Ariana Grande

MORE BY PERSEPHONE

<u>Distorted Devotion</u>
Free-spirited Sarah lives life to the fullest. When a new love interest enters her life, she starts receiving strange gifts and letters. She doesn't want to relinquish her freedom or new love, but fears the consequences.

<u>Undying Devotion</u>
A long-term couple, Christy and Rick, live in a world of secrets. Their friends envy the bond they share, but remain oblivious to their lifestyle and how deep the bond lies. Until a turn of events has Christy wanting to open up.

<u>Darkest Devotion</u>
At an underground rave, the last thing either plans is a hook up. When he takes her home the next day, an unexpected confrontation threatens to keep them apart.

<u>Beloved Devotion</u>
Liz asks the love of her life, Tiffany, to marry her. When Tiffany

hesitates, but says yes, Liz is determined to learn why. As the pieces start to fall in place, Liz discovers she doesn't know her fiancée at all.

The Insomniac Duet

He was her high school bully. She was the outcast that secretly crushed on him. More than ten years later, he's her boss, completely oblivious to their shared past, and wants no one but her. More importantly, he doesn't understand her animosity toward him.

The Click Duet

High school sweethearts torn apart. When fate gives them a second chance, one doesn't trust they won't be hurt again. Through the Lens (Click Duet #1) and Time Exposure (Click Duet #2) is an angsty, second chance, friends to lovers romance with all the feels.

One Night Forsaken

One night. No names. No romance. Just fun. Nothing more–at least, that's what she tells herself. Until he appears in her coffee shop months later with that addictive smile. She swore off commitment. He vows to never love again. But the more they fight it, the more life brings them together.

Broken Sky

Their eyes meet across the bar, but she looks away first. Does her best to give him zero attention. But when he crowds her on the dancefloor, she can't deny the instant chemistry. After one night together, he marks her as his. Unfortunately, another woman thinks he belongs to her.

<u>Shattered Sun</u>

When your heart is split in two, how do choose who to love more? While Ben—her childhood best friend—and Travis—the hottest cop in Stone Bay—fight for Kirsten's affection, someone else has their eye on her. When she questions everyone and everything, Ben and Travis vow to protect her. In the process, she falls for both men. Before it's too late, she needs to decide which man she loves more.

<u>Fractured Night</u>

Shallow. Heartless. Egocentric. The top three words people use to describe Phoebe Graves. Somehow, I've always seen past her icy facade. Seen beyond her callous exterior. And those minor glimpses… they make me want her more. The moment my fantasies start becoming reality, I question how long it'll last before Phoebe abandons me for something bigger.

CONNECT WITH PERSEPHONE

Connect with Persephone

www.persephoneautumn.com

Subscribe to Persephone's newsletter

www.persephoneautumn.com/newsletter

Join Persephone's reader's group

Persephone's Playground

Follow Persephone online

instagram.com/persephoneautumn

facebook.com/persephoneautumnwrites

tiktok.com/@persephoneautumn

bookbub.com/authors/persephone-autumn

goodreads.com/persephoneautumn

amazon.com/author/persephoneautumn

pinterest.com/persephoneautumn

threads.net/@persephoneautumn

ABOUT THE AUTHOR

USA Today Bestselling Author Persephone Autumn lives in Florida with her wife and psycho cat. A proud mom with a cuckoo grandpup. An ethnic food enthusiast who has fun discovering ways to vegan-ize her favorite non-vegan foods. Most days, you'll find her with a tea latte or fruity concoction in her hand. If given the opportunity, she would intentionally get lost in nature.

For years, Persephone did some form of writing; mostly journaling or poetry. After pairing her poetry with images and posting them online, she began the journey of writing her first novel.

She mainly writes romance and poetry, but on occasion dips her toes in other works. Look for her non-romance publications under P. Autumn.

ACKNOWLEDGMENTS

To my family! Thank you for continually supporting, encouraging and promoting my passion for writing books. Without your constant cheerleading and praise, I don't know where I'd be. I love you hard! xoxo

Kate Farlow! Your cover design skills always take my breath away! I've stumbled over how to make the cover of this book something readers want on their shelf. I'm absolutely in love with this stunning cover. Thank you!!

Ellie and Rosa… Thank you for fixing all the punctuation either I or my computer can't get right (bet it's the computer), for your feedback and suggestions. My books wouldn't be as magnificent without you!

Author friends… You know as much as I do, this business is not easy. At all. Thank you for all you do—from reading my words to sharing my content to lending an ear. We're better together than apart. Love you all so much! xoxo

To every person who reads one of my books… THANK YOU!!! Thank you for taking a chance on my books. For choosing me. Your continuous support melts my heart and makes me emo. Being an author is hard. But you help make it easier. xoxo

www.ingramcontent.com/pod-product-compliance
Lightning Source LLC
Chambersburg PA
CBHW061609190726

48288CB00007B/2249